# HELLDORADO

# HELLDORADO

## BAD TIMES BOOK FOUR

## CHUCK DIXON

LMBPN Publishing
PMB 196, 2540 South Maryland Pkwy
Las Vegas, NV 89109

First US edition, June 2020
eBook ISBN: 978-1-64202-848-5
Print ISBN: 978-1-64202-849-2

1

## THE RUNAWAY

She would not be owned. Rather, she would run.

The slope was covered in berry bushes and vines that choked off every trail but those traveled by the smallest game. The earth was soft with the passage of so many hooves and paws, and so she avoided the trails. Instead, she followed the path of a dry stream upward, stepping from stone to stone. She'd leave no sign for the hunters to follow. And there would be hunters.

The night was cool at the start of the season of planting. A bower of branches sheltered her from a cold wind falling off the ridgeline. She wore only a loincloth tied at the waist with a leather belt. She would have risked discovery by taking her cloak of thick bison hide. There was only time to gather a few things that might not be missed at first: a knife, a waterskin, a small sack of dried fruit and meat. The knife was a skinning tool with a long thin blade of hammered metal fitted into a handle of horn. It was a sorry weapon but would have to serve.

Her long black hair was gathered at the back of her head, held in place by her most prized possession: a wooden clasp cleverly carved by her father and gifted to her when she was a small girl.

She gripped the knife in her fist as she climbed, holding it before her against whatever the dark might hold. She kept the lake behind her until she reached the ridgeline. Even on this high ground, the roof of thick brush blocked out the sky. Shafts of silver light came down through the screen of new leaves. They served to deepen the dark around them. There was no way down on the lee side, so she followed the narrow ridgeline until she found an open space where the wind had scoured a high spot clean of vegetation. A broad table of rock lay naked under the light of the moon and stars. She stood for a moment, looking down from her windy perch. The air was wet and chilled, and she hunched with her arms across her breasts to look at the world that lay ahead of her. This marked the farthest N'itha had ever been from the people, and the most she had ever seen at one time of the land that surrounded their home. Before her, she saw that the land fell away toward more water, either another lake or a branch somehow connected to the water she left behind.

The water shone white in the moonlight, rimmed all around by tall trees.

She looked back but could not see the home of the people under the thick cover of brush. Trails of smoke rose above the tall trees from the sentry fires. They looked like wispy threads at this distance. She had traveled far and well since slipping from the home of the Earth Mother when the moon first began to fall toward the far hills. They might pursue her, but they would never find her. She would keep on through the night and through the day leaving as little trail as she could behind her. They would not catch her, and even if they did, she would never return alive to the home of the people. N'itha would plunge the skinning knife into her own throat before she would be taken back to Koto and be wed to him.

The thought of that bloated, greasy swine's hands on her sickened her. His eyes filled with cold lust, his tongue sliding over fat lips each time he looked at her. To be consigned to his loathsome custody and, she imagined, loathsome desires was unthinkable.

Whatever other fate awaited her in the unknown land below her, it would be preferable to being the bride of the Earth Mother's son. She might starve, or be eaten by a great cat or bear, or wander until she went mad, or fall prey to the flesh-hunters. Any end she could imagine would be better than lying with Koto until the next planting season. It was enough to be free at this moment in the dark night.

She found a game trail below the shelf of rock and followed it to the base of the slope. The thick bramble hedges gave way to a forest of old trees. N'itha moved more cautiously. The cold made the night silent. There was no wavering thrum of insects and toads, no calls of birds, to cover the noise of her passage. Nor was there the sheltering cover of the brush to hide her movement. This was the hunting ground of the bear and the cat. The grunt of the bear she knew well. She strained her ears to listen for it. The cat moved quietly until the final rush. N'itha could feel the yellow eyes filled with malevolent hunger watching her from the dark. She gripped the bark of a tree, willing herself to join its shadow, and shivered with fear more than the chilled air.

Anger welled within her. Anger at her father for meekly surrendering her to the Earth Mother. Anger at the Earth Mother for choosing her to wed her son. Anger at the Sky Mother and her demands that the price of a good harvest was the life of a girl who had once loved her so.

Most of all, N'itha burned with anger at herself. She had accepted that she might suffer for her choice, and now she cowered like a child in the woods. She might sit here, shrunk small and terrified of imagined predators until the hunters found her and dragged her back to Koto. Better to give herself to the great cats. Better to be torn to bloody shreds and her guts scattered over the forest floor. Her suffering would last only moments rather than the endless nights as a plaything to the Earth witch's disgusting progeny.

She pushed away from the tree to trot down the hillside into the gloom between the trees. The gloom turned to mist as the sun rose over the peak behind her. The land leveled out at the floor of the lake valley. N'itha came to the edge of a marsh and was forced to change her course to her left to follow the dry ground. With the warming rays of the sun, the sounds of the forest returned. Birds cawed and twittered. Squirrels thrashed in the branches overhead. From somewhere beyond the marshes, the trumpeted calls of an elephant reached her. She crouched in the shelter of a deadfall while a line of moose, moving with remarkable quiet, marched across her path.

Her feet were sore, and eyelids heavy as the sky lightened more and more. Her belly snarled. She needed food and rest and began searching for a hiding place to lie awhile and close her eyes.

N'itha stopped at a trilling sound she'd not heard before. Somewhere behind her the crunch of a step on brittle leaves. A grunt followed. A hoot sounded off to her right. Another answered it to the left. She turned her head to see a shadow streak between tree boles.

Only one animal hunted like that.

Man.

She thought at first it was hunters sent by the Earth Mother, but they would not move so cautiously. They would boldly stalk her and run her down. These were men unknown to her, and that sent a thrill of fear through her that washed away her weariness in a single stroke.

N'itha sprinted forward, followed by rising calls of hoots and barks. They grew more frequent to either side of her. She could see black shadows racing through the trees to be lost from her sight each time she turned her head. Her hand ached with the grip she kept on the knife handle. Her breath came in gasps. Her legs burned with the fire of exertion. Still, the voices closed in all around her from the curtain of sun-dappled green.

Her path led to the edge of the marsh. To turn to avoid it would bring her into the arms of her pursuers. To go forward would slow her progress until they caught her.

N'itha stood in the ankle-deep muck and turned her back to the reeds with the knife blade held before her in both hands. She would die here and draw the blood of the strangers as she did so. A calm came over her as she stood crouched and ready for what manner of man might come out of the surrounding forest.

A squat figure holding a spear was the first to emerge into the light. It was furred over every surface with sloping shoulders descending to either side from a thick neck topped with a broad head from which deep-set eyes studied her over the point of a stone-tipped spear. A wide mouth opened to reveal ranks of yellowed teeth filed to razor points. The creature, hardly a man, barked a single basso sound to bring more of its kind out from the trees.

They were flesh-hunters. The near-men who were so often the subject of stories the hunters would tell around the fires at night. N'itha knew them only as figures of nightmares. They were smaller than in the pictures she made in her dreams but more fearsome than she'd imagined. Their number grew until they approached in a half-ring to jabber at her and to one another. N'itha retreated into the reeds up to her calves in muddy water. They poked their spears in her direction and hooted, daring one another forward into the clinging muck.

A new voice sounded from the tree line at their back. The near-men stopped advancing on her and turned to watch a man join them on the bank of the marsh.

A man, an actual man, standing upright. He had hair on his chest and arms only. Atop his head, jet-black hair was pulled back into a long tail. His face was clean-shaven. He moved with a limp, favoring one leg. He wore a strange skin of mottled green about his waist and legs. His feet were shod to above the ankles in black moccasins of a design N'itha had never seen before. In his hands, he held a weapon of black iron. It was too short to be a spear and had no edge or point. The man shooed away the flesh-hunters with an angry growl and then stood as though transfixed by the sight of N'itha. He spoke in words that clearly meant something but held no meaning for her.

"Holy shit. Where'd you drop from, honey?"

2

## UNCLE MO

"Come see the baby," Caroline Tauber said.

"I'm wrapping up a few trials, and I can get away in a week. Maybe two," Morris Tauber said.

"You're leaving tomorrow, Mo."

Morris *was* anxious to meet his newborn nephew for the first time but was dismayed that his sister insisted he come ashore to do so.

After all, he tried to explain to Caroline, the Tauber Tube was his own baby and required constant attention.

"The Tube is *our* baby, big brother," she reminded him over the sat phone connection. "Parviz and Quebat can look after it along with the reactor. You need some time away from your work, and you need to start acting like an uncle." Parviz and Quebat were the pair of Iranian expatriates who looked after the stolen mini-nuclear reactor they maintained aboard the leased container ship, *Ocean Raj*. The two were under a *fatwa* from the mullahs in Tehran both for fleeing Iran's advancing nuclear weapons program and for remaining outrageously and defiantly gay. Though, as they reminded anyone incautious enough to make the mistake, they were *not* "a couple."

"And how does an uncle act, Sis?" Morris asked.

"Well, he doesn't hide out below decks in a rusting container ship. He's more fun than that. He brings gifts and acts avuncular."

"Very helpful."

"I'm going to make this simple for you, Mo. Arrangements have been made. Pack a bag and the passport under the name Kenneth Armbruster of Halifax, Nova Scotia. A seaplane is coming to pick you up tomorrow morning to take you to Rimini where Dwayne and I have rented the most secluded little villa."

"I can't make it tomorrow. I'm in the middle of calculations that—"

"You're just going to have to recalculate them anyway after what I have to show you." Her tone was the same as when they were kids, and she found out what he was getting for Christmas.

"What are you talking about, Sis?"

"Samuel gave me some research materials on chronal manifestation fields that you're going to want to see."

"Research from where?"

"The future, stupid. Don't you want to see how our work was refined and applied by minds other than our own?"

After a pause, he said, "What time is the seaplane coming?" He could see her smug smile on the other end of the phone as clearly as if he were there.

"Eight your time." She hung up, cutting off her own laugh of delight.

The next morning, he landed in the harbor at Rimini. A cab was waiting for him at the end of the pier of the seaplane dock. It carried him over the Tiberius Bridge and along a road that followed the Fiume Marecchia before turning off onto a road lined with orchards of olive trees to a crushed stone turn-around before a whitewashed country house of Neapolitan design.

Dwayne met him on the drive to pay the cab driver a fistful of Euros. He caught his brother-in-law up in a bearhug. Caroline had a lunch of cold prosciutto and salad waiting on a veranda from which they could look at the sea visible over hills dotted green and white.

"Is my brother somewhere in there?" she said, touching the bush of his new beard and recoiling in exaggerated surprise as though a bird had flown out of it.

"I'm keeping it," he said with defiance.

"Well, as long as it doesn't scare the baby," Dwayne said. Morris wasn't terribly shocked to find that his nephew, born less than a month before in relative time, was sitting up and making noises that almost sounded like words. His experience with infants was limited, to say the least. He wasn't at all sure what babies were supposed to do or when. Stephen seemed alert enough for his age certainly but was fixated on sticking his own fingers in his mouth more than anything else. Perhaps he favored his father over his mother, Morris suspected. He kept that thought to himself.

More surprising to Dr. Morris Tauber were the reams of spiral-bound volumes his sister had waiting for him on a table in a library room.

"What are these?" He riffled pages to see rows of complex formulas and columns of dense text.

"The materials I promised you," Caroline said.

"In print? On paper?" He picked up one thin volume entitled *Mica Prima* by Kosimo Trivenchy.

"You expected it on a flash drive? Believe it or not, there are compatibility issues with a parallel universe. Their 'windows' are still something you look out of when you're inside. Besides, Samuel was concerned with having these books in any kind of medium that could be duplicated and disseminated easily."

"So, I can take these back to the *Raj* and read them?

"No, you can't, Mo. Samuel trusted me with these, and I promised they wouldn't leave my sight."

"I have to stay here?" Morris said with dismay.

"Yes, bro. You have to stay in a six-bedroom Italian villa, enjoying the sun and the breeze off the Adriatic in the company of your brand-new nephew and getting to read the most mind-blowing scientific treatises you will ever see in your lifetime. Poor baby." She tsked.

"If I have to, I suppose," Morris said with a sigh.

"I see I forgot to turn on the sarcasm indicator," Caroline said and left him with the books.

---

The baby was asleep for the night. Mom and dad were drinking glasses of Chianti on the balcony, enjoying the moonlight over the harbor below when Morris burst upon them.

"Have you read this stuff?" he said breathlessly. He was waving a spiral-bound folder.

"Morris, you need to do something about the beard," Caroline said with a wry smile.

"Yes. I'll trim it in the morning. Have you read this material?"

"Not as fast as you, apparently. There's a lot to digest there, and the language is—"

"To hell with the language. The ideas are so clearly put forward in the numbers. The applications of our theories take the technology in so many different directions. The ramifications are limitless." Morris sounded almost giddy. He even accepted a glass of Chianti from Dwayne which he chugged down like a frat boy.

Caroline shrugged. "You were always the numbers guy, bro."

"We have to get back to the *Raj*. There are changes to be made. So many adjustments and alterations, and I'll need some new hardware."

"We'll talk about that en route," Caroline said.

"En route? En route to where?"

"Well, as close as we can get the *Ocean Raj* to Las Vegas," Caroline said.

Morris looked to Dwayne for help with this riddle. "We're going back to get Rick Renzi," his brother-in-law said and held out a second glass of the rich red wine.

## 3

## THE OCEAN RAJ

"Does the eye hurt?" Dr. Paphos asked.

"The one that's gone?" Jimmy Smalls asked.

"Yes."

"How can an eye that's gone hurt?"

"You are a soldier. That much I learn from your *et wasz*—your tattoos. You must know soldiers who have lost a limb, an arm or leg, who still have sensation in the *ackrodees-ti*—the amputated member."

"Yeah. I know a couple guys. One guy lost both legs in Iraq and swears he still has athlete's foot. I don't feel anything except some pain around the socket," Jimbo said.

"You will need reconstructive surgery to the orbital rim if you wish to be fitted with a glass eye," Dr. Paphos said.

"The patch will do for now."

"Without the surgery, you may suffer further complications to the sinuses. Infections and such. The fracture was quite severe."

"The ladies like the patch, doc. But send me some suggestions for good surgeons for when I have some downtime."

The Cypriot doctor promised to do so and left a supply of

primo painkillers and antibiotics. Jimbo paid him with a stack of Euros and saw him down the gangway to the launch that would take the GP back to Lanarca.

A man with a mane of dirty blond hair and the build of a featherweight all-in wrestler waited at the top of the gangway for Jimbo. Byrus was a Macedonian pit-fighter the Rangers had brought back from ancient Judea. He was wearing the same blissed-out smile he'd been sporting ever since the day he arrived in The Now.

"All okay, baas?" Byrus said. He'd picked up the common Ethiopian term for superiors and more rudimentary English in the month since they'd come back from the past.

"Fucking A, Bruce," Jimbo said.

"Fucking A." Byrus' grin broadened, and he fell into step behind his master.

Jimbo admitted that he really hadn't thought it through when he insisted that Byrus return with them. There was no question that the pint-sized surfer dude had saved his life and kept him alive until they could be extracted. The massive injury to his face and eye left Jimbo defenseless for almost a week following their run-in with a Roman century. He still had trouble with vertigo, and adjusting to two-dimensional vision was a bitch. He owed the little man, no question of that. But it might have been better if they'd given him a shitload of gold coins and left him *in situ*.

Only, Byrus was technically a slave and a wanted man. And wanted in Roman Judea meant being nailed to a cross upon capture. The best getaway Jimbo could imagine was putting two thousand years between Byrus and rendering unto Caesar.

And it was all cool at first. Byrus reacted to the world of, to him, the far future like a kid experiencing Christmas every day. So far, he'd been quarantined to the *Raj*, now anchored out in the Aegean in international waters. But even the old container ship was a world of marvels to him. Microwaves, refrigerators, televisions, sat phones, and all the other everyday miracles that the world took for granted were works of magic to Byrus. The concept of time travel was impossible to get across to him. There was a knowledge and language barrier that nobody on the team knew how to get past. Byrus thought he'd been taken to the home of the gods and they let it go at that. If he wanted to think he was hanging with some of Zeus' close pals, then so be it.

Jimbo worried about his little displaced buddy's future. They couldn't keep him on the boat forever. And if the *Raj* blew his mind, what would his first glimpse of a big city do to him? Any city for that matter. Detroit would look like Olympus to Byrus. It was all about perspective. Lee Hammond was creating a bullet-proof identity for the Macedonian, but where was he going to fit in? And, the bigger problem, how to detach him from Jimbo's side.

It was reasonable that Byrus would stick close to the most familiar face in this most unfamiliar environment. The little guy was rarely out of sight of his one-eyed Indian brother. Even giving him his own cabin didn't create separation. Jimbo woke up the first morning to find Byrus asleep on the deck at the foot of his bunk.

"He's like a pet," Jimbo said to Chaz Raleigh. They sat fishing off the lower stern deck, sharing a bucket of long necks.

"He's like a slave, bro," Chaz said.

"I don't own him. I don't want to own him," Jimmy said.

"That's not how he sees it. He's a slave. Been one all his life. No one's freed him. He just switched masters."

"I don't want a slave."

"Props to you, bro."

"I want him to have his own life. I mean, I'll look after him. I owe him that. He's my responsibility."

"Now he *is* sounding like a pet."

"So how do I explain that to him that I don't own him? How do I free him?"

"Has to be a way to get it across to him. I'll do some

Googling," Chaz said.

Chaz Googled and found a helpful suggestion. He located a member of the *Raj's* crew who was a skilled woodcarver. Chaz gave him the image printed up from the internet search. The guy went down to the ship's workshop. He came back in a few hours with a full-scale version in mahogany.

———

That night they had dinner in the galley presided over by Boats, the *Raj* skipper. The former SEAL was still favoring the leg that had been pierced through-and-through by an arrow on their latest trip to the past. He took the head of the table and sat with his healing leg propped up.

Lee Hammond, Bat Jaffe, *Raj's* first officer, Geteye, Jimbo, Chaz, and Byrus sat around the table, digging in. After a meal of salad, pasta with shrimp, and lots of wine, the ship's cook carried in a cake decorated with Roman columns of white icing and Byrus' name spelled out in chocolate. The cook set it down in front of the Macedonian who looked perplexed at the smiling faces around the table all turned his way.

Jimbo reached under the table and brought out a wooden sword, a replica of a Roman gladius. He held it out to Byrus, who stared at it with wide eyes. His perpetual smile faded away. Tears welled in his eyes as he took the sword in his hands. He wrapped arms around Jimbo's chest and lifted the larger man off the deck with a roar of triumph.

"Shit. The little man sure likes that sword," Boats said.

"It's a symbol of his freedom. It was given to gladiators in the arena to take away their slave status," Chaz said.

"So Bruce is a free man for the first time in his life," Bat said.

"Yeah, but I don't think Jimmy's free of him," Lee said, looking at the Macedonian clinging to the Pima in a serious man hug.

Eventually, Byrus recovered from his bromantic moment long

enough to cut messy slices from his cake with the wooden sword. Then they finished the wine, switched to tequila and all got very, very drunk.

## TRAVEL WEST

The *Ocean Raj* rolled on gentle waters twenty miles west of San Clemente. California "sunshine" was pouring down in buckets on the decks from lowering skies.

The trip through the Panama Canal went smoothly. Ships in transit don't get as much scrutiny as those stopping at Atlantic or Pacific ports. Boats still had his papers from the company he leased the ship from, and the last time they were in any port was the year before in Alexandria. The manifest was unchanged and contained no reason for suspicion.

The pilot crew boarded to see them through the locks. Panamanian customs did a cursory check that missed the Conex containers of firearms and explosives. They also missed the mini-nuclear reactor humming away deep in the hold. Radiation screening was done by *Servicio Marítimo Nacional* at the container port. Since the *Raj* wasn't picking up or dropping off any cargo, they got a pass on the rad check.

The real trick to smuggling was never putting into port.

Quebat and Parviz stayed drunk the rest of the ten-hour trip through the canal.

Their course registration was for the Pacific off the California coast. The cover story was that they were doing some bullshit tectonic study of the Mendocino fracture zone paid for by a bull-shit nonprofit foundation funded by the secret sale of prehistoric gold made to Russian mobsters.

Pirates once stood at the wheel of a three-master. These days they served as chairmen for charities and sat at the end of board-room tables.

Boats let many of his Ethiopian crew go with a hefty cash bonus in Euros in their bags. He kept on his first mate Geteye and four other crewmen. As big as the *Raj* was, she required only a few able hands to get her from A to B. Jimbo, Byrus and the two Iranians stayed on board as well. The Iranians kept watch on the reactor. Jimbo and his sidekick cooked meals for everyone when they weren't fishing or running laps around the deck.

The rest flew to L.A. and would rejoin them when the weather cleared.

"This Renzi guy must mean a lot to you and your team," Boats said to Jimbo. They shared a leisurely watch on the bridge. Boats, smoking a Cuban, sat in a command chair with his feet up on a control console.

"He's a brother. A pain in the ass but a brother," Jimbo said, his eyes on the water streaming down the viewports at the front of the bridge.

"How'd you come to leave him behind?"

"The field was closing, and we had bad guys on our asses. He stayed back to cover our exfil."

"These bad guys. Some kind of monkey-men, right?"

"Badass, man-eating motherfuckers. Shorter than Bruce but mean as hell. And there was a shitload of them."

"But Renzi survived. How'd that happen?" Boats took a long drag.

"Because Rick Renzi is the most stubborn son of a bitch who ever lived. Couldn't even die when he was supposed to. We were all sure he bought it."

"His bones say different."

"Caroline Tauber says the remains we found are Renzi's, but he was at least sixty years old when he died back in The Then. That gives us a second chance to go after him."

"That Caroline is some kind of woman," Boats said, releasing a stream of creamy smoke to billow against the port glass.

"She's also married to Roenbach, sailor."

"Oh, I was just admiring her mind, brother."

"Really?" Jimbo said.

"Sure. Sure. You may not think it to look at me, but I'm an intellectual," Boats said, grinning teeth visible through a thick of shrubbery of beard from which emerged a rich fog of Havana smoke.

# ANOMALIES

"Morris isn't going to like this," Caroline said.

"That's why Morris isn't here, honey," Dwayne said. "Your brother is a worrier."

The team was meeting in a chartroom of the *Ocean Raj*, most of it anyway. Chaz Raleigh had arrived with Dwayne Roenbach, the Tauber siblings and little Stephen by shuttle out of Catalina earlier that day. Lee Hammond and Bat Jaffe were staying behind a few days to see the sights in Southern Cali. They kept Dr. Morris Tauber from the meeting by assigning him babysitting duties in order to "bond with his nephew."

On the broad chart table before them was a drone Jimbo had ordered over the net. An Avi-Dex 5000s, a high-end model with all the candy. Chinese manufacture with full HD video capability, sixty-minute battery life, and an airspeed of sixty knots. The squat barrel-shaped body was suspended from four powerful rotors. Tiny and fast and light, with a diameter of under a half meter, and portable. The heaviest portion would be the two batteries. The drone set them back fifty thousand. Jimbo was studying the thick manual that came along with it. Chaz was booting up the controller.

"It's all high-grade plastic and steel," Caroline said, shaking her head.

"Yeah, an anachronism of mass destruction," Jimbo said.

"A chronal catastrophe," Chaz parroted.

"You forgot, 'an anomaly that would change history as we know it,'" Jimbo said.

"Funny," Caroline said. "But this stuff my brother warns you about is very real."

"I think they were quoting you, honey," Dwayne said.

"Fine. But you lose one of these in some prehistoric valley ten millennia ago, and we'll all be reading about it on Facebook tomorrow."

"It's a three hundred mile plus hike from the nearest landfall we can make to the area of Nevada where Rick Renzi's bones were laid down," Dwayne said. "The terrain between here and there is nothing like it is today. We need to find the best, straightest path for getting in and getting out," Jimbo said, "We could waste weeks going around water or marshlands that aren't there now. Or even longer following dead-end passes through the San Gabriels. The drones will show us the way ahead."

"There's no other way?" Caroline said.

"This has the least impact of all the other options we talked about," Chaz put in.

"What options?" she asked.

"Dwayne suggested using ultra-lite aircraft."

"Cochise here wanted us to bring along horses. Of course," Dwayne said.

"I still say a dirigible would be kick ass. We'd get there in a day. No chronal footprint." Chaz shrugged.

"You tell my brother any of those ideas, and he'll have three kinds of kittens," Caroline said.

And kittens there were when Morris popped into the chart-room with a bawling, squirming Stephen in his arms. The baby had handfuls of Mo's beard in his fists and was pulling hard. Morris arrived in time to see the bright yellow drone hovering a foot off the surface of the chart room table, and Jimbo and Chaz fighting over who'd get to fly her next. "What in God's name is that?" He shouted over the whirr of the motors and pointed an accusing finger at the offending machine.

Stephen stopped crying to reach his fingers out for the remote in Chaz's hands.

"We're going in heavy, Mo. You know that, right?" Dwayne and Caroline had Morris sat down with a bottle of Maker's Mark.

"I didn't think about it. I sure as hell didn't think you'd be taking your own unmanned aircraft," Morris said with a glum expression.

"We got our collective asses kicked once before back in the same country. That's not happening again. We go in armed to face stiff odds."

"And wildlife," Caroline put in.

"That's right," Dwayne said. "The guys are going through the books we picked up. There's some predators where we're heading. Big ones. And lots of them."

"And you can't move blind. I get it." Morris winced at his second sip of aged bourbon.

"We've gotten good at retrieval protocol, mostly. We make picking up after ourselves part of our mission chores. We won't leave the drones behind. I guarantee it."

"The guys are actually reading books on prehistoric Mammalia?" Morris said.

"It's mission prep," Dwayne said.

"I'm not so sure how much they're actually reading," Caroline said, freshening her brother's drink with a healthy slosh.

"You see the teeth on this fucker?" Boats said. He held open a book called *My Book Of Prehistoric Monsters* to a colorful two-page spread of a furry beast the size of a house devouring a caribou on a grassy plain.

Byrus looked up from the stack of *Penthouse* back issues he'd been studying. He knit his brows at the picture.

"Farther back you go the more things can eat you," Chaz said, squinting at a page of his own book showing a painting of a herd of mammoths crossing a primordial valley teeming with life. It brought back memories of the teams' own encounter with the same breed of elephants on their first trip back through the Tauber Tube.

"Or stomp you to shit," Chaz added.

"Every animal we encounter will be bigger than anything we see these days. Even animals we're familiar with will be a hell of a lot meatier. There'll be rabbits that can kick your ass." Jimbo looked up from a thicker, more serious volume than the children's books the others were browsing.

"Why's that?" Boats asked.

"Well, if you *read* these books you find out that we're going back to a warming period between the last major ice age and the final minor one before the current period we're living in. The air is hotter, wetter, and thicker. Like summer in New Orleans all the time."

"That makes them bigger?" Chaz said.

"Just like the tits on a waitress I met at Mardi Gras two years back," Boats said.

"Tits!" Byrus shouted, holding up a glossy foldout of a blonde Pet reclining on the hood of a Porsche.

"His English is coming along," Chaz said.

"I'll find images and specs for the critters we might run into, arranged by region and period," Jimbo said. "A lot of the ones in these books will be extinct already. But there's still some dangerous ones we'll need to watch out for. I'll have profiles and scans for the tablets we'll be taking with us. We're probably looking at a dense wildlife population. The most effective preda-tors haven't shown up on the continent yet."

"What animal's that, Smalls?" Boats said.

"Cochise is talking about his great-great-great grandpa." Chaz smiled.

"Damn straight," Jimbo said, returning the grin.

## VESPERS

"You off daddy duty, Daddy?" Lee Hammond said.

"Stevie's down for the night. So's Caroline," Dwayne Roenbach said.

They were alone on the lower aft deck, sheltered from the weather by the deck above, and watching light rainfall dapple the water under muted moonlight. A cooler of iced Dos Equis sat on the deck between them.

"You sure your head is into this?" Lee said.

"Why wouldn't it be?"

"You have a wife. A son. You've already been through enough of this shit as it is."

"So, I'm supposed to retire?"

"Hell, no. But you have people now. I figure you're going to be thinking about them more than you're thinking about the op."

"How long have we known each other, Hammond?"

"A long fucking time."

"Long enough for me to know that it's always about Lee Hammond. In the end, after all the bullshit, it's going to be all about your favorite person." Dwayne grinned.

Lee looked away.

"You really like this girl," Dwayne said.

"Yeah. Bat's cool. I like her," Lee said, turning back to look at the rain on the sea.

"And you're looking to get out."

"No. That's what's different. We've been together a few months, right. Usually, at this point, I'm looking for a way out. Shit, I'm looking for a way out the next morning, trying to get my boots and car keys together without waking her up."

"So, you *really* like her. This time it's different." Dwayne smiled.

"Yeah. It's different."

"It's probably because she can kick your ass."

"Don't think I haven't thought of that," Lee said, offering one of his rare smiles.

"Well, at least you're not leaving her behind. I might stay if it wasn't for Rick. And Caroline says she wants me to go back and get him, even if she doesn't mean it. She thinks she owes Rick, too. We all do, right?"

"Then it's back to the valley of the shadow of death tomorrow for both of us."

"And we shall fear no evil," Dwayne said.

"For we are the baddest motherfuckers in the valley," they said in unison and clinked bottles.

The rain died away, and the moon came out from behind the clouds to turn the sea to silver without further comment from either Ranger.

## TRANSIT EAST

The transition went like clockwork.

The field opened in a flash of blue lightning that lit the sea for a mile around the *Ocean Raj*.

A cloud of mist spread over the black water.

In the same place one hundred millennia in the past, a forty-foot inflatable raft emerged from a cloud of white mist into a sunny afternoon and calm seas. They were taking a full complement with them this outing: Dwayne Roenbach, Lee Hammond, Charles Raleigh, James Smalls, Bathsheba Jaffee,

and the two men known only as Boats and Bruce.

Once everyone had recovered from the physical effects of the transition, the brand-new Titan rigid-hull raft moved at forty knots over the smooth surface. They'd all been through the manifestation field before and found that the more often they transited, the less effect they felt. The only ones heaving over the side were relative newbies Bat and Byrus.

Dwayne used a specialized transmitter to text back through the still open field:

**HELLO FROM THE PAST**

**WEATHER CLEAR. EN ROUTE TO MALIBU B.C.**

An answering text followed:

**TRNSMT STAR READINGS WHEN POSSIBLE LOVE FROM BABY AND ME**

The boat's cabin and hull were painted in dazzle stripes of desert colors, camouflaged to help conceal it once they reached shore. They needed to leave it behind when they started their hike inland. There were no eyes that might see the anomalous craft and record the sighting in words or pictures. They were firmly in prehistory. The first cave drawings were many thousands of years to come.

Boats stood on the open bridge piloting the boat and scanning the sea all around through mirrored Ray-Bans. Chaz held onto a railing by him, feeling the spray.

"No dinosaurs, huh?" Boats asked.

"You read the same books I did, brother. In the big picture, we just took a baby step back in time. We're still way closer to T-Mobile than T-rex."

"Shit," Boats said, disappointed.

The shoreline they approached bore no resemblance to any section of the California coast any of them had seen before. Gentle rollers lapped the edge of a vast beach. The long expanse of sand sloped slightly for a mile or more to a range of dunes that stretched to the horizon. The only inhabitants were shifting masses of birds trotting along the surf or resting in mobs on the sand. The arrival of the team disturbed the birds who took to the air to resettle out of reach.

The birds were in a great variety of sizes, though most were either white or gray like the species of shorebirds the members of the team were more familiar with. Most were larger, the smallest on the scale of a gull all the way up to long-legged critters taller than Dwayne.

The remains of crabs lay in scattered heaps on the sand and floated at the edges of the rolling water. It was these the birds were gathered to feed on. They were enormous crabs with bodies two feet across. Blue-hued claws, bigger than a man's hand with legs a yard long. There were no live ones in sight. From their coloring, they were obviously sea crabs. Most of the team had seen monster land crabs in Thailand and other places around the Indian Ocean. These prehistoric crustaceans dwarfed those.

"What a stank! Man, I am never eating seafood again," Chaz said, waving a hand before his face.

"I wouldn't want to have been here when these things were alive," Bat said.

"I'm more concerned with what killed them," Jimbo said. "It wasn't these birds. They came in for the leftovers." They took a fresh look at the carcasses that littered the sand at the water's edge. Their thick shells and claws were smashed open, and legs were torn from their sockets. "Could be a mass death from illness. Let's worry about it later. We need to secure the boat," Dwayne said.

The team worked to haul the Titan well away from the surf and into the first range of dunes. They staked it down in place between two tall hummocks of sand. They'd make camp tonight, allowing themselves time to gauge how far high tide reached inland.

Without being asked, Byrus began dragging driftwood to their camp to build a fire.

Gear was offloaded and parceled out. The main unit weapon was the modified M4 the team was most used to, only these models were high-end custom weapons with reinforced actions and receivers and chromed barrels. Dwayne and Boats had 20mm grenade launchers mounted on theirs. Sidearms leaned toward the heavy Dan Wesson .44 Magnum revolvers. Lee opted for the S&W Model 500 in .500 magnum. In addition, Boats had his Mariner twelve-gauge and Jimbo his Winchester bolt action chambered for the powerhouse .458 Winchester Magnum round. Also, an assortment of knives, tomahawks, and hideaways. Bat would never give up the .38 snubby she kept squirreled away in a pocket of her Molle vest.

Only Byrus was without a firearm. He chose for himself a broad-bladed bowie knife from Jimbo's collection as well as a tomahawk, a twenty-first century model with a high impact Rynex handle mounted with a broad titanium blade on one side of the head and wicked chromed spike on the other. His main weapon of choice was a spear with a six-foot shaft. It was made of ash with a carbon steel tip in an elongated spade shape. It was what he was comfortable with, the assault weapon of his day.

Chaz busied himself with unpacking the drone and had it airborne within moments. The whirring machine soared up into the cloudless sky, sending high definition images back from the three cameras mounted on its belly. Bat leaned over his shoulder to look at the tablet mounted atop the controller. Chaz steered the drone out past the dunes to where the sand gave way to low scrubby pines and rocky ground. From a thousand feet, they looked down at a large mass of shifting shapes moving between the low trees. The drone dropped for a closer look, and the shapes took the form of animals moving leisurely over the rough ground in a loose herd.

"Bet you that's what had the crab feast," Chaz said.

"Whoa," Bat said, looking at the mass of ridgeback pigs bristling with hair with stripes running down their flanks.

"Can't tell scale here but some of these look big. See the tusks on that piggy?" Chaz said.

"Swine fed on shellfish. That's super double not kosher," Bat said.

Chaz shared the intel with the others.

"That fucker is a half-ton at least." Jimbo pointed at a huge tusker bucking along a shallow ravine.

"How far is that?" Dwayne said.

"A klick. Closer to a klick and half," Chaz read from the

screen on the controller. He initiated the drone's autopilot to return to him.

Dwayne said, "We make a wicker of driftwood either end of this hollow and build the fire high. We should be all right."

"We better hope that herd is gone in the morning," Jimbo said.

They set up camp and ate a meal of lasagna and fresh salad packed for them by Oromo, the *Ocean Raj's* cook, as a farewell gift. It would be the last fresh food they'd have other than any game they picked up along the way. From this point on, it was freeze-dried meals, protein bars, and trail mix.

When full night came, Chaz took the star readings. The algorithm Caroline Tauber had come up with placed the date at five years and three months and four days after the last time they departed prehistoric Nevada.

"Renzi's been alone here for five years without a drink," Jimbo said.

"He's probably running the place by now," Lee said. Lee and Chaz took first watch while the others slept.

They took up posts atop the dunes and listened to the calls and cries of animals both familiar and unknown. Each scanned the surroundings with night vision lenses. Glittering eyes looked back at them from beyond the glow of the fire. Humped shapes skittered across their vision from dune to dune. A whoop was cut short in an agonized gurgle, and all went silent for a while. It was a prehistoric buffet going on out there.

The following morning came muggy with clouds of outsized flies that had the team slathering on DEET.

"Would it help if we drank this shit?" Boats said, crushing a winged pest on his arm.

"If we'd gone with my dirigible idea, we'd be flying above these fuckers," Chaz said.

They secured the boat in place with staked lines and covered it over, using camouflage netting reinforced with wire cables. There was no way to keep curious critters off it, but the netting would resist the largest and most destructive of them. Jimbo had used his sextant the night before to record the boat's location and shared it with the others in case they got separated.

They rucked up with all their gear. Weapons and ammo packs and backpacks filled with food, medical supplies and changes of socks and underwear. They'd share the burden of the drone case between them by taking turns. Each had a CamelBak for water. They didn't anticipate any kind of firefights, and so did not bring along any kind of body armor. Their clothes were summer weight BDU pants, t-shirts, tank-tops, and boonie hats and ball caps except for Byrus, who wore a pair of surf shorts in an outrageous aloha pattern of orchids and pineapples.

Byrus also wore a pair of New Balance cross-trainers. A lifetime of running around barefoot had broadened his feet to the point where no boot would fit him comfortably. Though he topped out at just over five feet, he wore a size-fourteen sneaker.

Jimbo and Byrus trotted out to take point and headed inland along their chosen route.

## 8

# ALL CREATURES GREAT AND VERY SMALL

Two klicks into the dune banks they ran into the wild pigs.

The porkers did not impress. The largest of them was about the size of a miniature poodle. They charged up a track between dunes snorting and grunting. Jimbo and Byrus pressed to either wall of the gully to let the herd of forty or so stampede by.

Shouts then laughter came from around the turn behind him. Jimbo knew the team would ride his ass for days for this one. He made a mental note to activate the scaling option in the drone's imaging program.

After a few hours of hiking, the sandy ridges gave way to low pines and clumps of razor-sharp grass. The ground sloped up to the hills and the peaks of the San Gabriels. The clouds were darkening and dropping to the crest line ahead. There was a breeze climbing up off the ocean with the weather. The rising wind caused the bugs to subside from a constant to an occasional annoyance. Jimbo and Byrus stopped and waited for the others to catch up. The Pima stood watching a herd of the biggest caribou he'd ever seen in his life moving lazily through the trees to the east. Nothing was in the right scale here. The 'bou were the size of draught horses, and the pigs looked like toys.

Byrus gathered brush and wood for a fire. He had a blaze going by the time the main body of the group arrived.

"I like those hams, baby. Two of 'em would make enough for a sandwich," Chaz said.

"Talk about baby back ribs." Dwayne grinned.

"They were cute," Bat said and clapped a hand to her mouth.

"Take a look up there if you like your game super-sized," Jimbo said, pointing at the herd feeding in the trees a hundred yards from their position.

The large animals burst into sudden movement. As one, adults and calves went from a trot to a full gallop and were away out of sight into the dark of the woods. Their passage could be felt as a tremor through the soles of the team's boots.

"We spooked them," Dwayne said.

"Not us. They knew we were here. They're downwind. Smelled us before they saw us. Something else got them running. Something we didn't see." Jimbo had his eyes to the binoculars always handy about his neck.

"One of those things we saw in the books," Bat said.

The water pot by the fire was coming to a boil. They parceled out food packs.

"Put that shit away. I got fresh." Boats caught up from walking drag to join them in the clearing. He held up the carcass of a wild pig in one bloodied hand.

---

The pig was skinned and gutted and on a spit over the fire within minutes.

Wiping his hands clean in the sand, Dwayne said, "That was the goddamned sweetest ham I ever tasted."

"I could eat another one. Swear to God," Chaz said, standing and tossing a finger sized rib to sizzle in the dying embers.

"Sure you don't want a bite?" Lee held a rib out to Bat.

"I'll stick to my chili," she said, raising a spoon from the steaming plastic pack in her lap.

After they finished, Byrus scattered the fire on the sands as directed by Jimbo. The team rucked up.

"I don't like that sky." Dwayne nodded at the bank of black clouds dropping down to the peaks.

"It'll be a relief from the bugs," Chaz said.

Boats sniffed the air. "No thunder. We should be okay in the trees."

"Bat and me will take point. That suit you?" Lee said to Bat Jaffe.

"Sure. I want to see what got those big deer hustling like that." She slung her rifle across her midriff. The pair started off toward the taller trees at the far end of the clearing while the rest adjusted gear for the long afternoon hump.

"I'll stay on drag," Boats said.

"Leg bothering you, sailor?" Dwayne said.

"I can hack. I won't slow us down."

"Let me know if it gets any worse," Dwayne said even though he knew the former SEAL could be marching on bloody stumps and never let him know. He'd keep an eye on Boats.

They both smelled blood before they came up on the kill. The caribou was an enormous doe lying on its side.

Black flies swirled over it in a dense swarm. A rear leg was broken. White bone gleamed from torn flesh. The guts had been ripped from the abdomen in a wide swath that dampened the forest for twenty feet behind the animal. Its shattered rib cage was spread wide like a grisly pair of wings.

Bat crouched away from the carcass. She waved a hand before her face to part the fog of flies. They were well up the forested slope, the trees were old-growth redwoods with boles thirty feet in diameter at the base. The forest floor was a spongy loam of fallen needles and fungus growths. Shelves of fungi climbed up the bark of the trees. Under the stink of blood and tripe was the musky smell of old rot always present in rain forests this thick.

"Look at the size of this female," she said. "How big are the bucks? We can't stay here. Whatever killed this will be back."

"Uh-huh. I only want to wait for Jimbo to catch up," Lee said. He held his rifle raised while scanning the gloom all around. The dark sky above turned the forest to a world of shadows. The patter of rain was reaching them where it dropped through the branches high above.

Jimbo trotted up, with Byrus behind.

"This is a cat kill," Jimbo said. "Big cat. Snapped the 'bou's leg, bringing him down. That took weight and force." The rain was coming down steadily now, dissipating the worst of the insects. Byrus stood by, his ever-present smile gone now as he watched the woods around them with a head cocked to listen. His fists gripped the shaft of his spear well past mid-length. With the length of the razor-sharp blade, the Macedonian had a good five feet of stabbing reach.

"How do you know it's a cat?" Lee said.

"Bite marks on the head. The skull is crushed. Whatever did this, took the caribou's whole head in its mouth to use as a grip while it clawed out its guts. That's how cats kill."

"Is it still here?" Bat said.

"Oh yeah. It's making up its mind about us," the Pima said.

"Best guess?" Lee said.

"Upwind. Above us. The sign is all one cat. My theory is they hunt solo like our tigers or leopards. If they move in prides, we are seriously fucked."

"We're talking a sabretooth, right? Like in the Ice Age movies?" Bat turned her head on a swivel to look up the hill.

"Never saw them," Jimbo said.

"Cartoons. They're cute," Bat said, his eyes on the gloom between the trees.

"We need to move, and we need to stick together doing it. We need to move downhill and join the other guys." Jimbo backed down the slope, rifle raised to port, eyes trained over the front sights.

## 9

## STALKING HORSE

Dwayne halted with Chaz behind him. They could see the others turned back and moving downslope toward them at a run. he rain was pounding now, creating a susurrating din that made the world close in around them. Both Rangers raised rifles. Something was up. It all felt wrong in a sudden moment of change.

A movement to the left. Something was rushing between the trees, and Dwayne swung his rifle to cover it. A tawny shape burst from the shadows between the thick boles. It was streaked with white and black stripes from its thick neck along its barrel chest and heavily-muscled haunches. It had impossibly large yellow teeth and black-rimmed eyes. The creature ran full-out toward the Rangers. A high scream plunged to a thunderous roar as the cat raced over the ground in leaps and bounds.

There was no running away. Dwayne dug a boot sole into the sandy soil and dropped the sights on the enormous animal racing to fill his entire field of vision. He sent a long burst of rounds directly at the pair of eyes now wide and staring, eyes filled only with hunger and rage. The world slowed down as everything happened at once. He sensed rather than saw Chaz rooted close to his right also firing full auto. The heat from a muzzle flash swept over Dwayne's face. Over the noise, he could hear Chaz shouting wordless sounds.

A tremendous weight struck Dwayne hard and fast. He felt sudden vertigo as his boots left the slope. A feral smell filled his nose and mouth. Dwayne could feel himself falling and falling and was gone in an instant riding a bright white flash of pain down into darkness.

He came to with voices all around. He tried to move and felt agony claw at his side. He sucked in a lungful of air, and the pain climbed up to his neck and down to his groin like a lance of fire.

"Slow down, bro. You broke some ribs." Chaz's voice. "I'm alive, right?" Dwayne's voice was a dry croak. He opened his eyes to see the fluttering glare of a campfire.

"You're alive. Got you taped up tight. Giving you the good stuff to cut the pain. You might want to take air in little sips for a while." Chaz was adjusting an IV drip hanging from Byrus' spear stuck in the ground. Dwayne was propped up on a pair of packs. Rain spattered on a groundsheet slung above him. The downpour was a steady drizzle now.

Bat was by the fire. A big blaze stacked with timbers.

Boats was dropping new logs on top, causing white embers to rise in the dark. They were back down on the sandy clearing where they'd had the last meal he could remember. The others were unseen. They'd be away from the glare on watch.

Dwayne wondered how long he'd been out. He tried to form the words to ask Chaz. The world went all fuzzy around the edges, and he was gone again on a delicious current of painkillers dripping down the IV tube to become a consuming torrent.

---

The cat was a sabretooth. A male. An adult from Jimmy Smalls' educated guess based on the teeth. And the teeth were a wonder.

Two big tusks yellowed to an amber color. One was blunted where the point broke off in some struggle a long while back. With Byrus' help, Jimbo pulled them from the jaws of the carcass as a trophy. He presented them to a bleary Dwayne the following morning.

"These are yours, dude. You earned them," the Pima said, placing the curved fangs in Dwayne's hand.

"What did I do?"

"You did everything right. You stood your ground and unloaded. It's your damned Viking luck that two rounds went into its heart. It was stone dead when it hit you."

"I was aiming at its head."

"Yeah. That was dumb. That cat's skull bone is two inches thick. All you did was gouge its fur."

"I'll remember that next time," Dwayne said with a weak smile.

"It's my fault, Dwayne," Jimbo said.

"What?"

"I was thinking like a soldier instead of an Indian. We shouldn't have been walking point and drag, all spread out like that. We're not walking a battlefield. We're walking a hunting ground. We need to stay tight from here on."

"We lost a day, right? Let me wire my shit up, and we'll get back on the hump tomorrow." Dwayne winced as he tried to lever himself to an upright sitting position.

"You're not going anywhere but home, asshole." Lee was standing over him.

"Fuck you," Dwayne growled between clenched teeth, trying to get to a knee.

"Sure. You will fuck me. You'll fuck us all if you come along. We have a hard week-long march ahead of us at the outside. And a week back, maybe with pursuit on our ass the whole way. We're not taking you with us to turn that into a month-long clusterfuck while we nurse your broken ass along."

"There's truth in that." Dwayne nodded, resting back with teeth gritted against the fire wrapped around his ribs.

"Fucking A. We're moving east. You and the sailor head back to the beach," Lee said.

"Boats? You'll need him. I'm only a half-day from the raft."

"And how are you gonna drag it to the surf? You're busted up. You keep playing, and you'll wind up with a snapped rib in your lung," Chaz said less harshly than Hammond.

"I want you and the sailor off this op," Lee said. "That lame asshole and his bum leg were going to hold us up anyway. You cripples need to go to the showers and let us finish this."

"Yeah. Fuck. Yeah. That's the right call. Damn it," Dwayne said and spat. He didn't like giving in, leaving a fight, but this wasn't about him. It was about the unit. Pride was a killer. He had to tamp that shit down.

The others split out the bulks of Boats' and Dwayne's ammo and food packs, leaving them enough for the march back to the beach and to hold a camp there until they could get the field open again. Jimbo had already set up a recorded repeat transmission for them once they were back in range of the manifestation field area and the *Ocean Raj* thirty miles out at sea and a hundred millennia away.

Chaz had last-minute medical orders for Dwayne. "The painkillers should serve double duty as a cough suppressant. Take it easy walking back, frequent stops. You don't want those ribs slipping out of place. They're green breaks. There's no blood in your spit or piss, you're good as long as you don't do anything stupid."

"Like let a giant pussycat fall on me?" Dwayne said with a grin. Even smiling hurt.

"Like that. Let Boats make the decisions, all right? You're going to be goofy for a while."

"How fucked is my life that I'm letting that nut call the shots?"

"That hurt, bro," Boats said with a grin.

The two groups rucked up and made their farewells. The larger unit moved away toward the redwoods in a tight wedge formation. The two remaining went at a slower pace back toward the dunes. Boats dragged their packs on a travois rigged up from some sapling boles, leaving twin gouges in the sand. Dwayne walked before him at an easy pace, rifle ready and eyes focused on the tops of the dunes marching ahead of them to the surf. The fangs of the sabretooth were tucked into a cargo pocket of his pants.

———

From the dark within the tree line, two yellow eyes watched the herd of strange creatures divide. Two had cut themselves away, moving on two legs.

The female tiger lay unmoving, filling her eyes with the vision of the pair of wounded animals moving back toward the water. She filled her nose with their strange scent, the oily smell of blood and sweat and a heady mix of spice and musk. A scent unknown to her but sharp enough even to cut through the smoky fug from the guttering embers of the fire she'd watched them build the night before.

The two were out of sight in the low pines below. The others were gone into the woods up the hill. She slipped low from the ferns at the forest edge, keeping the fronds of saw grass between her and the tree line. Past the fire, the scent of animals grew stronger. Salty with a sharp tang of something unknown to her memory. And something else, an odor as familiar to her as her own. The slightest tinge of the aroma of her mate slain the day before.

She rose to lope through the grass following the twin lines in the sand with the determined pace of a predator wary of a new breed of prey.

## 10

# REVERSE ENGINEERING

Seas were at four feet under a rising wind and falling barometer. Enough to make the *Ocean Raj* pitch uncomfortably. Acting skipper Geteye got them underway in a roundabout course at ten knots, enough to make the ship's stabilizers kick in and settle the decks to a comfortable roll.

Caroline Tauber awoke from her nap when she felt the rumble of the engines through the frame of her bunk. She called the bridge to ask why they were accelerating. Geteye assured her that they would remain on station. They were on a circular cruise to nowhere.

She was awake now and decided to stay that way. The nap had been troubled with what she called work dreams. In her dream, she was working out problems on a whiteboard. The equation kept erasing itself somehow, and she raced to rewrite the symbols and numbers before they vanished again. But each time she was near to a conclusion, the board was wiped clean again by an invisible hand. It was a familiar anxiety dream for her. It usually meant she was close to some kind of breakthrough.

The main crew cabin had been transformed into a playroom for Stephen. Caroline found her son laughing at Quebat, who was in a faux argument in rapid Persian with a squirrel hand puppet. Parviz lay on a lounger, apparently engrossed in a SpongeBob cartoon on the television mounted to the bulkhead.

The pair made perfect babysitters. Maintaining the reactor that was humming away below decks wasn't much to occupy them. It could be done remotely from anywhere on board. The Iranians were bored out of their minds and eagerly volunteered to watch over Stephen whenever Caroline needed a break or to work. It was the perfect distraction for them, and the boy adored them both.

"Are you guys okay?" she asked.

"We are fine, Caroline," the squirrel answered in falsetto.

"You sure? Because I wanted to get some work in."

"We were going to give the little one lunch then down for a nap," Quebat said.

"Hummus and mashed carrots," Parviz said, turning his eyes from the television.

"Sounds yummy. So, you're good?"

"All is good. You work. We'll watch Stephen," Quebat said.

She kissed her son on the top of his head and made her way below decks to the lab area.

---

"This may get techie," Morris Tauber cautioned.

"I'll try and keep up," Caroline said.

"I'll break it down for you."

The sarcasm in her reply had eluded her brother. It always did.

Morris tapped some keys and brought up a schematic crowded with call-outs. A window was open with a dense column of numbers and symbols scrolling down it.

"The papers that Samuel gifted you have opened my mind to

some new possibilities. This is a manifestation frame I've been working on," he said.

"It's a cube," she said.

He nodded. "A perfect cube."

"So your improvement is changing the manifestation array from round to square."

"No. No! It's not a change to the tube. This is dedicated to digital transmission only. We use this to communicate with the guys instead of opening up the larger field. Less juice and a constant signal."

"What are the dimensions?" She leaned in to study the image.

"A cubic meter. Even less. Totally contained."

"And the operational window?"

"Perpetual. In theory. It doesn't rely on the gigajoule push the main Tube does. It's a soft opening allowing only two-way transmission of voice and data. We could keep it open for uninterrupted communication with anyone in the field."

"And this can be done? What changes would need to be made on the other side?" Caroline's excitement grew.

"Zero. We open it up and start transmitting." Morris smiled, pleased to see his sister's keen interest.

She gripped his shoulder and nodded, eyes on the animated schematic turning on the screen.

"This is great, Mo. A real breakthrough. What can I do to help?"

"Well, I haven't made it upstairs in a while. I could use a sandwich."

He rocked forward under a sudden slap to the back of his head.

"Engineers. Get your own goddamn sandwich," Caroline said. She prodded him out of his chair to take his place at the keyboard.

## 11

# THE WAY AHEAD

The drone settled back to the ground, almost at Jimbo's feet. He shared the data he'd recorded with the team.

"This pass is the most direct route. See it there? The opening is four klicks east by south of here." He traced the snaking pathway between peaks with his finger on the screen.

"We'll have to pathfind it," Lee said.

Jimbo nodded. "No GPS in The Then. The only satellite up there is the Moon."

"Tree cover goes all the way to the peaks. Looks like Burma," Lee said.

"Feels like Burma. Thicker air. Warmer and wetter. The canopy goes all the way to the top."

"No relief from the bugs then." Bat waved a hand to part a cloud of gnats.

"We can make another ten or fifteen. Thirty for the day.

Make camp on higher ground," Lee said.

"And wring out our undies," Chaz added.

The dense air and high humidity were taking a toll. Their CamelBaks were near empty, and they gobbled salt tabs like candy. The branches above dripped with fresh rainfall, nowhere near enough for a refill. Jimbo used his nose for water on the march up the slope but found only a few stagnant pools. At one pool, they startled a herd of animals that looked like short-haired alpacas with drooping proboscises. The odds were good they'd find a spring or stream further into the San Gabriels. If not, they'd have to stop and waste march time looking for potable water alongside trails.

"You ever think of a unit name? I mean, what do we call ourselves?" Bat said from a broad shelf of rock, waiting for the others to catch up.

"Like the 'Time Rangers' or some shit like that?" Chaz handed the drone case up to her.

"Yeah. A little *esprit de corps*. A patch or something," she said.

"We just call ourselves 'the guys,'" Chaz said. He levered up onto the ledge, helped along by a hand from Bat.

"Well, that's not exactly accurate anymore, is it?" She smiled.

"You need to forget about a unit patch, babe. This outfit is need-to-know," Lee said, clambering up after Chaz.

By late afternoon they were well into the mountain range along the selected trail. It turned out to be a dry wash with stunted pines growing close on either side. The climb up was an exhausting series of steps from one ledge of stone to another. The sky cleared, and the sun could reach them now. Each of them had their own cloud of evaporating sweat rising off their clothes. Only Byrus seemed unaffected, hopping from rock to rock and barely breaking a sweat.

Jimbo stopped and spat a pebble from his mouth. He hooked his thumbs in his ruck straps and lifted them off his shoulders for a few seconds of relief. He sniffed the air, taking a deep breath through his nose. He opened his mouth and let it out to take in a slow, shallow breath over his tongue to taste the air.

"Water," he said and pointed right into the trees.

"We'll follow your nose," Lee said.

The team moved into the trees where the shade provided some relief from the heat but not much. It was green and dark with a thick odor of rotting wood from the surrounding foliage. Their heads moved on swivels, on constant watch for movement of any kind.

Bat was startled when a shadow separated itself from the immense bole of a sequoia. She hissed to the others and raised her rifle. The shadow rose on hind legs to a height of ten feet or more. It was covered in thick fur. Its massive body tapered to a narrow skull and teeth chomping lazily. It leaned on the bark of the tree and regarded her with gleaming dark eyes. Bat turned her gaze at a deep purring sound and saw that others of this same species were all around them quietly munching on fungus they stripped from the bark of the trees with foot-long claws and curved flat teeth.

"Sloths. They're not interested in us," Jimbo said in a low voice. Byrus stood by him with eyes wide, whites showing all around.

The giant creatures lost interest in the strangers and returned to feeding as the team moved by in single file.

A twenty-minute hike brought them to a large pool at the base of a rock face fed by a spring. Creatures fled into the thick carpet of ferns on their approach. Bat spotted one before it vanished, a wingless bird about two feet in height. A ridge of iridescent blue feathers ran along its spine. They left three-toed tracks in the thick mud around the basin.

Jimbo tested the water and announced it drinkable. Chaz knelt on a moss-covered slab of rock at the edge and dunked his whole head in the ice-cold pool. They ran it through a filter to refill their CamelBaks and reserve canteens. They drank their fill and topped off all the containers before departing.

"Where are we, Zim?" Byrus asked as they returned to the

trail. The Macedonian could not get his tongue around a soft "J" sound so "Zim" was the best he could do.

"It's called California. The other side of these mountains is Nevada. That's where we're going," Jimbo said.

"Not Tartarii?" Byrus said, his head turning and eyes sweeping the trees before and behind them.

"No. Tartar-eye? What is that, Bruce?"

"Land of dead men. Many *chamaloph*. Many *zhulomiphica*." Byrus searched Jimbo's eyes with fearful wonder.

"You mean Tartarus. Like Hell. An evil place," Jimbo said. Byrus nodded.

"It's not like that, Bruce. Everything is cool, okay? Fucking A, all right?" Jimbo clapped a hand to his neck.

"Fucking A," Byrus repeated without conviction.

They regained the trail and continued their inland march.

---

"Nothing like a day at the beach," Boats said.

"And no surfers. What beach you think this is?" Dwayne said.

"Hermosa? Redondo? Wait long enough, and Brad Pitt will give you a million bucks for where you're standing." Boats shrugged out of his t-shirt and Molle vest.

The SEAL was setting up the transmitter while Dwayne unpacked goods that they'd need including groundsheets and food packs. They found an open section of sand above a tidal pool with a clear field of view in all directions. Rollers were coming in with crowds of birds hopping and skittering in the shallows. It was a short walk to the concealed boat and they were well clear of high tide. It was as good a place to wait as any. With any luck, the field back to The Now would open, and they'd schedule an extraction.

"Don't push it, soldier. You're busted up, remember?" Boats said.

"I sit too long I'll get stiff. Better to stay on the move," Dwayne said. It had been a long, painful walk, but he wasn't about to give in to it.

"I hear you. You listen for any calls while I go to the boat. There's a freshwater tank. We'll need it."

"I can manage setting up some sun cover before you get back."

"Sounds like a plan," Boats said and set out along the sand for the dunes. He had his shotgun held easy in one hand, and both their CamelBaks slung over his shoulder.

The SEAL climbed the slope of sand and down into the gully between two high dunes. Little birds, gray and white, fluttered out of the grass. They kept up a chittering sound in protest at his passage and continued with tweets and trills, creating a vivid soundtrack all around. He followed the winding floor of the gully north until he came on the covered shape of the raft, undisturbed since they left it. He pried up a few pegs and lifted the camo cover. Some lizards slithered from inside to run away into the brush.

Boats was filling the CamelBaks from the reserve freshwater tank on the side of the Titan when he sensed a change around him. The shotgun was in his fists before he realized it. His eyes scanned the ridgeline. He asked himself what was different.

The birds.

The birds were silent now.

He dropped low and eyeballed the ridgelines on either side of the gully.

A shape rose from the peak of the inland dune away to the south. Fifty yards. Maybe less.

It was a big cat sliding cautiously into the gully. It was like the one Roenbach brought down but sleeker. It was shy of the half-ton weight of that monster but not by much. The thick tuft of white hair at the throat was missing on this one.

A female.

The mate of the cat they'd killed.

Boats jerked upright, shotgun to his shoulder. He loosed a load of double-ought, but the creature was already on the move. Pump and pull. A rifled slug raised a gout of sand behind the tiger as it raced up the slope back the way it came. He chambered another round, but his target was slipping over the ridge and out of sight.

The SEAL didn't stop to see what the cat did next. He had to get out of this slot where he was blind in two directions. He slung the CamelBaks and climbed up over the seaward dune and down to open sand where he broke the land speed record for running backward while covering his own ass.

Dwayne was up with his M4 at port and covering Boats' six as he approached the camp by the tidal pool at a limping run.

"I heard your shotgun," Dwayne said.

"That big cat you offed? He had a girlfriend, and she is a stone-cold bitch," Boats said once his breath had returned.

## 12

## BAD NEWS

"You need to see this, Morris," Caroline Tauber said.

Mo moved from his workstation with a great deal of reluctance to look over his sister's shoulder at one of those click-bait "news" websites on her monitor.

"Seriously, Sis?" He sighed.

"Look," she demanded.

He leaned closer, lowering his glasses to scan the text below a picture of a smiling kid in glasses and a hipster goatee holding up a slab of petrified dirt the size of a dinner plate.

"Oh, no," he said.

# GOOGLED

I t was a slow news day.

That's the only reason the news outlets picked up a story more suited for the wackier of the tabloids.

Lawrence Fonseca, a student at Ball State University, claimed that a fossilized bird track in his collection had been altered in a rather amazing way. The tracks were of bird called a *rhea mexicanus*, a type of prehistoric ostrich common in the southwestern United States and throughout Central America in the Pleistocene period, and now long extinct.

Larry found the perfectly preserved pair of tracks on the floor of a wash following a heavy rain. It was on a high school trip to California with a paleontology club he only joined because he was smitten with Felicia Danby, the club's vice president. The oversized chicken tracks caused a lot of excitement in the group and brought Larry a lot of attention. Felicia even let him get to third base in her tent that night.

The admiration of the club fellows and Felicia's affection for him faded once they got back to Evansville. All fame is fleeting, he found out. No one really cared all that much about some zillion-year-old chicken prints. He had the flat square-ish section of limestone mounted in a shadow box display case. It went along with him to college where it sat on a shelf with his Ninja Turtles action figures and a signed Derek Jeter baseball. It was a conversation starter, but the conversations never went much further than "that's cool." After a while, Larry stopped pointing it out to visitors to his off-campus apartment on the second floor of a duplex on Winthrop Road.

Until a girl he met in his Organizational Principles of Business class promised to come over and make him a spaghetti dinner. Larry went into a flurry of dusting and vacuuming and general cleaning in preparation for her arrival. Mostly the tidying amounted to stowing all of his unsightly shit in Rubbermaids down in the chicken-wire "locker" in the basement that came with the apartment. Removing his collectibles from the Ikea shelf in order to dust it, he came across the shadow box containing the pair of primordial bird tracks.

Only it was different now.

Overtop of the millennia-old tracks was the unmistakable imprint of a waffle-stomper boot sole. He could even clearly read part of the company logo preserved in the prehistoric mud. He Googled "boots, hiking, brands" and identified it as a women's boot made by Vasque. Size eight.

Larry did what any millennial does when confronted by the confounding or the discovery of anything of even mild passing interest. He took a picture of it and put it on Facebook. His friends' responses predictably ranged from "WTF?" to "What have u bin smokin?" But the post was re-posted over and over until it reached the section of the internet community fascinated with Big Foot and Area 51. A bored reader at Associated Press picked it up, and the next day a local TV station came and put Larry on the air holding up his amazing find mixed in with B-roll lifted from Jurassic Park. It was all enough to get him laid a couple of times, and his curiosity ended there.

He forgot all about it until his phone rang at two in the morning.

"Lawrence Fonseca?" A woman's voice.

"Yeah. I'm kind of busy." He was cramming for a final in accounting.

"I wanted to talk to you about what happened to you last week."

He panicked. Was this about Angela or what's-her-name, the spaghetti making girl? Was this an angry mom?

"The fossil. The one you claim changed overnight. I wanted to speak to you about it. I represent a foundation with an interest in that area of study."

"Oh, okay." Larry sighed in relief.

The woman on the other end of the line, who Larry decided sounded way sexy now that he knew she wasn't a pissed off parent, asked about where he'd found the fossil originally. He told her generally. It was at the south end of a park in the San Gabriels four summers ago. She asked details about the original bird prints and the new boot print. She asked if it had been tested in any way, such as carbon dating.

"Naw. I just put it up on Facebook. Talked to some TV people. No one asked to look at it like that," he said.

"I'd like to do extensive tests on it to prove its authenticity."

"Oh, it's authentic, all right. I thought some of my friends were fooling with me. But, trust me, none of them are smart enough to fake something like this."

"I'll be sending a representative to see you in the morning. Will you be home?"

"I don't have classes until afternoon but, hold on, you want to take the fossil?"

"To study, yes."

"I'm not so sure about that. I don't want to just give it away like that," Larry said.

"Oh, we're prepared to buy the specimen from you," the cool sexy voice said.

"Yeah? How much?"

"What do you owe on your student loan?"

"That much?"

"Will our representative see you in the morning?"

"Bet your ass, lady," Larry said, grinning.

The line went dead.

## 14

## THE CIRCLE OF FIRE AND BLOOD

"I can handle this part on my own, Dwayne," Boats said.

"What am I supposed to do? Sit here shitting my pants until the cat comes back?" Dwayne took overwatch.

He perched atop a dune with his M4 charged and a scope attached. Below him, Boats worked at cutting away scrub pines and dragging them back to their camp. It was part of the strategy they'd worked out together. They agreed that the sabretooth was not going to let them go. As long as she stayed on the stalk, they couldn't move the raft down to the surf. They were in her hunting ground now. If they were ever leaving this beach, the she-cat had to die first.

Boats chopped and dragged double time, making brush piles on the sand around their camp. The sun was dropping. They needed everything in place before dark. No one knew the hunting habits of these cats. They were extinct long before any written language was created. No one had recorded observing them in the wild. The Ranger and the SEAL would be learning as they went along. But it was a good guess that this animal hunted like other big cats.

By night.

They needed to contact the *Raj* and get home. The clock was ticking. Dwayne would never let Boats know, but his ribs hurt like hell. It hurt every time he drew in a breath. He'd be no good in a protracted fight. And he'd seen enough battlefield rib injuries turn to pneumonia to not kid himself about his chances if he didn't get some help pretty soon. The bandages were holding him in place, and he had his Molle vest cinched as tight as he could stand it. But he knew he needed more extensive medical attention. The sooner they killed this cat and got the raft deployed, the sooner they could radio back at the first field opening.

His eyes swept the dunes for movement. A flurry of birds rose in a rush from between dunes. Dwayne trained the rifle their way, focusing through the scope on the ridgeline. The birds flew honking overhead to drop in a group to the shallow water of the tidal pool. There was no movement from the deepening shadows in the gulfs between the sand peaks. The tops of the thick brush swayed. That could have been the evening wind building off the Pacific.

Dwayne turned at a low whistle. A new spear of pain shot up into his armpit. He swallowed it down. Boats stood at the foot of the dune with the shotgun in his fists. The SEAL nodded toward the camp and raised the pump gun to cover him as he came down from his perch. They both backed toward the camp, eyes locked on the dunes for any motion in the growing shadows. The sea was swirling copper and cream under the lowering sun behind them throwing their shadows long on the sand.

Boats had six stacks of brush and dry seagrass spaced around their camp. As it grew darker, they lit them using splashes of tequila from the SEAL's ever-present flask. The fires threw off little light but lots of greasy smoke. That was the idea.

"You don't mind being bait?" Boats said.

Dwayne stood in the center of the circle of smoldering piles. "It's me she wants. It's my scent she followed."

"Then let's go hunting," Boats said and slid the night-vision gear down over his eyes. He was wearing the full array of four lenses that made him look like a big bearded bug. He backed away toward the surf and the outer dark.

"Uh-huh," Dwayne said and fixed his own binocular NODs lenses down.

The dark and the smoke were both wiped away as filtered through the lenses. A digitized image area showed him the world in high-contrast monochrome. The dunes looked like ranks of drifted snow now. He turned back and forth, panning and scanning. Tiny eyes glowed like pinholes in the greater wash of glare. Some kind of nocturnal feeders, dozens of them, prehistoric possums curious about the new scent on the beach.

Dwayne's hands were slick on the grips of the shotgun. He blinked sweat from his eyes. Even the night wind off the water did nothing to relieve the cloying humidity. Jesus, it was hot here. The sand beneath his feet was cooling, but the air was so damned thick. Breathing was like drawing air through a straw. He forced himself to breathe shallowly to keep the view through the lenses steady.

The plan was simple. The fires would provide enough light to throw off the she-tiger's night vision and the smoke would interfere with her sense of smell. The NODs should allow them to see her before she saw them. And they'd need every foot of distance that advantage could provide them. The male that collided with Dwayne was half a football field away when he came into view. It was only pure dumb luck that let Dwayne nail the bastard. That kind of luck was scarce.

The pairs of eyes dotting the shadows at the foot of the dunes vanished in an instant.

The possums were on the move all at once.

A gray shape topped a dune far to his right. It dropped away into a gully and appeared again crossing a hummock still to his right and closer in. He trained the front bead of the Mariner on the next closest ridge of sand where the shape might reappear. It surprised him by flashing over the dune just left of his aiming point. It was the cat all right. Less bulky than the one he'd killed like Boats described. That probably meant the she-cat was faster. He recalled from nature specials he'd watched as a kid that the female was often the more skilled hunter. One row of dunes separated them, and when she came out on the open sand, she'd be less than a hundred yards from where he stood.

He waited, eyes locked on the high drift. Shifting left and right over the front sight of the shotgun. He kept his finger resting on the trigger guard. Dwayne was only supposed to discharge the twelve-gauge loaded with slugs if the cat made it into the ring of fires. He was bait. The kill shot belonged to the SEAL watching from somewhere in the dark. The wind shifted, and piney smoke found its way up his nose. He shut his eyes and fought down the urge to cough. His throat spasmed. He swallowed hard. One cough would bring an agony that would drop him to his knees, making him helpless. He lowered his head and bit down hard to fight the reflex back. His eyes swam with tears that blurred the image coming through the lenses. He tore the NODs rack from his head.

A rifle shot sounded behind him. Then a second and third.

"Contact left!" Boats' voice boomed behind him.

Dwayne turned in time to see the tiger loping easy through the wreath of smoke. The cat stopped as though surprised to see him. Its tawny fur was matted with dark blood along one side. It shook its head, causing crimson-flecked foam to fly from its fangs before setting its baleful gaze on Dwayne. The eyes were the size of silver dollars in the flickering light and a hand-length apart. Even though it was smaller than the male he'd faced earlier in the day, Dwayne was taken aback by the size and power of the animal. It seemed impossibly huge.

The muscles quivered along its flanks as it lowered its head.

Dwayne didn't bother raising the shotgun to his shoulder. He fired and pumped and was about to fire again. Something struck him between the shoulders, and he fell hard to the sand on his right. A fresh spear of pain burned into his side.

He was fighting to remain conscious. Boats stood over him, bellowing to match the roar of the charging cat. The M4 in his fist was stabbing the night with flame. In the quivering light, the eagle tattooed on the SEAL's arm looked like it was flapping furiously to stay aloft.

Dwayne saw it all strobing in slow motion as he struggled against the night closing in around him. The night won in the end as the dark shut everything out except the staccato explosions and animal shrieks. Even they died away into the silence, leaving him to wonder which predator was making those ungodly noises.

He rose out of the darkness to the sound of lapping water. He lay back on a surface that was gently rising and falling. With an exhausting effort, he raised his head. Boats stood above him, piloting the Titan under a blue sky.

"Your blood," Dwayne croaked.

"What's that, brother?" Boats turned from the wheel.

"Thought it was your blood. On the cat."

"I winged it on the fly. Put one through a lung."

"Oh," was all Dwayne could manage.

"Sorry for checking you, bro. You were between me and the target."

"We're going back?" Dwayne's mouth was all cotton.

"Yeah. The Taubers have a little surprise for us." The SEAL grinned.

Dwayne pursed his lips to speak. His tongue felt like it had an anchor lying on it.

"Hey, I shot you up with painkillers. Why don't you let me do the driving while you enjoy the ride?"

Dwayne decided to do just that.

## 15

# HARD CHEESE

"This is your kind of country, Jimmy," Chaz said.

Jimbo shook his head. "Naw. No horses."

"Looks like horse country to me," Chaz said. "Beautiful horse country, but no horses. Not here. Only horses in the world right now are in Asia. The ones that were here were the size of dogs. They died out millions of years ago. I saw them in the books."

"So we walk." Chaz shrugged.

"That's what soldiers do. Hump. Hump. Hump." Jimbo led the way.

The team reached the open country after two days of picking their way through the San Gabriels. Heavy rain turned their chosen trail into a rushing mountain stream. They climbed above it to follow a goat track through a higher altitude. After two nights of wet camps, they came down the other side in the general area of what would be Victorville someday. Instead of a high desert of rocks and sand, there was a rolling prairie of tall grass that stretched east as far as they could see.

It rained. A lot. The only difference was whether it rained all day or part of the day. Even on the days that began dry with clear skies, by afternoon, clouds would form against the distant Pahute

Mesa and drop anything from a light drizzle to a steady down-pour on them. Water wasn't going to be a problem for them here. Every depression turned to a waterhole, and every waterhole presented its own dangers. The rich grassland was home to hundreds of species of animals. The variety of avian life alone was a distraction. Birds of all sizes and colors moved over the stalks in dizzying patterns, snapping up bugs or feeding on seeds. Wingless species hopped and skittered underfoot.

Of the larger creatures, the mammoths were easiest to avoid since the team could spot them moving slowly, towering above the tops of the grass. Chaz and Jimbo had experience with the huge elephants from their first trip back to The Then. They adjusted their path to give the shaggy monsters a wide berth.

The drone revealed other wildlife hidden by grass or grazing deep in hollows. There were camel-like herbivores and tiny deer. They even saw something that could be best described as a furry rhinoceros. The most problematic was a species of long-horned bison. They looked like a Texas steer crossed with a buffalo. The scale app on the drone put them at ten feet at the shoulder. Monsters.

Jimbo worked the controller to drop the drone for a closer look. A big bull raised his head from grazing to see what was buzzing just above him. The eyes of the animal were rimmed in white and staring right into the drone's lens. The bull snorted and bucked and turned its head to gouge the air with its six-foot horns. Jimbo pulled the drone up to take in a broader area. The bull bucked and kicked and gored the cow closest to it. The curved horn stabbed deep into the cow's ribs. Gushing blood, it took off into the heart of the packed herd. That began a general panic that set the herd running.

Though the stampede was miles away, the team could feel a tremor through their feet.

"Which way are they moving?" Bat asked, glancing east toward a cloud of yellow dust rising in the sky.

"Away from us. We're okay here," Jimbo said, eyes on the monitor set on his controller. He pulled the drone up to one thousand feet. The charging bison filled the screen, countless animals on the hoof rushing over the rough ground in an unstoppable panic. The herd numbered in the tens of thousands. The head of the stampede was twenty acres across. Nothing in its way could possibly survive that panicked flight.

Lee said, "We're going to have to keep an eye on them. Any way to predict their movements?"

"Well, even though most critters here are bigger in size than we're used to, they have smaller brains than the animals we know. They're more primitive, more specialized. The simplest way to think about it is to think of the animals we know only back here they're bigger, dumber, and meaner," Jimbo said, eyes on the horizon watching the drone grow from a speck against the sky.

"So, best advice?" Lee said.

"We make avoiding the herds of those bastards our first priority. We get in the way of one of their rushes, and there's nowhere to run and no place to hide." Jimbo brought the drone in for a landing.

"Anything else we need to look out for?" Chaz said.

A yipping sound came from the other side of a hummock. It was joined by others and grew to an extended howling sound that receded away toward the cloud of dust dropping away to the north.

"Everything." Jimbo shrugged.

---

They chose the crest of a hill to make camp. The high ground provided them some protection from whatever prowled outside the feeble light of their campfire. Beyond that, the tundra was a flowing silvery sea under a half-moon hanging above, magnified by the dense atmosphere to appear unnaturally large.

The campfire was a sad thing. Byrus built it for them from greasewood he uprooted from around a muddy wallow. It provided more smoke than fire. When it burnt down to embers, the heat was just enough to warm the water they needed to rehydrate their meal packs.

Lee stood first watch using NODs lenses.

"What can you see?" Bat asked. She'd come from the fire to hand him a mug of lukewarm coffee.

"Some kind of dogs. They checked us out and went back into the grass," Lee said.

He didn't tell her they left two of their number behind. The pack numbered at least the forty-four he could count. Two males sat at the foot of the hill with glowing silver eyes fixed on Lee. They had lean bodies like coyotes and broader heads with short snouts packed with teeth. They sat panting in the heat and sniffing the air as if they were waiting for a treat.

"This is a lonely place," Bat said, patting down grass with her boots and taking a seat by him.

"You like lonely places. I've spent more time camping in Godforsaken places with you than I did in the Army."

"That's different. I can be in the mountains or the desert and know there's still people, cities, malls."

"Your problem is there's no shopping here?" Lee said. He turned to look down at her, ghostly in the artificial light coming through his lenses. She punched his knee playfully.

"Don't be a smartass. You know what I mean. This place. It's alien. Or *we're* alien in it. There's nothing we know here. In the whole world, there's no one like us and won't be for a long time. It's not like when we went back to Roman Judea. There were people there."

"They weren't like us, Bat."

"Sure they were. They were like us in every way that's important." She turned to look up at him, a purple shadow against the black sky.

"I guess that's why we're here." Lee turned, twin lenses flashing.

"Yeah?"

"Imagine how lonely Renzi is," he said.

---

"You think we'll run into more of those big cats?" Chaz said, scraping the last of some rice pilaf with chicken from the pack in his hand.

"I'm sure there's some out here. Not sure they'll mess with us," Jimbo said. The Pima sat sharpening the long blade of his knife on a whetstone. Byrus laid curled up and fast asleep by the fire, his hands wrapped around the haft of the spear.

"Why not?"

"That male tiger Dwayne killed? It had a bad tooth. Remember the broken tusk I pulled? Probably sick with pain. Thing like that slows a predator down. They take to hunting smaller prey or wounded animals."

"I think I read that somewhere." Chaz nodded and took the last spoonful in his mouth.

"There's so much game on the ground here. Like a buffet for an animal that big. They'd rather bring down one of those buffalo or a camel than mess with us."

"We're like that last piece of cold pizza in the fridge when your hangover's so bad you can't think of leaving the house," Chaz said, licking the spoon clean.

"Week-old piece of pepperoni with the cheese hard as clay left in the box on the counter."

"That bad?"

"Man survived because we emit pheromones that smell bad to most animals. The only animal that can really stand to be around us are dogs. The only animal that will eat us is one that's too old, too sick, or too slow to kill something else." Jimbo aimed a stream of spit onto the sharpening stone.

A series of yips turned into a mournful keening somewhere out in the dark.

"Like those dogs?" Chaz said, nodding toward the sound as more throats joined the invisible chorus.

"No, brother. Those dogs will try for us as soon as they get their courage up." Jimbo slid the blade back and forth across the stone in a whispering rhythm.

Byrus, lying near the fire, farted long and loud without waking.

Jimbo winced. "Well, maybe not Bruce."

## 16

# THE BABYSITTER

The chopper, an Alouette painted in an outrageous scheme of Day-Glo lime green and screaming blue, settled onto the makeshift helo-deck that the *Raj's* crew fashioned from plywood and bolted down atop the mountain of Conex boxes stacked on the main deck.

Dwayne fought about getting on the gurney, but Caroline insisted.

"You want me to knock you flat with some more painkillers?" she said.

"All right. I'll be a good patient," he said and allowed the paramedics off the chopper to strap him in tight.

A call had been made to a reliable off-the-books clinic in Mexico. They had a team ready to take x-rays and scans and fit Dwayne with a cast if needed or surgery if it came to that. Caroline had a handbag full of cash and was going with him. First, she had some directions for Boats.

"The line is open now for a constant, direct digital signal through a permanent field opening," she said hastily.

"You rig that up since we left?" the SEAL said.

"By our reckoning, it's been two weeks since you manifested.

We had downtime to do some tinkering. Morris came up with the idea. The next time the team checks in tell them about it. It allows for voice, text, and data and operates just like any transmitter."

"Morris can run me through it."

"Morris is away for a few days. Something came up he has to take care of. Thanks for bringing Dwayne back in one piece." She rose on tiptoes to kiss his furry cheek before running for the open bay door of the chopper as they finished loading her husband. The EMY+Ts helped her on board and pulled the hatch shut.

Boats backed away from the cyclonic prop wash and watched the chopper go nose down south for the Mexican coast over the horizon.

"Shit. I forgot to ask who's taking care of the baby," the SEAL said.

## 17

## MEET MR. TAAN

Morris Tauber found the address on a street shaded with mature junipers and poplars, filled with older houses converted into apartments between squat apartment buildings from the Seventies.

He chose a route from the airport that would take him through the Ball State campus on his way to Larry Fonseca's place. Morris had never seen a state college before. His scholarships had taken him to the top schools in the United States and Europe. He drove past the usual neo-classical piles of marble and brick built a century ago.

There were also rec centers and natatoriums and an outdoor rock-climbing center. All was surrounded by acres of parking lots that reminded Morris more of a mall than a center for higher learning. He honestly couldn't recall if any of the institutes he'd attended had any form of recreation. His grueling lecture and lab schedule had consumed all of his time,and whatever was left over was spent at the library or on his laptop. Oxford might have had a miniature golf course and a go-cart track, and he'd never have known it.

He pulled the rental car into an empty slot before a two-story duplex. He pressed the button for apartment number three. The slapping of bare feet on stairs and the door was yanked open by the same young man who appeared smiling in pictures in all the stories about his amazing discovery.

"Yeah?" Larry Fonseca said. He wasn't smiling now. His eyes were sunken and rimmed red. He wore a stretched-out concert t-shirt and sleep pants.

"I called earlier? Kenneth Armbruster," Morris said.

"I already sold it," the kid said and started to close the door.

"Already sold it?" Morris almost shouted it.

"Sorry." The kid shrugged and continued to push the door closed.

Morris put a hand out to press the door open.

"You told me you'd sell it to me. I thought we had an agreement."

"You got outbid. What can I say? Sorry." The kid put a shoulder to the door, and it slammed hard enough to make the frame shudder. Footfalls climbed the stairs within.

Morris stood uncertain about what to do. Should he knock and bring Fonseca back to the door? Would the little bastard share with him the identity of the buyer?

He stepped off the front stoop to return to his rental. Maybe if he offered Fonseca some of the cash from the stash packed in the steel briefcase in the trunk of the rental. Maybe then he'd cooperate. He now regretted not making a cash offer over the phone. The stupid kid probably sold it on eBay for peanuts. Morris was willing and able to go to seven figures.

With a fresh gush of courage, he turned to go back and pound on the door to number three until the kid came back. He wasn't going back to Caroline empty-handed. Dwayne and the others could brave the horrors of the past and come back victorious. He should be able to fly to Indiana and back to buy a paleontological oddity.

"Dr. Tauber?" a polite voice said behind him.

An Asian man, Chinese or Japanese, in a splendidly tailored dark suit, stood on the walk with hands folded before him. He smiled at Morris from behind tinted glasses.

"You are Dr. Morris Tauber? Am I correct?" The man spoke in perfect English with a disconcerting trace of an Australian accent.

"Um, I am," Morris answered.

A black SUV with deeply tinted windows sat on the street athwart the parking space where the rental sat. Morris turned from the polite man with the Paul Hogan accent.

A second Asian man, a much larger one in an equally splendid suit, emerged from around the corner of the duplex to block his way. This man was not smiling.

Morris stood between the men as they closed on him. He held up his hands.

"Look, I don't have it. The kid said he sold it."

"He did. He sold it to us," the smiling man said.

"Okay. Then we're done here, right? I'll just walk away."

"We would be pleased to offer you a ride," the smiling man said. Behind him, a third man in a dark suit opened the rear door of the SUV and stood by with hands at his sides.

Morris thought about arguing that he had his own ride, but decided it was irrelevant to the conversation.

He went with them without protest.

Larry Fonseca watched from the window of his bedroom as the Chinese guys loaded the bespectacled, bearded guy into the back of their Suburban.

"He's gone. I did what you asked. We're done here, right?"

The two well-dressed men who'd been keeping him company since last night stood now. They wore vinyl gloves that he hadn't noticed before.

"Oh shit," Larry said.

## 18

# MONSTERS OF THE SWAMP

"*Ocean Raj* to the Lone Rangers."

Jimbo was surprised when the radio squawked to life with Boats' voice coming from the speaker. The drone was hovering at its maximum altitude of five thousand feet to act as a relay antenna to extend the range for their latest attempt to reach the ship out in the Pacific a thousand millennia from when they were.

"Is that you Boats?" he said keying the set.

"Bet your ass, Cochise. Surprised?" The voice was coming through in digital clarity.

"I wasn't expecting to reach you live."

"We're live twenty-four and seven, bro. The Taubers built a brand new rig that keeps a hole punched to your twenty on a permanent basis."

"The field is open all the time?" Jimbo said and turned to Chaz who was squinting at him puzzled.

"Just a small window. Enough to transmit and receive. We can be in constant contact. What's your sit-rep?"

"We're past Barstow halfway to Fort Irwin. Remember that place?"

"That shithole? I did desert training there. What's it like?"

"Nothing like you'd remember," Jimbo said. The team had reached the top of the broad mesa leading to the higher country of Nevada. He could see the endless expanse of the primordial prairie they'd spent two days crossing. Ahead of them was a forest of beech, poplar, and tall pines. The landscape bore no resemblance to the arid wastelands of the Mojave Desert that would one day be here.

"You're making good progress. Any complications?"

"A wild dog pack followed us most of yesterday. We turned them back with a twenty mil. Haven't seen them since," Jimbo said, recalling the harrowing day of watching the extended pack loping along their flanks as they marched. By evening, the dogs were coming close enough to smell, growing bolder as the sun went down. Lee let a 20mm grenade loose into the thick of the pack. It sent a half-dozen dogs flying to bits. The others took off in a race with their own asses. Lee sent a second grenade looping after them to let them know the first one wasn't an accident. They camped that night without hearing a single bark from the pack.

"You guys extracted okay, right? How's Dwayne?" Jimbo asked.

"He's with a doc in Ensenada. He and Caroline should be back on board in the next few days. You going to be able to stay in contact?"

"Only when I have the juice to send up the drone. Once a day at most. I have to bring it down now to conserve the battery."

"We'll be here listening. Happy hunting, chief. Hope you find your friend soon. *Ocean Raj* out."

"Rangers out." Jimbo broke the connection and set the drone on a return course earthward.

The trees of the forest atop the mesa thinned out toward the end of the following day. The ground was pitching away into a valley below. The hillside was dominated by thick hedges of berry bushes that Jimbo warned them against picking. The drone revealed that the bush country went on for miles to the east. It was impassable on foot with growth above eye level and spiked with long thorns. An impenetrable barricade of vines alive with the chittering and caws of birds overhead and within.

They camped at the edge of the wall of berry bushes and awoke the next morning to find themselves in the center of a herd of moose quietly munching on the fruit and leaves along the hedge line. Jimbo was on morning watch and never heard the enormous creatures moving toward them through a soupy morning fog. He moved among the team, waking them as gently as he could, and whispering a warning to break camp without startling the herd.

The largest of the moose were twelve foot at the shoulder, and some had racks of antlers easily that wide across. The calves were the size of modern adults. They turned their heads lazily to watch the Rangers, Bat, and Byrus move at a slow walk in a line through them. With little curiosity, the antlered monsters surrendered to the lure of the sweet berries and returned to feeding.

"Jesus, I thought regular moose were big. Those were Moosezillas," Chaz whispered when they were well clear of the last of the herd.

"We are damned lucky the females had calved. If we showed up in mating season or when the cows were carrying, we'd be dead now," Jimbo said.

"They're so cute," Bat said.

"Cute, my ass," Jimbo said. "One of those fuckers would stomp you to a greasy spot. They're calm as hell most of the time but can be killers depending on the season."

The team stopped long enough to wolf down some protein bars and secure their gear after the hasty decamp. Jimbo unpacked the drone and sent it aloft to find a dry wash that led through the thick brush in a generally northern course into rocky ground and down the back slope off the mesa.

The trail was narrow and covered over in spots by a bower of bushes. The hedge around them blocked any movement in the air. Even though the path was an easy one and carried them downhill, they were gasping for air and drenched in new sweat. In addition, the insects were even more punishing here. They became used to the constant buzzing cloud around them and the feathery touch of wings on every inch of open skin.

Swarms of birds hopped from branch to branch on either side of them, cackling defiantly overhead or from the protection of the thicket of thorns. At one point, they had to halt entirely to allow a herd of wild pigs, the same kind they'd met in the dunes, to trot before them before disappearing again, grunting and squealing, into a gap in the bushes.

"What do you call a herd of pigs? Herd isn't right, right? That's for cows?" Bat said.

"I've heard drove or passel," Jimbo offered.

"In Alabama, we call a bunch of swine a sounder," Chaz said.

"I call it barbecue," Lee said.

---

They emerged from the thicket where it ended in broken ground falling away from the mesa. A welcome breeze rose up the slope. They stripped out of their packs and took seats on flat rocks strewn among the field of scree. Below was a flat plain with forested hills rising miles beyond. The broad valley, torn in the earth by the passage of glaciers in an earlier epoch, was thick with vegetation. The afternoon sun created a silvery sheen in the open areas between copses of thick cane growth.

"It's a marsh. It stands between us and the lake where we left Rick," Jimbo announced to the team as he eyed the screen on the drone controller. Byrus crouched by him, gripping the haft of the spear and sniffing the air.

"Is there a way around?" Lee peered over his shoulder at the miles of wetland stretching beneath the drone hovering stationary a half-mile out over the valley.

"I can't tell how deep it is or what the bottom's like. It could be a flood plain or swampland. No way to tell from here. Best plan is to follow the ridge we're on south to try and find a way around it." Jimbo jinked the drone onto a southerly course to where the valley narrowed.

"They're crossing it," Chaz pointed down to where a line of figures moved across the shallows.

Jimbo raised his glasses and found a long column of some species of camel plodding through the muddy water that reached midway up their legs. The single-file herd left a wake of mocha latte mud behind them as their feet disturbed the silt floor of the wetland.

"They weigh more than us. That means the bottom is solid. The water would be thigh deep for us." Jimbo lowered his scopes and turned to the others.

"Okay. If it takes a couple of days off the march, I say we go wading," Lee said.

"Zim," Byrus said and pointed the tip of his spear down at the camels.

Dark shapes were gliding through the shallows on a direct course toward the line of camels. Partly submerged, they moved at speed on a deliberate path to intercept the column. Seven or more of them were piloting from the reeds out into the open water.

"Alligators?" Bat said.

Jimbo found them through the binoculars. The shapes were black and, judging from the scale of the camels, were six or more feet in length with shiny, sleek coats. Their heads were blunt, and they lacked the elongated bodies of gators or crocs. Their passage created nothing more than gentle ripples in the dark water. The animals glided without effort and no visible means of propulsion. They were moving fast to close with the unsuspecting camels crossing the marsh at a leisurely walk.

The torpedo shapes struck the center of the file of camels. Three animals went down shrieking in churning water that turned to pink foam in an instant. The panicked camels before and after the stricken members of their herd bolted away from the slaughter to flounder in deeper water. The predators were on them in seconds. White teeth flashed. The greater weight of the attackers bore them under the water.

"Beavers," said Jimbo, eye to his scopes.

"Bullshit," Lee pulled a 30x scope from a pouch on his Molle.

The herd was down in seconds. Splitting up only brought the end faster. The lumbering camels fought to make progress in the water while their killers moved at astonishing speed. One adult and a calf struggled onto a bar of mud to get out of the water and escape the carnage. The sleek furred killers rushed from the water and up onto the bank. These were leaner, more muscled animals than the species the team knew from documentaries on tv. The adult camel bleated and kicked as two beavers leaped to bring it down with claws and teeth. The calf screamed in a cry in an eerie mimicry of a human baby. A beaver clamped its razor-sharp incisors on the yearling's leg and dragged it back into the water where both vanished in a welter of bubbles and spray.

The water grew still except for expanding ripples of foam. The bodies of camels, some surrounded by greasy pools of their own bowels, floated in the crimson mire. Their attackers drifted back the way they came, not staying to feed.

"Giant beavers. Fuck me." Chaz sighed.

"It was my people hunted them to extinction. Now I understand why. Imagine a world full of those bastards," Jimbo said.

"They wasted those camels. Killed all of them, and they're not eating them," Bat said, eyes locked on the torn bodies moving past them on a sluggish current heading south.

"They're defending their habitat," Jimbo said.

"You mean they have a dam?" Chaz said.

"That's what flooded this valley. We follow the current to the right we'll find it," Jimbo said. He turned to see Byrus staring at the carcasses floating by. Some were getting hung up in the reeds where billows of insects were already gathering to feed. The Macedonian's mouth was hanging open.

"Tartarii," Byrus said in a hoarse whisper. The Pima didn't correct him this time.

## 19

# IN FLIGHT

I t wasn't his first ride in a corporate jet. However, it was his least fun ride in a corporate jet.

The Embraer Legacy 650 climbed to thirty thousand feet, pressing Morris Tauber gently back into the plush suede leather seat. Whisked away by mysterious Asians in a state-of-the-science private jet. It was all starting to feel very James Bond. But Morris wasn't feeling very Sean Connery. "Do you like the ride?" the smiling man in the tinted glasses asked from the swivel seat across from him.

"It's comfortable," Morris admitted.

"This is one of the finest executive jets you can buy. Made in China. Jackie Chan owns one. Who would have thought the communists could build a ride with this kind of luxury?"

"So, you're not a communist?"

"Taiwanese. Of course, even the communists aren't all that red any more, am I right?"

One of the men from the SUV, the driver, came down the aisle offering a tray with tall glasses of iced tea. Morris took one and waited until the smiling man took one before sipping.

Chilled with a fresh lemon slice and honey. The driver returned with a tray of cookies. Macadamia nut with white chips.

"This isn't a coincidence. My favorite iced tea. My favorite cookie," Morris said.

"We pride ourselves on our research, Doctor," the smiling man said.

Morris replaced the cookie he'd chosen on the tray and searched for his inner Connery. "I'm not going to tell you where they are. I won't betray my sister or my friends," he said with all the gravity he could muster.

The smiling man's smile faded to a frown. He wasn't angry. He was disappointed.

"I don't wish to threaten you," the man said. Morris said nothing.

"Coerce you? Yes. Gently. You were not forced to come with us. No one has done so much as touch you, Dr. Tauber."

"I'm free to go then?"

"After a while. After we have talked." The man's smile returned.

"Then what do you want? Why go to all this trouble?"

"To make you, and your people, an offer."

"What kind of offer?" Morris' eyes narrowed. "A job, Dr. Tauber." His host was Jason Taan, CEO and principal shareholder in Dex-Tan Industries, a diversified engineering firm specializing in water management and dam construction projects worldwide. They'd recently moved into building supertankers with the purchase of a Dutch shipbuilding firm.

"As you can see, I take a hands-on approach to my business," Jason Taan said.

"You have no connection with Sir Neal Harnesh?" Morris asked as they shared a meal of shrimp cocktail and a salad of chilled arugula.

"He is a competitor in areas where our businesses intersect.

That's why we purchased company files stolen from the database of one of his subsidiaries by a hacker. We wanted a dekko at how he was pricing some of his contracts."

"In the area of?"

"Oil transshipment. I'm not sure if you're aware of it, but India and China are in a fierce struggle for energy resources to fuel their growing economies. We are looking to be competitive now that Dex-Tan has moved into the construction of super-tankers."

"And did you find what you were looking for?" Morris said, gesturing with the tail of a shrimp on the end of a fork.

"Not at all. The database we purchased was from a separate corporation not associated with either shipbuilding or oil pipe-line construction. An outfit called Gallant Limited.

Are you familiar with it?"

"Yes."

"You worked for them for a number of years. Along with your sister. Then you suddenly severed your relationship with them, and not by mutual accord. The files we have detail the theft of some very dodgy items from the company inventory. And the company's efforts to find you and recover those items has been interesting, to say the least."

Morris swallowed. "I suppose."

"Sir Neal very much wants his nuclear reactor back," Jason Taan said with obvious amusement.

"He does."

"And his time machine." Jason Taan held up a glass for his driver to fill with champagne.

Morris raised his eyes to see Taan smiling at him.

"Yes. I know all about it, Dr. Tauber. What's more, I believe it. As fantastic as it all sounds, I believe it."

"Uh-huh." The shrimp was turning to chum in Morris' stomach.

"Don't worry, Doctor. I don't want to steal your device. I only want to borrow it."

Jason Taan laughed openly at Morris' reaction to that.

## 20

## THE LAKE

They reached the dam before noon the next day.

It looked more like a massive natural deadfall than a planned structure. The trunks of whole trees filled a narrow gap in what was once a tributary feeding a broad river. The wall of logs was reinforced by a tangle of tree limbs piled behind it to form a barricade created from dozens of habitats. The domes of individual lodges dotted the organized mess. Jimbo counted fifty-two. That was well over a hundred of the buck-toothed monsters out of sight beneath the water or in their nesting chambers. The two hundred foot long dam breast was held in place by tons of packed mud. The dam was old enough that a thicket of reeds grew through the construction, further camouflaging it as a natural obstruction.

The blockage reduced the river's flow to a trickle that ran down through gaps in the ten-foot face of the timber weir. The effect over the years since its completion was the swamping of millions of acres at the base of the mesa. The day before they'd passed hundreds of independent lodges. For that reason, they kept to a high trail to avoid the miles-long beaver colony. Any threat to that colony would be met with violence. They had no desire to share the fate of the camels.

The team moved down to follow the gravel bed of the river. A stream trickled at the center with weed-choked slopes describing where the water once rose up the banks before the dam stopped the flow. Birds hunted for grubs in the mud. Some fluttered aside as the group approached. Wingless birds stalked clear and stood watching the four men and one woman pass. The largest of the flightless birds were eye-level with Lee Hammond at six foot four. They were dove-gray with long necks and hooked beaks. Scaly red legs rose atop powerful feet with three toes ending in wicked black claws, hooked and razor-sharp. Their heads tilted and turned, eyes locked on the strange column moving among them.

"Never had a chicken size me up for dinner before," Chaz said.

A short drone flight revealed that the river turned south, then hooked hard east where it joined an elongated lake. Jimbo and Chaz recognized it as the body of water from their first trip into the past. The cliff wall where they'd found Caroline Tauber held captive was another day or two from where they stood. It was here they hoped to find Rick Renzi.

The battery life on the drone was low. Jimbo didn't want to risk losing it and called it back. The solar panels hanging off his ruck would need the rest of the day to restore the extra battery secured in his pack. And that was if the sun stayed out the rest of the day. The sky was clouding up to the north.

"It's like an all-year monsoon season here," Jimbo said, restoring the drone to its protective case.

"Between the rain and the sweat I don't think I'll ever get dry again," Bat said. She took off her hat to slap away flies.

"Bruce has the right idea," Chaz said, pointing.

The Macedonian squatted in the mud in his colorful shorts and mirrored shades. He looked like a hipster Tarzan.

Crouched on the bank of a pool, Byrus slapped handfuls of mud on his arms and legs. The others joined him and coated any open skin area with the cooling mud. It brought relief from the biting insects until it dried and flaked off.

The following day, the dry bed broadened into what was the delta area where the river joined the alluvial lake. The narrow stream ran along the center of acres of sucking mud. The team found a narrow trail along the foot of a granite cliff face. They stayed on that until it widened and led along an incline into deep pine woods. Sunlight off water led them through the trees to a ledge above the lake.

"It's not the same as the last time we were here. The surface level's lower," Chaz said.

"It's those damned beavers," Jimbo said.

"Those damned beavers and their damned dam," Bat said, but only Byrus found it funny.

"Dam dam," he chuckled.

The sun was dropping, and the shadows between the trees grew blacker. They decided they were worn out for the day and made camp on the ledge. Byrus built the fire as usual. Jimbo and Chaz sat down where they were and were instantly asleep against their packs.

"Care for a swim?" Lee said.

"You read my mind." Bat stripped off her sodden t-shirt and ran ahead of him down a game trail toward the beach. A bank of shale and sand led down to the water's edge.

Lee and Bat stripped off the rest of their clothes and laid their rifles atop a flat dry rock then, naked, raced one another for the water. It was wet, but that's all the relief it offered. The water temperature was the same as the air. It felt like a lukewarm bath. They waded to a place where the water was to their armpits. Lee snagged one of Bat's wrists and pulled her to him. They kissed and touched a while until interrupted by the bark of some unknown animals invisible in the trees above them.

"Look, this is all very romantic but…" Bat said, her cheek on his chest.

"Yeah. I'd feel better closer to the rifles myself." Lee released her.

Wading back through the still water they saw two figures crouched in the shallows, bent to drink. The pair straightened and then stood upright on two legs, shoulders hunched. The setting sun glinted off large discus eyes under heavy brows. Yellowed fangs were bared in protruding jaws. They silently followed with their eyes as Lee and Bat walked easily from the water to the rock where the rifles lay. The Ranger and the commando ran the last few strides to snatch up the M4s and swing the sights to where the pair of hominids had been crouched a second before. All that remained were eddying ripples from where the pair of watchers left the water's edge to disappear into the trees.

"You know those guys?" Bat said breathlessly.

"I've met a few of their cousins," Lee said.

"That means we're getting close."

"Yeah. Sure does. Closer to what, I'm not sure."

They dressed in a hurry and hustled back to the light of the campfire now glowing atop the ledge.

## THE BLUE MAN

The drone buzzed the lake at five hundred feet.

The lake had decreased in volume since they'd last been here. Broad flood plains lay exposed, and all around new-growth trees encroached where once there was open water. Dropping lower, the drone found what was left of proto-human settlements. They were collections of collapsed huts in roughly circular patterns around the remains of communal cook fires. The sites were overgrown with weeds. Totems made of bones leaned crookedly or had fallen to the ground.

The rain went from a light mist to a driving downpour on a stiff thirty-knot wind. Jimbo brought the drone back to base. Bat Jaffe and Lee Hammond sat under the shelter of a tarp strung between trees and reviewed the video on a tablet.

"It looks like an extinction event," Bat said.

"There were thousands of the little bastards when we were here before," Lee said.

"Did the receding of the lake cause this?" she said.

"We caused it. We were the extinction event," Lee said.

"We offed hundreds of their males getting out of here," Chaz said from where he was helping Jimbo pack up the drone.

"And you think your friend is still alive here somewhere?" Bat said.

"The fossil record does not lie. His bones were in the cave where we found the golden idol. The bones of an old man," Lee said.

"High-def video doesn't lie either. Keep watching," Jimbo said, moving over to join them.

From the camera point-of-view, the drone swept over the treetops until it reached a broad bay formed in the shadow of sloping ground that rose at a severe grade to the top of a mesa. At the foot of the bay was a sheer cliff face. Huts were collected at the base of the rock, only this time they were standing and clear of growth. Columns of smoke rose from fires. Small figures could be seen moving.

"Look there. On the beach. Freeze it." Jimbo touched the screen to zoom the image in. White stones were arranged in a pattern on the black shale sand. They spelled out in letters ten feet in height:

*RLTW*

"Rangers Lead The Way," Jimbo said, grinning.
"Son of a bitch," Lee said under his breath.

---

Knowing they were close to the end of the trail acted like a restorative to the team. They picked up the pace along a game trail through the trees above the coastline around the lake. They walked single file with three paces between them, and Byrus was literally the point of the spear.

"Renzi is going to shit when he sees us," Chaz said.

"Or he's going to be pissed at us for leaving him back here this long," Lee said.

"He never expected to see us again. As far as he understood the rules," Jimbo said.

"Remind me again of the rules," Bat said from where she walked drag.

"Originally," Jimbo said, "the Taubers couldn't open a field farther back in the past than their last field. So each new opening had to be closer to the present. Each new opening closed a door on going back any farther."

"And that's not true anymore?"

"Not since Samuel dropped some new knowledge on them. The transit field has a localized effect. So long as we could manifest outside the zone of the last field opening in this era, we could punch a hole through the barrier created by our last transits. Get all that?" Jimbo turned to glance back at her.

"I think so. And Samuel is the son of the guy we're here to rescue. His grown son from the future," Bat said.

"Yep."

"I must be nuts because this is all making total sense to me," she said.

"Welcome to our world," Chaz called back.

Bat hiked on as she considered that, eyes on the men ahead of her when not sweeping the trees for movement and sound. This place, this time, and the fact that she was in this impossible place thousands of centuries before her own birth should be unsettling. It should be turning her head inside out. Instead, she found it somehow reassuring. It was a new dimension in her reality and further proof of the wonders of creation. Sure, it was a pair of rebel scientists who made this journey possible by breaking all the rules, but it was God who made the rules so that they could be broken. Bat Jaffe was buoyed in spirit by this proof that all was possible even if she couldn't get her head around it all.

A movement, no a *change*, off to her right made her swing her rifle up.

Over her sights, she saw a figure standing upright and still by the bole of redwood fifty paces above the trail.

A man, an actual man, coated head to toe in blue. He stood, naked but for a cloth tied around his waist, and watched her expressionless with dark eyes. Bat stood fixing her rifle sight's center on the silent man. He parted his lips to reveal jagged teeth stained black. It was not a smile. It was the leer of a predator.

Bat's eyes left the blue man long enough to glance at Jimbo, at the back of the line of march, receding away from her down the trail. She began to speak. She turned eyes back to the target.

The blue man was gone.

She swung the rifle left and right. The hillside above was empty of men, blue or otherwise. She lowered the rifle and rejoined the Rangers at a trot.

Bat didn't say anything to the others. She wasn't sure they'd believe her. She wasn't sure what she saw herself.

2 2

---

SHANGHAIED

"Morris! I'm so sorry I haven't called. Dwayne is in recovery after surgery, and I haven't had time to call you on the *Raj*."

"I'm not on the *Raj*, Caroline."

"Things taking longer in Indiana than you thought?"

"I'm in China."

"Excuse me?"

"Shanghai, to be precise. I'm a guest here at Dex-Tan Marine Fabrications."

"A guest? What the hell, Mo?"

"Someone else had an interest in that fossilized footprint. We got outbid, and they got me in the deal."

"Harnesh?"

"A competitor. He has a lot of compromising data he picked up along with a lot of data retrieved in a major hack on Gallant. Mr. Taan knows all about the Tube and our experimentations with it. He's got us boxed in."

"To what purpose, Mo?"

"Well, refreshingly, he only wants to increase his bottom line. He's not looking to change the world."

"Are you free to talk?"

"I'm free to do anything except leave. They have me in a very nice executive suite here. We can talk freely. There's not a lot they don't already know about us. And seeing as they have us at a disadvantage already, there's no need for further secrecy."

"You're not in any danger?"

"Unless you include being bored to death."

"That doesn't mean they won't crank it up, Mo."

"I'm aware of that. Mr. Taan has made his wishes and conditions plain."

"If I ever want to see my brother again, they want the Tube."

"Only for a little while, Sis. A one-off deal, as Mr. Taan phrases it."

"They all say that. What does he want from us?" Morris Tauber laid out in detail the demands that Mr. Taan was making of them.

"Holy shit," she said after breaking the connection.

## 23

## THE ALTAR OF MA

"You have that feeling?" Chaz said.

"I've had it all afternoon," Jimbo said.

It wasn't anything they could see or hear. The sense that they were being followed and watched was unmistakable. It intensified as they neared the location of the cliff settlement. And there was the smell, a tang of something in the air.

They stopped in a quad with backs to one another. Byrus stood apart in a crouch, spear in his fists and head raised to sniff the air.

"Are we sure these assholes won't kill us before we reach Rick?" Lee said, eyes darting left and right in a search for targets.

"Or kill him? Have you thought of that?" Bat said.

"They've been holding him prisoner this long? Could they be saving him as a hostage?" Chaz said.

Jimbo shook his head. "I wouldn't count on them having their shit together to that degree."

"Ambush?" Lee said.

"Not from our experience. These skinnies are closer to animals than they are to us. They see us, they attack us. For some reason, they're hanging back," Jimbo said.

"Are you sure it's the same bunch as the ones we saw by the water?" Bat said.

"Who else would it be? We're only a few klicks from Bedrock. We're in the cannibals' neighborhood," Lee said.

"Just saying," Bat answered. She had not told them about the blue man. She still wasn't convinced that the man wasn't a result of exhaustion and shadows.

"Nothing to it but to do it," Jimbo said and motioned for Byrus to lead the way. The others followed.

"No one's home," Jimbo said, lowering his scopes.

The team was concealed in the brush along a tree line, deep in the shadows where they couldn't be seen. The settlement lay below, a sloppy ring of thatch huts around the smoldering black stain of a community cook fire. Not so long ago, they'd seen a man murdered there, then butchered like a hog by a mob of man-eating savages. Now it looked abandoned. Nothing moved but for a few of the runty breed of mean-ass dogs the skinnies kept as pets. Not a single proto-human was in sight.

This was the place where they'd found Caroline Tauber held captive on their first operation back through the Tube to another time. There was the sheer cliff face at the back of the settlement with the cave where Caroline had been held prisoner, The cave where they'd found a fortune in gold artifacts. The cave that was Richard Renzi's grave and could be again if their mission failed.

There was a new addition to the scene. A cairn of stones piled six feet high in a rough pyramid. At its peak sat an artifact of rusting steel.

"The Ma Deuce. You see it?" Chaz said. "Damn," Lee said, eye to the scope in his hand.

The heavy .50 caliber machine gun rested on its tripod at the summit of the cairn. It was orange with rust.

"It's a shrine," Jimbo said.

"What the hell's been going on here?" Chaz breathed.

There was movement down in the village. A single figure

limped from the collection of huts and waved a hand overhead. A few of the dogs trotted alongside the man.

"You pussies going to hide up there all day?"

Rick Renzi folded his arms and waited for his brother Rangers to reach him.

---

"What the fuck? I thought you guys couldn't come back," Rick Renzi said, grinning once the man-hugs and back-pounding were over. Rick was tanned and muscled. His hair had grown down his back, and he was sporting some serious choppy sideburns. Except for what looked like a badly healed break to his leg, the prehistoric past had been good to him. He wore a kind of leg brace of leather bound with thongs around his bare calf. He had on forest camo BDUs sliced into cut-offs, and his desert issue combat boots, now held together with straps of skin. The cut-offs were faded and patched with leather. A holstered .45 hung from a belt around his waist.

Bat and Byrus stood apart. They were not included in this very close circle of friendship and also they wanted to keep an eye on their surroundings. This all seemed alien to them.

"You know science. Always changing. One day an ice age and the next it's global warming." Chaz grinned back.

"You can take me back, right?" Rick said, searching their faces.

"Sure. If you're up for a week-long hike. We even brought a taste of home," Lee said and rooted in his pack to produce two items. A fifth of Jack Daniels and two cartons of Marlboros.

"Don't need the smokes. I've had plenty of time to quit. But you better believe we'll crack this Jack, bro." Rick accepted the gifts.

"What's your situation here, Renzi?" Chaz said, looking around him at the empty settlement.

"Well, I finally found a job that suits me. I'm a *god!*" Rick said, exploding into his signature braying laugh.

"Where's your followers?" Jimbo said.

"They're shy. Can't blame them after what happened last time guys looking like you showed up. They'll come out when I tell them it's safe."

"They've been taking care of you all this time?" Chaz said.

"You wouldn't believe it. Look, I'll tell you all about it. You can catch me up on what's been happening. But first, I want you to meet my wife." Rick grinned wider at the way the others exchanged astonished glances.

## 24

## LONG DISTANCE

"Ranger Zulu to *Ocean Raj*. Are you reading us, *Ocean Raj*."

"Five by five."

"Can we talk in clear?"

"We're on a unique frequency, Jimbo. No one's listening in."

"That you, Dwayne? You recovered?"

"Been back a week my time. Ribs are mending. Concussion cleared up. What's another bruise on my brain, right? What's your location?"

"Cannibal Lake. Bedrock. Mission accomplished. We found Renzi."

"Holy shit. That's great. What's the sit-rep?"

"Well, he's still a raging asshole. Otherwise, he's fine. Lording it over the man-eating motherfuckers like a dollar-store Caesar. We're taking some downtime and moving out tomorrow."

"Listen up, Jimbo. I need you guys to double-time it to extraction. We have a situation of our own here."

"Thought you guys could dial the calendar any way you like. What's the rush on your end?"

"I'll fill you in when you get back. You have enough on your plate. Just no side trips, all right?"

"Straight as an arrow back to the beach, Dwayne."

"Godspeed, brother. *Ocean Raj* out."

"Ranger Zulu out."

## RICK TELLS HIS STORY

With a great deal of coaxing and a brand of sweet talk the Rangers would never have thought him capable of, Rick Renzi urged a woman to step out from the shadows of the cave at the base of the cliff face.

"Come on, Neeta. These are friends. My very good friends."

N'itha stepped into the sunlight, eyes wary. She wore a beaded buckskin skirt that reached her knees and a necklace of gold and turquoise pebbles about her throat. Except for those items she was naked. Her skin was olive-hued and her hair black as night, worn gathered behind her head in a wooden clasp. She was slender and small-breasted and a few inches shy of five feet tall. Her dark, almond-shaped eyes shifted warily over the strangers from under loose strands of bangs shading her brow.

"She's beautiful," Bat said in a whisper.

"Isn't she? I bet you fuckers thought I hooked up with one of those butt-uglies." Rick grinned broadly and drew N'itha to his side where she smiled shyly. Rick was the shortest of the Rangers at five foot eight, but he was easily a head or more taller than his bride.

"Where did she come from?" Chaz said.

"I found her."

"Just like that? Where does she come from? Are there other people like her?" Jimbo said.

"Don't know. Don't care. Me and the boys found her lost in the marsh and brought her back here. I didn't make her stay. She doesn't want to go back where she came from, so we started playing house."

"And here we were worried about you," Lee said.

"Hey, it's all good. You guys rest up a day or two and me and Neeta will pack up and head back to the USA."

"You and—" Chaz started.

He was interrupted by Rick letting out a loud ballpark whistle followed by commands that sounded like he was imitating a pit-bull. One by one, hominids emerged from the surrounding huts and trees. Adult males and females and children. They looked as they did when the Rangers last saw them, bestial and primitive but more docile than before. Only a few were armed with spears which they carried easy over their shoulders like tools rather than weapons. Around the throats of the men were necklaces strung with some items that clattered and jangled as they moved.

Empty .50 caliber shell casings pierced and strung on leather thongs. The symbol of their god Rick Renzi.

That evening saw the strangest dinner the team had ever experienced. After stripping down and bathing in the warm lake water, they ate strips off a roast deer stuffed with wild onions and greens along with bass fresh-caught out of the lake that day. Renzi had taught the skinnies to fish once he got them over their fear of the water. The new Mrs. Renzi supervised the meal preparation and served everyone on the team from wooden trays of meat and fried yams. Dessert was sliced fruit served in carved wooden bowls. The fruit was topped with honey and crushed cinnamon.

Whatever else had changed in the valley, the skinnies' table manners were vastly improved. Humans were off the menu in this brave new world.

Some of them, especially the kids, rushed to grab anything the Rangers discarded. Empty food containers or wrappers. There were fights. Especially over the cartons of Marlboros that had been cast aside. A skinny that Rick had renamed Homer after Homer Simpson was the eldest of the tribe. Homer was balding on top and had a long upper lip that recalled the cartoon character. He claimed the Marlboros for himself and pulled one of the cardboard cartons apart. The shiny packs fell to the sand. He ripped one open with his teeth and sniffed the broken cigarettes inside before sticking them in his mouth to chew thoughtfully.

"Let me help you out there, chief," Rick said and peeled the cellophane from a pack to open it properly. He lit a cigarette with a stick from the fire and took a long drag before handing it over. Homer stuck it between his lips and sucked back smoke in mimicry of his deity. The skinny hacked and coughed before throwing up violently by the fire. He tossed the lit cigarette aside with a screech of rage.

Rick returned to the others and dug into the freeze-dried food packs, gorging on chili-mac and pasta with sausage. Hard candies were handed out to the skinny kids who acted like children everywhere, tussling over who got the most and crowding the Rangers to beg for more. Rick scattered them with a string of barks and grunts that sent them fleeing from the firelight.

The team caught Rick up on what he'd missed since they'd left him. He had a hard time at first with the idea that he'd been here five years, and for them, only a year had passed. They shared it all with him. Stealing Sir Neal Harnesh's nuclear reactor and going on the run, the return to the cave where they found Rick's skeleton and a half-ton of gold waiting, Dwayne and Caroline's trip back to the ancient Aegean and locating a fortune in pirate gold. And how Dwayne and Caroline were married now, under an alias, and had a six-month-old son.

"I thought you said you left here a year ago? How can they have a six-month-old kid?" Rick asked.

"They stole some time on us. It's complicated," Chaz said.

"Fuck it then. How'd you lose the eye, Cochise?" Rick said.

"A Roman took it when we went back to save Jesus," Jimbo said.

"Save Jesus? No shit?"

"No shit," Chaz said.

"You learned their language?" Jimbo nodded toward the skinnies seated around the fire cracking scorched bones with rocks to get at the marrow.

"More like sounds. There're no real words to it. None I can make sense of anyway." Rick shrugged.

"And Neeta? You can communicate with her?" Bat said.

"Look, why don't I start at the beginning?" Rick said. And between pulls of Jack Daniels, he did just that.

"I was covering your withdrawal back into the mist. The skinnies were fucking everywhere. Coming out of the trees for the slope. Climbing up on my flanks, both sides, I was traversing the fifty left and right, and the Ma Deuce was getting hot. I could light a smoke off the barrel. I ran through that last can of ammo in a heartbeat and got up to get clear. I didn't get far before they were on me from all around. I don't remember a lot after that. At least for a while.

"I woke up back in the cave, the one back there, the same one they were holding Caroline Tauber in. The skinnies carried me back there. I was sick as a dog with a concussion, and I had a fractured bone in my leg along with cuts and bruises all over. They beat the shit out of me up on that hill, but they didn't kill me. I'm still not real sure why. They don't really have a way of telling me. Near as I can make it out, they think that if they killed me it would enrage the other gods who were my friends and they'd come back and finish the job they started. That's why they hid when you showed up. But now we're all friends, right?

"There's no way I'll ever know how long I was in that cave passing out from pain. Hell, I might have been in a coma for all I know. I can remember some of their women spooning some kind of soup into my mouth. Turns out it was made of game meat, wild onions, and cannabis. There's primo weed growing in a field above the cliffs. They were keeping me stoned out of my mind until the swelling in my head went down. Staying on a perpetual week-long high might have saved my life. I don't know.

"The pain in my head went away, and my vision cleared. It was time to deal with my leg. I could manage to hop around even though it hurt like a bitch. I drove a peg into the ground and tied one of my shoelaces around it and my ankle and pulled the leg bone as straight as I could stand it. The bone went back under the skin but not all the way back in place the way it should. I splinted it and wrapped it and found a branch I could use as a sort of crutch. The leg is fucked up, but I manage.

"So I settled down to my new life on the planet of the midget apes. And if I was going to have to live here, it would be on my own terms. There were some objections from the new head asshole. I took care of him with a little help from Sam Colt then the majority voted me god-for-life. I put them to work cleaning up the place, and I taught them how to fish. Even taught the kids to swim. I tried to teach them to farm, but they don't get it. Guess they can't see the reason for it when there's berries and root vegetables growing everywhere.

"I do keep bees though, I built some apiaries for the honey. My ma used to tell me my grandpop kept bees back in Capua. Maybe it's in the blood. Funny, right? Me, a beekeeper.

"It went on like that, getting by, getting high. Until this past spring when I found Neeta. She was running away from her people somewhere over the ridgeline to the north. Her daddy wanted her to marry some guy, she didn't want to and ran off. I took her in and, honest-to-God, as horny as I was after four years, I didn't make any moves. It was all her idea. It was like a courtship, with flowers and all that shit. So, we set up house, and that's the way it's been for most of the past year."

"So, on top of everything else, you're a bigamist," Chaz said.

"I guess, but technically I married Neeta first, okay? Like a million years before I ever met Lynn, so this is like my first marriage, really. You guys took care of Lynn and my kids, right?"

The Rangers looked at one another. Rick didn't know he had a new son and that the team knew his adult version from the future. It seemed like too much at once. They silently agreed to let that intel wait for another time.

"In some ways, they've been taking care of us," Chaz said.

Rick narrowed his eyes at that.

"Dwayne's been handling it out of your cut," Chaz said.

"He gives Lynn an allowance. They don't have any worries. And since you just vanished, there's no connection to us and the shit we pulled to piss off Harnesh and his people."

Jimbo added, "She's been good about it. Didn't buy anything flashy, stashed some in college accounts saying she won it at a casino. She did right by you and the kids."

"Yeah, I was a fucking lousy husband. I'm glad she's okay. She was always so much better than me."

"We need to talk about your new wife, bro," Lee started.

"Oh, and I taught the skinnies one more thing." Rick stood up from where he'd been sitting by N'itha.

Unsteady on his feet, he waved the mostly empty bottle of Jack to the mob of hominids squatting around the fire. He grunted and thumped his chest with a fist. They turned all eyes to him as he began to recite in a rhythmic chant:

*"They call me Ranger Rick*
*Got skills that are sick*
*And I'm Army all the way*

*Like a bullet to a gun*
*A gun to a bullet,*
*I mean I rock prehistory*
*It ain't no mystery*
*I'm the baddest fucker*
*You ever seen*
*Got my bitch Neeta*
*And no one's sweeta*
*Waking up*
*Before I get to sleep*
*'Cause I'll be rockin' this party eight days a week!"*

He nodded his head, chin to chest as he rapped and punched the bottle in the air to the rhythm in his head. The skinnies all around loudly called back in time with his pumping fist as he led them in the chorus. It was a series of practiced, coordinated animal barks and hoots.

*"No sleep till*
*No sleep till Brooklyn!"*

"That's some old-school, right there." Rick grinned at them and dropped back into N'itha's waiting arms.

On the other side of the fire, Homer was lighting his third Marlboro after recovering from his initial reaction.

# CARDS ON THE TABLE

"Explain this to me," Mr. Taan said, holding up the square of calcified mud preserving Bat Jaffe's Pleistocene boot print.

Morris Tauber looked out a window wall in the luxury condo provided for him by his captor. The sun was rising through a murky layer of smog and fog, hanging low over Shanghai harbor. Massive freight cranes down on the piers stood above the layer of gray mist covering everything in a sooty blanket. They were already dipping and rising, looking like giant birds fishing for breakfast through the mist. Taan relaxed behind him in an opulent conversation pit upholstered in highly illegal elephant hide.

"I'm not sure how much I should tell you," Morris said, sounding petulant to himself.

Taan laughed without malice, with honest amusement.

Maybe it's Stockholm Syndrome, Morris thought, wary of being played but unsure of how to prevent it. How much would he do, could he do, to save himself from harm? He was no tough guy like Dwayne and the others. But there was Caroline to think of. The thought of his sister gave him strength. He would aspire to her brand of stubbornness. It was in their DNA, after all.

"I already know most of what you wish would remain hidden, Morris. I know you have stolen a nuclear reactor and that has you in trouble with Neal Harnesh and who knows how many governments and international agencies. I know that you have the technology to travel back in time and return safely. I can hardly believe that I just said that out loud. Those are only the broad strokes. What harm is there in sharing something that is strictly theoretical in nature? I'm merely curious."

Morris sighed. "What is it that you want to know?"

"About this. How does this happen? One day it's one thing, and the next day it's another." Taan turned the tile of stone in his hands.

"The events of the past are mutable. What has happened before isn't locked in place forever. It can be changed."

"But doesn't that alter the present? Toss a spanner into the great cosmic clockwork?"

"I used to think that. I know better now. So much is predetermined by…I'm not sure what. Small, isolated changes have no discernible effect on the present. Bradbury was wrong."

"Bradbury? A scientist?"

"Ray Bradbury. A science fiction writer. He posited that the slightest change to events that have already occurred can effect catastrophic changes in the present. Someone steps on a butterfly and the world is altered when the travelers return to their own time." Morris warmed to his subject, overcoming his reticence to share anything with this man. Next stop, Sweden. All out for Stockholm.

"I'll have to read that. You specified 'small, isolated changes.' What about more profound alterations of established history?" Taan said.

A servant, a middle-aged European man in a dark suit, silently appeared from another room to set a silver tea service down on a Queen Anne occasional table.

Morris stood silent, waiting for the man to depart.

"Franz is Serbian. He doesn't speak English," Taan said. Franz did not even respond to his own name as he poured one cup of tea then another.

"Well, take the stone there. For a hundred thousand years, it was a pair of bird tracks in the mud of a riverbank or something. By chance, they were preserved by replacement minerals over centuries and centuries, and, against all the odds, were found by a high school student on a field trip."

"Yes. Go on please," Taan said. He lifted a cup of tea on a saucer to offer it to Morris. Franz bowed slightly and departed as silently as he'd arrived.

"And for all those centuries it was just a pair of bird tracks. First lying in the desert in California and finally on a shelf in a dorm room. Unchanged. Unaltered. Until a member of our team walked in the mud along that same riverbank and stepped on the bird tracks. Now, that boot print is history. That boot print is the record. What happened then, all those years before, is not as it was. It is now changed forever."

"And that change is reflected retroactively from that time to this." Taan nodded over his steaming cup.

"Well, whatever the opposite of retroactive would be, I guess." Morris shrugged and picked up a silver creamer to add a dollop of skim milk to his tea.

"We'll need a whole new lexicon for this branch of science you and your sister have created. But that was a small event. The passage of a single extinct bird long dead. Of no importance. A fart in a hurricane. What about larger events? What if you went back and killed Einstein? Or caused Napoleon to win at Waterloo? Or China to win a World Cup in football?"

Morris said nothing. The casual mention of his sister chilled him.

"Is that possible? To cause a more momentous shift in the path of history?" Taan feigned interest in a bit of fig cake he'd picked from a plate on the tray, waiting for Morris' response.

After a moment, Morris said, "Then you could, theoretically, change the course of history and, tail wagging the dog, the present and future."

"You say, 'theoretically.' Your eyes and manner tell me otherwise. I am a very good poker player and you, Dr. Tauber, have a lot of tells. You know that this is all more than just two guys talking, isn't it? You *know* that catastrophic changes can be made."

"Well," was all Morris could manage in reply.

"That's what Sir Neal is up to, am I right? I know that old bastard. I've had dealings with him. A pain in the arse, and not half mad. He takes no prisoners and probably had grand plans for your device before you, and your band of villains snatched it away."

"Let's say he saw the Tauber Tube as a means to an end."

"To conquer the world? Like a James Bond bad guy? That's just like that audacious bastard." Taan was amused.

"More like remake the world to his benefit."

"I don't care for remakes. That's not my interest in your device." Taan smiled.

"What *is* your interest? What is it you *do* want, Mr. Taan?" Morris asked, seated now on the opposite side of the upholstered pit. Oddly, the Bond reference gave him new confidence. If this was to be a game of wits, then wasn't he fully armed? His PhDs had to mean something, right?

"Simple. I want you and your people to go back and get something for me. Something forgotten, something I need. It's purely for profit, a business venture. I have no desire to rule the world. My current holdings take up too much of my time as it is." Taan set down his cup and settled back in the cushions.

"And until you get it, I'm your prisoner."

"Prisoner? Have you been coerced? Was a gun held to your head? A knife to your throat?"

"Then I'm free to walk out of here?"

"If you wish. Though how far will you get? There is no record of you entering China. That's going to be hard to explain at the airport."

"I'll go to a consulate," Morris said as he stood up from the sofa section.

"Which one? The American consulate as Dr. Morris Tauber? Or maybe the Canadian embassy as Kenneth Armbruster of Halifax?" Taan said with the smug assurance of a man laying down a royal flush.

What now, Mr. Bond? Morris sat back down.

"All I'm asking of you and your group is a little bit of your time. And you are in the unique position of having all the time in the world at your disposal," Taan said with a candid and earnest note in his voice.

How candid and how earnest Morris could not discern. "And you will be compensated. Richly compensated. It's all business. I am not asking for something for nothing, Dr. Tauber. That's not how I operate."

"Why should I trust you?" Morris said.

Taan picked up the stone tile from where it rested beside him. The record of a fleeting, inconsequential moment that occurred millennia ago. He lifted his hand and brought it down on the edge of the occasional table with some force. The tile shattered into a thousand pieces. A cloud of dust settled on the tabletop as a fine powder.

"Is that a good start, doctor?"

## THE HONEYMOONERS

"You sure you don't want to stay, Ricky?" Lee said.

"No fucking way."

"Wasn't it you who always said you'd rather reign in Hell than be just another asshole in heaven?" Chaz said.

"I used to say a lot of bullshit. But tomorrow me and Neeta are coming back with you to the land of cheeseburgers and cold beer." Rick drew N'itha closer to him. He whispered, his lips close to her ear. She lowered her eyes and shared a shy smile with them.

"Say what now?" Chaz said.

"She can't come back with us," Lee said, nodding toward N'itha.

Rick was suddenly sober and up on his feet.

"You brought *him* back!" Rick pointed at Byrus crouched among some of the hominid kids, pulling faces for them and making them fall around giggling.

"Bruce is different. He saved my life," Jimbo said.

"Who's he? Some Spartacus looking hippie motherfucker? You think Neeta didn't save my life? You know how many times I thought of hanging myself or drowning in the lake? You know what it was like thinking I was the only man on Earth? You left me behind, brothers, and you can leave me behind again if she doesn't come with me."

Rick paced before his fellow Rangers spitting the words at them. The skinnies around the fire were hooting and baring teeth.

The team felt several hundred pairs of eyes fixed on them. They were messing with the man-god of a half a thousand man-eaters.

"Stand down, bro," Chaz warned with open hands held up.

"You know she may not even be human," Bat said. Rick jerked to a stop and turned on Bat Jaffe. N'itha's wide eyes went from her mate to the strangers and back.

"And where'd they pick you up, honey? Who the fuck are you, bitch? Neeta's human. She's probably the most *human* human I ever met. You think she's one of these monkey motherfuckers? You think she's got a tail?"

Rick stepped closer to Bat. Lee Hammond stood to block his way. The hooting grew louder. Male skinnies stood up, barking.

"You need to step it down," Lee said low. "You may not have as much control over this little clubhouse as you think. I'd hate for us to have to kill all your new friends." He stood to block Rick but did not raise a hand to him.

"Okay. Okay." Rick lowered his voice.

"We'll talk it over. We'll work it out. You know we will."

"Talk all you want. I'm not coming back without her," Rick said, eyes locked on Hammond's.

"I know that you boneheaded son of a bitch," Lee said.

"Okay," Rick said after a tick.

They shook hands, and the skinnies settled back down to their places. All was right in Heaven and on Earth once again.

All but N'itha, who left the light of the fire to move silently into the shadows. The party broke up early with the first sign of silver moon over the trees. The Rangers were beat, and looking forward to their first full night's sleep in what felt like forever.

"Weird shit. This was the scariest place I could ever think of. Now I feel safer here than any place in the world," Chaz said, bedding down by the fire.

"Let's hope they don't change their mind by breakfast time," Jimbo murmured, rolled over on his side, and was asleep in seconds.

But no one was having breakfast.

Hours before dawn, Rick Renzi woke with a fiery headache to find his second wife was gone.

## THE OCEAN RAJ

Taking Stephen for a walk was a twice-daily tradition that served as a welcome distraction for both of them.

Caroline and Dwayne took turns pushing their son in a stroller on a circuit around the main deck once in the morning and again in the early evening, taking advantage of the cooler air at those hours. Dwayne's ribs were mending, and all signs of concussion were gone. He was anxious now to get on with what came next.

"Four days back to the extraction point for the team. Maybe one more if Renzi's not in top condition," Dwayne said. They stood on the aft deck, listening to the slap of water on the hull far below. The sun was dropping below the horizon, turning the sky orange, then pink. Stephen was asleep. The walks knocked him out every time. The regular roll of the deck worked like a lullaby.

"He's never going to get seasick being raised out on the water like this," Caroline said.

"You're changing the subject."

"I'm avoiding the subject. There's a difference."

"I thought you'd be anxious to get this latest operation over with. We have to deal with whatever Morris has gotten into."

"Of course, I'm worried. But these walks are a reprieve from that. Taking care of Stephen is relief from thinking the same thoughts over and over until I can't sleep or think of anything else." Caroline sighed.

"Sorry. I can't help talking shop," Dwayne said.

"Of course, you can't. You're a man. You're a fixer. You're focused on challenges and solutions. There's nothing I can do to get the team back any faster or bring my brother home. So I'm treasuring these little moments."

"I'll shut up then."

"You can do better than that. You can hold me." She leaned against him, so he could put an arm around her, each of them with one hand to the bar of the stroller in which their son napped.

On the way back to their cabin, a figure stepped toward them along the deck. The crew was down to bare bones, and they seldom saw their fellow shipmates except at meals. As the man approached from the evening gloom, they both recognized that he was not Boats or Geteye, the pair of Iranians or any of the crewmen.

"Caroline. Dwayne," said Samuel Renzi, stopping before them.

They invited their friend into their cabin, but he wished to speak to them on the open deck. He gave no reason, but they had long ago stopped asking questions of Rick Renzi's mature son who visited them from the past or future at times of crisis.

"Your father is alive. The team found him. They're heading back with him," Caroline said.

"I'm grateful. I wish I was here only to express my gratitude," Samuel said.

He looked older than the last time Caroline saw him in Paris only a few months ago and, before that, in the same city more than a hundred years prior. Rick Renzi's son lived *through* time, not *in* time, as he'd explained to her. His life was not lived in a linear fashion. This visitation was from a Samuel in his late forties. There was a touch of steel-gray to his hair, and lines were beginning to form around his eyes and mouth. He stood apart from them, never touching them or any object. His hands were always gloved, and he wore his customary black-on-black clothing, fashioned to allow him to travel without drawing attention to himself from one time, one world, to another.

"So you've got bad news," Dwayne said.

"I'm here to guide you and warn you," Samuel said.

"Tell us what you can," Caroline said.

"The capture of your brother will take you into the past once more. He is your brother, and so you must deliver him from his abductors. I understand this. Only take caution with these men. They are rivals of Neal Harnesh, and he seeks what they seek."

"We'll be running into Harnesh again?" Dwayne asked.

"He will have agents in place where you are going. Do your best to avoid contact with them. Stay wary. And it is vitally important that you travel there with as little impact on the technology and culture as it is possible to be. It is a time closer to your own, and therefore more fragile to any interference from your era."

"Where is it? When is it?" Caroline said.

"China, during the later years of the Qing Dynasty. The city of Nanjing in the year 1864."

"Another treasure hunt?" Dwayne asked.

"It is more significant than that, but, essentially, you will be seeking a great treasure." Samuel looked away for a moment regarding the dark stillness of the sea all around them.

"This is all kind of vague, Sam. Can you give us a little more than that?" Dwayne said.

"I do not mean to be obtuse or mysterious. As you already realize, there is a great deal of flux in these matters. Suffice it to say that, if you succeed you will foil another of Neal Harnesh's schemes to reshape a future where he determines the course of human events."

"Well, there's that, right? What about Morris? Does succeeding mean he goes free?" Caroline said.

"You will need him with you to perform this task. You must convince his captors of this. And he must stay with you when you make your escape. This is vital. He's already gained knowledge from the writings and files I gave you. He will use this knowledge to create the means of your escape."

"That's all you can give me?" Caroline said, masking her impatience.

"You know that time is malleable. Morris must think outside of the limits he has placed on his work and on his thoughts," Samuel said and turned his gaze to the child breathing softly in the bed of the stroller.

"Damn it. We need to know what you know," Caroline said and reached out to grip Samuel's wrist. Her hand passed through his forearm as if it was smoke. He raised his gaze to meet her eyes. Those peculiar eyes, green as aged copper. She felt a cold shiver rise up her spine as she jerked her hand back through a translucent field that shimmered and rippled and once again took the form of Samuel's arm.

"Well, that answers a lot of questions I had," Dwayne said, eyebrows raised.

"Any more information could prove misleading. I will try to return as I gain more exact data to share. If I cannot, it is of paramount importance for you to remember that you must get free of your brother's captors upon conclusion of your mission. You must distance yourself by any means. Any means." Samuel said the last with an uncustomary degree of emphasis.

With that, the man in black vanished into the gloom as if he were never there.

## FAREWELL BEDROCK

A search of the skinny settlement and the near shoreline of the lake turned up no sign of N'itha other than a line of petite footprints in the sand that led into the tree line to the west. That trail soon died on the needle littered floor of the deep woods. They gathered back by the communal fire.

"She was running when she left," Jimbo said. The Pima had learned tracking from the elders in his tribe. He'd hunted in the Arizona desert from the time he could walk.

"She didn't just go for a walk?" Chaz offered.

"A walk? A fucking walk? You've been in that bush? Would you take a walk by yourself? And she took all her shit with her. It's like when Lynn left me, only she took my car," Rick shouted at everyone and no one.

"Why would she leave? Could she understand what we were talking about last night?" Jimbo asked.

Rick lowered his voice. "I don't know, Jimmy. She knows some English. Maybe enough to get an idea of what we were saying."

"She ran away because we were arguing over her. She heard her name. She saw your face," Bat said.

"Yeah. And you suggesting she's some kind of animal didn't help, honey," Rick said. He glared at Bat.

"Where would she go?" Jimbo said.

"Back to her village. Where else? We can catch up to her if we move now," Rick said.

"You know where the village is?" Lee said. "Somewhere over that way." Rick waved a finger north at the hills turning purple in the pre-dawn light on the other side of the lake.

"We're not doing this. It's still dark, and she's got hours of head start on us over strange country," Lee said, stepping up to within arm's length of Renzi.

"I told you, I'm not leaving without her."

"You're leaving with us if I have to drag you by your balls the whole way."

"You don't understand. She's engaged to some dickhead over there. He takes a new wife every year, and when spring comes, they kill the new wife to help the crops grow or some shit. If Neeta goes back there, they'll marry her to the fucker then fucking kill her."

"If that's true, then why would she go back, Renzi?"

"Because she heard us talking. Because she knows I won't go with you guys without her. She did it for me, man."

"Then that's on her," Lee said.

Rick stepped forward to move past him. Lee grabbed a wrist and yanked him around and slid an arm around his throat.

Choked out, Rick dropped to the sand unconscious. "Secure him, Chaz. He'll thank us for this when it's all over," Lee said.

"You know that's bullshit. He's not big on forgiveness," Chaz said.

"Poor baby. Let's get a few more hours' sleep then get the fuck out of here." Lee moved off toward the camp the Rangers made at the base of the cliffs.

Chaz wrapped lengths of duct-tape around the unconscious

man's wrists and ankles. He hoisted Rick up in a fireman's carry to follow Lee.

"This doesn't feel right," Jimbo said.

"We did bring your buddy back," Bat said, nodding at Byrus.

"Are you saying that was a mistake?" Jimbo looked toward Byrus who was running on the beach growling and play-chasing some hominid kids.

"Hey, I'm on your side. Take the prehistoric princess back with us. True love and all that." Bat shrugged.

"Yeah. Doesn't feel right," Jimbo said.

"It's not right. Lee's calling the shots."

"Is he? Your man is solid on tactics. No one better. But he has a problem with strategy."

"I see what you mean."

"He'll be pissed," Jimbo said grinning.

Bat returned the grin with gusto. "Let him be."

***

"Lee. You need to get up. *Now*, soldier," Chaz said, sitting at a safe distance from the sleeping Ranger.

Lee Hammond sat up, fully awake. He rubbed his legs, still aching after the punishing week-long hike. Getting older was a bitch. The mileage of eight deployments as an Army Ranger and the weirdness with the Taubers didn't help.

"Rick's gone," Chaz said. Strips of neatly cut duct tape lay in the sand near them.

"Shit! That one-eyed Apache motherfucker. It was him, right?"

"Yeah. He's gone, too."

"And Bruce, too, right?"

"Roger that. They took the drone with them. Your girlfriend, too," Chaz said.

"Shit!" Lee roared.

# LATE INTEL IS NO INTEL

"This is where I first found her," Rick said.

They were standing at the edge of a marsh after an hour of hard pushing. The sun was up. Mist rose from the forest of reeds before them. Birds screeched from within the tangle. Bigger creatures splashed away upon their approach. They were armed and rucked up. Rick had an M4 he'd managed to maintain and a hundred rounds for it. Byrus carried the drone case strapped on his back.

"How deep is it from here?" Jimbo said.

"The marsh runs right into this part of the big lake. It only gets deeper from here. And there's gators. Big ones."

"So she probably came along the bank. We find a game trail and follow it north to the hills. If the settlement is big enough, we'll find more trails as we get closer."

"And cook fires. We'll see their smoke in the sky," Rick said.

"I'm hoping we catch up to her or cross her path long before that," Jimbo said. "She was lost when you found her. Chances are she has no more idea of how to find her village than we do."

"Did you know there were people here before you found her?" Bat asked.

"We suspected," Jimbo said. "The gold artifacts we found were too advanced for the skinnies to make. There was no evidence that they had any interest in gold, let alone the means to render it. They had it because it was shiny."

"Like pack rats," Bat offered.

"The little fuckers used to raid when there were a lot more of them. At least I think that's what they were trying to tell me. They brought that big gold mama back with them a long time ago," Rick said.

Bat asked, "Do they paint themselves blue? Neeta's people. Do they cover themselves in blue paint?"

Jimbo and Rick turned to look at her.

"I saw, I think I saw, a man painted blue watching us as we got close to the village," Bat said.

"And you're mentioning this *now*?" Jimbo said.

"I wasn't sure I really saw it. He was there, and he was gone. I know there are people here now. I didn't before."

"Neeta never mentioned any blue people, But, shit, I don't know what the hell her people were like. I wasn't looking for in-laws," Rick said.

Jimbo took the drone case from Byrus' back and had the little machine aloft above the trees inside of a minute. As it buzzed skyward, it scattered big grey birds from the branches of the surrounding sequoias. He piloted it north and flipped on the heat signature option to look for a lone figure moving generally north of their position. Hot orange blobs showed up in packs and bunches. Birds, mostly. Jimbo adjusted the filters to take in only larger animals.

"You see her?" Rick asked, standing up on his toes to peek over the Pima's shoulder.

"It's a big search area, and I only have so much battery life," Jimbo said and jinked the drone east, closer to the lakeshore.

A singular reddish blob appeared inland of the north shore.

Jimbo switched to high definition and zoomed in. It was N'itha. She was armed with a skinny's spear and moving up a trail toward the ridge of a hill.

"That's ten klicks of broken country from here. How'd she make it that far in the time since she left?" Jimbo said.

"No way unless she cut across the lake," Bat put in.

"Fuck me. I taught her to swim," Rick said and left them to retrieve and repack the drone while he headed north along the edge of the marsh in a halting jog favoring his bad leg. The others rucked and followed.

They humped generally north using a divide in the range to reach the floor of a valley where they hoped to intercept N'itha. Their path took them dangerously close to a mammoth herd busily stripping limbs from a copse of the birch trees. Rick charged right through with the rest on his heels. He wasn't veering even for a mass of feeding elephants.

N'itha was lightly burdened, and they were rucked up. She could move faster. The girl also had the advantage of being a local. As she neared her village, her surroundings would grow more familiar. Her course would be true while they would be looking to cut her trail.

Drenched with sweat and hurting, except for Byrus who looked as if he could run another forty miles non-stop, the trio took a break at a stream. Jimbo sent the drone aloft and found N'itha climbing a rocky slope, hopping from one ledge to another like she was ascending a staircase.

"She's two klicks north and east and a thousand feet above us. Your lady is part mountain goat, Renzi," Jimbo said.

"This sucks. We can see her and can't reach her," Renzi said, lowering his head into the cool stream.

"Check this out," Jimbo said. He twiddled the controls, and the image of N'itha grew larger on the screen. Renzi stood close, watching the girl climb.

"What good's that do us?" he said.

"There's a speaker on the drone. I opened the line to it. Say something to her."

"Hey, Neeta! Neeta, honey! Slow the hell down, honey!" Rick shouted at the screen.

The girl stopped on a ledge and looked right at the camera. Her look of astonishment turned to fury, and she shouted at them from the monitor. An unintelligible stream of words came out of the speaker on the controller. Jimbo thought he heard a few clear Anglo-Saxonisms salted in there. He put it down to a year spent only in the company of Renzi, whose mouth was famous even in the Rangers.

"Come on, baby. Don't be like that. I need you, honey!" Rick said, edging toward whininess.

N'itha responded by picking up rocks and throwing them at the drone. Her aim was incredible. One rock soared close enough to momentarily obscure the image on the screen. She accompanied each rock with a shouted word. Both men leaned back as though the rocks might somehow come off the tablet screen and strike them. N'itha shrank to the size of a doll as Jimbo moved the drone up and out of range.

"This thing cost more than my last car, and she nearly totaled it with a rock," Jimbo said.

"What was that word she was shouting? She said it over and over," Bat said.

"It means 'turtle dick.' Apparently, it's the worst thing you can call someone in her language." Rick shrugged.

"That's pretty bad in *any* language, bro," Jimbo said.

They drank their fill from the stream. Jimbo brought the drone back and packed it away and back on Byrus' shoulders.

From the stream bed, they moved up the slope in the direction of where the girl was climbing toward the rocky ridge high above them to the north.

The day was wearing on. They needed to catch up before the sun fell, and the predators came out of their lairs to hunt.

## HISTORY LESSON

"So, the dude has been a hologram all this time? We've been taking advice from a theme park attraction?" Dwayne said once they were back in their cabin.

"You'll wake Stephen," Caroline said. She was making a fresh pot of coffee just to have something to do with her still-shaking hands.

"Was he ever real?" Dwayne said.

"Part of the time he must have been. I remember that he interacted with the physical world back in Paris. Opening doors. Loading a pistol for me. Chaz saw him driving a car, for God's sake. Though I've never seen him eat or drink anything." She set two steaming mugs on a table and took a seat across from Dwayne.

"Spooky shit," he said, idly pouring creamer into his mug until it was the consistency of milky mud.

"Remember Lynn Renzi told you about the time he visited her? He didn't knock at the door or ring the bell. She remembered that he never touched anything. He was a projection then."

"And in Paris at Christmas?"

"Probably then, too. He just came up to us out of nowhere and walked away when he was done speaking. I didn't see where he went. Did you?" She pulled her laptop open and was tapping away as she spoke.

"Googling astral projection?" he asked.

"Googling Nanking and 1864," she said, eyes on the screen.

"Another run for the gold. At least it's closer to home time-wise. It's got to be easier than the last few ops, right?"

Caroline's eyes grew wide, and she looked at her husband over the lid of the MacBook.

"What is it?" he asked.

"You really need to catch up on your Chinese history," she said.

## 32

# THE GRAVE OF THE SUN PEOPLE

N'itha was atop the mesa near her home. She recognized the yellow flowers growing everywhere. They would soon be heavy with seed, their stems bent under the weight. The seeds would be dried and stored in baskets. They were a favorite of the children who would eat them raw or as a paste ground by the women of the village. Her favorite was the balls made of honey and seeds that they made each year when the sun was at its lowest in the sky and the nights were longer.

She would not be alive to see that. She had seen her last winter in the company of her strange new mate. Her death awaited her in the valley beyond. She would surrender to the witch mother and die beneath her blade. She did not fear this end as much as she feared the grotesque attentions of Koto, the headman of her people, touched by the sun gods and bringer of the harvest. The girl crossed the field of flowers with a lighter heart. At least she knew the pleasure of having a loving mate who cared for her and was gentle and kind to her for the time they were together.

She'd defied the wishes of her father and the order of things as they had been since the time of her father's father and his father and back and back to the first fathers and the fire that brought forth the world and all that was in it. And she would never regret that defiance. There was no way to know the day she fled her home valley that freedom and happiness lay ahead of her. She'd believed her immediate fate was to be mauled and eaten by some predator or die of thirst or hunger, her body reduced to scattered bones by the animals of the forest. And she'd accepted that rather than wed the loathsome Koto. Instead, she'd been found by Rikki and taken to his home where they found pleasure in each other's company all through the summer until the birds of spring returned to tell her she must go home.

Just as her lover must return to his home, his world. His people had come for him. She understood enough of their words to know that she was not welcome in that world. And she knew her Rikki enough to know that he would stay here with the flesh-eaters, in a place that was not his home, just to be with her. She could not deny him the wonders awaiting him in the place of his birth, and so she had left him. Destiny would not be denied, and she would be dead by the time he could find her again.

Clouds moved in swiftly to hide the sun turning afternoon to evening. Thunder dispelled the silence of the fields of flowers swaying all around her. Driving rain fell with a sudden fury that broke the stalks of flowers with an insistent sound that rose and fell with the wind.

N'itha kept on even though the ground beneath turned to slippery mud. She came to the mesa's edge where the sudden rain swelled the washes with a torrent of muddy water. Following a ridge above a swampy swale, she came down into the woods above the cascade and was soon in the shelter of towering trees. Even through the downpour, she could smell the smoke of the village at the foot of the hillside.

Her village.

The scent was different now. The smoke smelled old, corrupted. It was not the scent of a cook fire, the clean aroma of dried wood. There was no hint of meat roasting or vegetables frying. It was more of a stink, unpleasant and rank. It grew stronger the farther she went down the hillside toward her home.

She crouched in the trees and looked toward the village across the broad fields that in the seasons before had been planted with squash and beans. They were fallow now, the empty furrows filling with rainwater. The fields had been prepared and not yet planted. Something was wrong.

Terribly wrong.

A white haze of smoke hung over the village. It shimmied and drifted low in the falling rain as though clutching the homes of her people in a ghostly embrace. She crept low across the muddy field, hidden by the shadowless gloom of the storm. She held the spear before her. Her eyes focused over the gleaming flint blade at the end. No sound rose from within the wall of woven branches that encircled her village as a protective fence to keep out predators.

The stench was stronger here. A nasty, noxious smoke of a guttering fire coming from within the fence line. As she approached, she saw that sections of the fence were torn aside or crushed low. No one had repaired them. She found her way through a gap to find a dead place.

No one greeted her. No one called out at her return. No dog barked. No child cried. The village was empty. The lanes between the huts were empty. Some of the huts had collapsed. Broken pots lay in the mud. A corral of piled stone had one wall shoved over. The goats penned within were gone. Most shocking was the state of the witch mother's home. The building, the largest in the village, was a charred ruin. It was the only structure with more than one level. It once sat on pilings of stout timbers with ladders angled to allow access. The earth mother once stood upon the broad veranda floored with adzed and polished planks to address the people of the village. Inside the pole and thatch dwelling were many rooms in which the witch mother kept her secrets as well as the offerings of the people.

It was all gone now. The once-grand palace of the witch and her son was a smoldering pyre. A few blackened poles remained, but the rest was a mess of cooling embers, the source of the pervasive stench. The lodge had burned bright and for a long time. These were the remains of a blaze many days old.

Something visited here only to destroy. Not just destroy but to take. There was not a single corpse in sight. No sign that anyone had ever lived here. Whatever force—man, god, demon or animal—that had done this left no trace of anyone who had called this place home. N'itha's mother and father, siblings, and friends were all gone as though they never lived. All that remained were ruined huts and the vestige of an inferno. The only sound was the rain falling on the sodden ground in a susurrus whisper that sounded to her like voices.

Voices of the dead.

It was a place of death. And something else.

She turned to run, away from this place and back toward Rikki.

To warn him, to tell him to go home and to go alone, to leave her. To tell him that she brought doom to her own people.

As if to make their curse upon her more emphatic, the sky gods opened the heavens wide. The rain became a blinding, pelting torrent that turned the world to a sea of cloying muck. A flash of lightning lit the firmament from horizon to horizon, turning the scorched frames of the homes around her into the skeletal silhouettes of unknown animals.

33

## THE OTHER MEN

The rain reached a near choking intensity. It drowned out every sound other than the constant beat of a billion tiny drums. Gusts of wind curved the downpour sideways in violent waves.

Jimbo lost sight of Byrus trotting ahead through a field of yellow flowers bending under the deluge crashing down all around them.

"Bruce!" he called.

Byrus trotted back, spear in hand, from the haze. "What's ahead of us? Up ahead!" Jimbo shouted over the din.

"Trees! Many trees, baas!" Byrus pointed the way ahead through the monsoon.

Rick and Bat caught up. Rick was moving slower now. The badly healed break in his leg created a painful limp over time. He was not complaining, but there was a pinched look on his face that betrayed the pain he was suffering. Bat Jaffe hung back with him.

"There's forest ahead!" Jimbo shouted and pointed.

"Thank God!" Bat yelled back.

They moved at the best speed they could manage across the slurry of mud and rain-crushed plants, and soon reached the shelter of the trees. The heat never abated despite the rainfall. A mist of evaporating water was rising from the forest floor even as the shower continued to trickle on them through the boughs high above. The wind died here. The sounds of the rain fell to a pattering murmur.

"It's pissing down! Jesus!" Rick said, leaning against the thick bole of a tree to massage his aching leg.

"You gonna be able to go on?" Jimbo asked.

"Don't ever ask me that," Rick said, eyes hooded.

"Okay, then. Noted. The only good news? This will be slowing Neeta down too."

Byrus raised his head and sniffed the air. He grunted to the others and pointed to his nose. Jimbo filled his nose and let it out over his tongue. He tasted the air as his grandfather once showed him.

"Woodsmoke. And something else. Something fishy," the Pima said.

"We're near the settlement. What do we do if Neeta beats us there?" Bat asked.

"Then things get messy," Rick said and pushed off from the tree to move on.

Jimbo adjusted his pack to set out. He felt Bat's hand on his arm.

"Jimmy. A blue man," she said, eyes wide.

Past her, he could see a man watching them boldly, standing in the open between two trees. He was naked except for the indigo dye that covered him from head to foot. In his fist, he held a peculiar cudgel: a round river stone secured to the end of a slightly curved wooden handle by shrunken leather bands. A killing tool. The man's black eyes regarded them with only mild interest. Jimbo realized he'd raised his rifle out of pure instinct and was viewing the blue stranger over his front sights. He felt cold fingers touch his spine when he met the other man's eyes.

He could tell by the confidence there that this man was not alone.

Bat's rifle was up and moving to cover the surrounding gloom.

"Guys! Hold up" Jimbo bellowed.

Byrus called back wordlessly. Jimbo saw him fall, struck by one of the stone cudgels. They were a throwing weapon as well. The curved handle should have told him that.

Blue men, dozens of them, and then scores appeared from behind trees all around and rushed forward throwing the cudgels overhand. Jimbo and Bat backed against the massive trunk of a sequoia. Jimbo dropped one then two with controlled three-round bursts. He could feel Bat against him covering the other face of the battle clock with three-round bursts.

A cudgel hit his rifle, then his arm. It went numb. The rifle dropped from his fingers as his hand went tingly then dead.

He pulled the Dan Wesson in a cross draw with his left hand. The big revolver boomed and lifted a blue fucker off his feet. A second shot turned another attacker's head to a spray of red mist. He was swinging his head back and forth, trying to cover the full one-eighty with only one good eye.

Stone cudgels smashed into the tree behind them, showering broken bark. The blue men pressed in with greater numbers.

Bat yelped. Jimbo felt her pulled from his side. He turned with the hot revolver in his fist. A cudgel in the hands of a snarling indigo man, eyes wild under a shock of bright red hair, smashed his gun hand. Jimbo fired the revolver inches from the man's skin. A hot shower of blood flew into his working eye, blinding him.

More strikes from bludgeons. Hands gripped him and dragged him down. They crushed him to the ground under their combined weight. His mouth and nose filled with the sharp fishy stink of them. He'd smelled them before he saw them.

Just like an Indian would, Jimmy Smalls thought as consciousness fled from him.

## HAMMOND'S HEROES

"Ho," Lee Hammond said, raising a fist.

"I heard it," Chaz Raleigh said, stopping behind him.

Lee stood, head cocked. "That's a mike-four. And another one."

"And a forty-four mag," Chaz said.

The sounds were rebounding off the hills rising above them. Dark clouds closed in over the top of the peaks. They were fast marching toward ugly weather.

The company was stopped on the beach at the lakeshore opposite the cliff settlement. About fifty skinnies were with them. Adults mostly and a few male boys. They were armed only with spears and flint knives, but six of them were burdened with the big fifty caliber machine gun and tripod. Chaz had tried to explain that there was no ammo for the Ma Deuce, but the little brutes wouldn't listen and shouldered the weapon and trudged on.

"To them it's magic," Chaz said.

"Whatever. If it helps them fight, we let them bring it," Lee said.

Others carried more useful burdens. Ammo and explosives.

Homer chose to hump Jimbo's Model 70 rifle. The Pima had taken only his M4 along with him. Homer wore ammo belts for the sniper rifle around his shoulders, looking like a Mexican bandit. He was puffed up and as proud as an Eagle Scout. He was being allowed to handle something that belonged to his gods. Lee had removed the 30x scope and slipped it into a pouch on his Molle. Jimmy Smalls would be pissed enough that he let a monkey-ass motherfucker carry his rifle. But the scope was the real money.

They were a good four hours behind Jimbo and his party, which put them seven or more hours behind the native girl heading for who the fuck knew where. The gunfire provided a general direction. They started the climb up the hillside away from the lakeshore and toward the long dark clouds and lowering black skies to the north.

"Hump it, you man-munching assholes," Lee growled.

Encouragement wasn't necessary. The gang of skinnies clambered up the hill on hands and feet. They handed up the Ma Deuce to one another over the rough patches. The pair of Rangers had to push hard to stay even with them. A hundred yards ahead, younger skinnies ran full out searching for scents like bloodhounds. They'd yip and hoot to be answered back by Homer, who had taken the role of war chief or top-kick sergeant for this sortie. He stood bandy-legged and growled orders to the others with a Marlboro clamped between corn-yellow teeth.

"He's chain-smoking those butts, bro. What's he going to do when the carton's empty?" Chaz trundled up the thirty-degree incline with some effort.

Lee blew hard behind him, bathed in sweat. "Grow his own for all I care."

They reached a ledge and took a breather. They'd come close to ten miles at a killing pace. Chaz sucked water from his straw. Lee broke out the salt tabs and protein bars. The skinnies kept on. Homer turned back above them to bark through a haze of blue smoke.

"Yeah. Yeah. We're coming, you hairy fuck. See how your wind holds smoking four packs a day." Lee waved a hand up at the gibbering skinny.

"That gunfire. You think they reached Neeta's village?" Chaz said.

"Maybe. Could be Rick's already got his girlfriend, and they're on their way back." Lee spat a stream of water into his hand and brushed it back through his hair.

"That's more luck than even Jesus will allow." Chaz smiled.

"And after all we did for him." Lee stood and started up the hill after the last of the hominids climbing toward the crest.

---

The storm passed over them, spending its fury on its way south, borne on gale force winds. The miserable march took them over one ridge then another and across a river valley to the wall of a mesa.

It was full dark when Chaz and Lee trotted up to where some skinnies were howling with excitement within a dense forest of old growth redwoods. The skinnies hooted and sniffed and capered around in the dark woods. They retreated before a bright LED lamp that Chaz flipped on. He trained it over the ground, finding empty brass glittering on the wet needles. There were drag marks, too.

Homer sniffed at a sticky patch on the bark of a tree and grunted. Chaz put the light on it and touched the stain. There was a fresh gouge in the surface of the tree where something struck it hard enough to tear off the thick bark and expose green wood.

"Blood," he said.

"There's blood here too," Lee said. "Bone fragments too. Must have been a lot if it's still here with all that rain. They got off maybe a mag of ammo judging from the spent rounds."

"And that's all they left. The brass. None of their gear's here."

"Could be they fought their way through. Packed out of here themselves. Runnin' and gunnin'."

"We'd have heard that."

"Yeah. We would."

"Drag marks in the mud." Chaz crouched and brushed the tracks in the spongey black ground with his fingers.

"More than our four. They took their own dead away, too."

"Dead or prisoners?"

"That Indian doesn't go that easy. Neither does Bat," Lee said.

"We go on?" Chaz said standing.

"We go on. Rescue or payback, we go on."

They moved north through the dark, reaching the ruined village lying still in the pearly glow of a quarter moon. It was twelve hours of hard pushing. The Rangers dropped where they were and were instantly asleep, trusting the near-men around them, like a pack of dogs, to wake them at any sign of trouble.

Their inner clocks woke them after an hour, and they were up and ready to go. Dawn was a few hours away. The skinnies rose around them, eager to get on the move—no sign that they'd slept themselves. They were on the hunt with their own personal gods and anxious to move on. The skinnies had fresh memories of the carnage these same men caused with the magical weapons. They were made bold by having this same power now on their side of the hunt.

And it *was* a hunt. War had no meaning to them.

Chaz handed out protein bars and candy that the skinnies took greedily and ate without taking the wrappers off. Homer crouched nearby, puffing a cigarette and watching the others eat breakfast.

Two young skinnies, Chaz named them Bart and Millhouse, came rushing into the dead village, whooping and shaking their heads to the north. They trotted away, running low, for the tribe to follow. The skinnies made off after them in a pack. Lee and Chaz rucked up to follow.

"Don't they ever sleep?" Chaz said.

"Close your eyes around here, and something eats you," Lee said, double-timing by his side.

"Come to think of it, that includes our current coalition. We could have woken up to *be* breakfast," Chaz said grinning.

"I still trust them more than I ever did the ANA," Lee said, a reference to the Afghan National Army. Both Rangers agreed that at least their present company had the excuse that they weren't human.

The sun was cresting the range to the east when the Rangers caught up with the pack. They were arranged in a rough ring thwart a well-traveled forest trail of packed earth, grunting and snorting at one another. The circular impressions of elephant tracks marked the ground along with fresh, more recent, prints from bare and booted feet. This was a pathway down to water or between grazing lands. They couldn't stay on it long.

Chaz broke through the huddle to see what they were yapping about. He picked up something glittering in the weak dawn light and held it up for Lee to see.

"This belongs to Bat, right?" Chaz said. A thin platinum chain dangled from his fingers weighted by a tiny Star of David in silver.

"Yeah. There's no way she lost it. She left it as sign."

"That means she's alive."

"She was when she left it." Lee turned to where the indefatigable Bart and Millhouse were running back the way the column had come. They were yelping and hooting. Something had them excited. The Rangers brought up their rifles and scanned the surrounding woods for mammoths. Nothing moved in the trees around them except some green and white birds fluttering from branch to branch, sending down silvery showers of water trapped in the boughs they landed on.

Bart and Millhouse returned, supporting a stumbling figure between them.

N'itha.

She fell into Lee's arms, succumbing at last from exhaustion.

## 35

# THE SKIN PALACE

They were force-marched through the night, driven on by prods from the wicked stone clubs.

The blue men tied their wrists behind their backs using twisted leather thongs. A connecting loop was cinched about their necks, forcing them to walk upright or choke. It was a ligature meant to strangle. It restricted their movement and left them easily controlled. A child could pull on the thong and cut off their air supply.

Jimbo managed a rough count of twenty or more armed men closely escorting them. There were even more in the surrounding woods and scouts running ahead. A dozen or more followed behind under the weight of the weapons and gear that they'd stripped from their four captives as well as the bodies of seven of their own killed back at the ambush. It was a platoon of as many as fifty men total that had overwhelmed them.

The skin of the men was dyed varying shades of blue, from azure to almost purple. It made it impossible to tell their race except that their eyes were dark and lacked an epicanthic fold making them Asian in appearance. The ones who were not entirely shaven had thick black hair matted atop their heads.

None of them had facial hair, and the older among them showed the whitish effect of skin damage where hair had been burned away again and again over the years.

He placed their median age at about twenty or younger. Kids. But in this environment, they might consider thirty to be a senior citizen.

The tallest of them was five foot four. Most were a head shorter than that. They were thin with layers of ropey muscle from hard work. Their legs were thickly muscled and showed all the signs of lives spent moving across great distances at speed. Jimbo figured that unburdened by their captives, they'd be running this track at a sprint.

It was hard to distinguish one of their blue captors from another since they kept moving and milling around him. Jimbo noted raised welts in ordered rows on their backs and chests. Ritual scarification. It signified rank or number of kills. No way to be sure. There was definitely a pecking order. One of the taller bastards had a pair of yellow buck teeth that stuck out prominently from his mouth. He gave the orders and generally gave the air of being the main shot-caller. Jimbo tagged him "Bucky." Another indication of his position was the layer of flab about his middle. He was the only one in the party above one percent body fat. That meant someone whose diet wasn't restricted due to his station. A boss.

His second-in-command was a toady with a permanent sneer and a brush of black hair atop his head. This one took an unhealthy interest in Bat and trotted close to her whenever possible, staring at her with his tongue out, working up the nerve to cop a feel. Jimbo tagged him "Biff."

And they all stank of fish. Fish that had gone bad. Like they bathed in kimchi. It came out worse the more they sweated. Jimbo realized the rain had covered the odor before. That was the only way these sushi-stinking fuckers had gotten the drop on him. Byrus had tried to warn him.

"Smells like pussy left out in the sun too long," Rick said in a growl.

They were all alive and able to walk. Jimbo didn't doubt for a moment that any of their party who'd been too injured to march would be brained by one of those clubs. Ricky was having the hardest time of it. Walking with his back straight was forcing him to put his full weight on his bad leg. He was obviously in pain and taking it out verbally on their captors. He kept up a constant commentary as he limped along. A caustic spew of the profane, vile, scatological and physically impossible that would make a drill instructor blush with embarrassment. His reward was a jab in the ribs with the end of a club.

Jimbo stayed close to Bat. He wasn't sure what he could do to help her, trussed as he was. The leather bands were tightly wound and triple thick. They were strong and expertly knotted.

The blue men took a great interest in Bat, sniffing and sneaking stroking feels before returning to the march. Something prohibited them from going farther, even Biff. One happy aspect of this clusterfuck. As bad as their situation was, rape wasn't an immediate worry for Bat.

Hell, Jimbo had been in the worst parts of the world back in The Now. If sexual assault was a danger for Bat, then it was a danger for them all. When things got this primeval, the only rule was that there were no rules. They'd be used and abused however, their new masters demanded. That meant there were some hard, existential questions ahead in their near future.

Bat Jaffe marched like an automaton. Her expression was vacant, giving nothing away. Not fear or anxiety or anger. She'd withdrawn either out of some mental breakdown, or to reserve her emotional strength for what came next.

Byrus ran second place with Rick Renzi for emotional displays. He growled and snapped and glared at the blue men that were urging them along the invisible pathway north. When he turned his gaze to Jimbo, there was a flash of terror in his eyes. As if to say, *This is Tartarus, baas. We are in Hell.*

One of the indigo bastards carried a hollowed-out horn slung by a strip of hide from his shoulder. It was about three feet long and twisted. From one of those giant bison they'd seen before—how many days ago Jimbo could not recall. As the sun came over the ridgeline, the guy with the horn raised it to his lips and blew a wavering note that rang off the rocks, and trees above them on either side. He would stop on the march now and then and send out a blast. On the fifth try, an answering peal reached them from somewhere ahead. Wherever they were going, their destination was only a mile or so before them.

The nearness of the end of the trail caused the blue men to push harder. They nudged the captives into a trot. Jimbo sent out a silent prayer that none of them would stumble. Their abductors would punish anyone who delayed them. Rick's breathing was labored. He was having the hardest time of it. They'd come all this way to save their friend and might have ended up dooming him.

The path sloped downhill. The silver sheen of open water was visible through the trees, glints of pearlescent light reflected back at them from the early morning sun. The trees fell away to grassland and reeds. Jimbo could see a rock face rising in the distance, a wavering smear of gray in the heat haze already building under the early morning sun. Big white birds rose lazily upon their approach to settle deeper in the wetlands all around them.

They were met by other blue men trotting through the rushes to join the returning party. There were whoops and hollers. The welcoming committee did a quick study of the prizes their comrades had found. One of them risked a feel of Bat's breasts. His hand was knocked away by a blow from Bucky's club. The snap of a bone in the groper's forearm could be heard even over the barking laughter of the others at his misfortune. The man pulled his wounded arm back and hugged it to him, his face paling under the dark dye.

The combined group headed off into the tall grass to a place where it thinned to a beach of sand and shale. It was the shore of a lake surrounded by thick marsh. The indigo men led their charges toward the foot of an earthen causeway that led across the bulrushes and open water toward that curtain of raised ground Jimbo had seen earlier. The causeway looked to be a natural formation of land, a finger of earth cutting across the marshland. It had been packed down to form a roadway. Further on it showed signs of having been filled in by hands other than Mother Nature's. It became more uniform in width. Four meters across. Along either bank of the passageway were the remains of stout baskets woven with sticks and filled with rocks and earth to create temporary dikes to allow the construction of the raised path. Engineering in the prehistoric age.

Jimbo could see more details of something at the end of the path. A humped structure of some kind was growing against the backdrop of the cliff face of red stone glowing rusty orange in the sunlight spreading to shrink the shadows from the ridges to the east. Atop the structure something gleamed dully, catching rays of light that created dancing speckles of white and yellow.

When the causeway broadened and he could take it all in, Jimbo slowed his step at the sight of what lay before him. The end of a stone hammer prodded his lower back, and he picked up the pace once more.

On a broad island or perhaps a beach at the base of the cliffs was a tall fence, constructed of timber posts with woven thorn branches strung between. The fence ran around the blue men's village. He could see the rooftops of thatched structures over the top of this barricade.

Beyond that was a much larger construction that towered over the rest. It was built of redwood timbers and covered over in a skein of skins stretched over a framework of what looked like the boles of saplings. It was designed like a Plains Indian's wickiup but on a massive scale. The entire structure looked like it covered several acres. The skins were from some of the larger beasts of the region, stretched and tanned with fur or wool remaining on the hides. Tall poles were set around the circumference of the structure with objects set atop them. It reminded Jimbo of flag poles set around a football stadium. Except each pole was topped with the bleached skull of an animal. He recognized bear, bison, tiger, and elephant.

These were a fearsome people. They'd found success in a hostile world. They dominated every species they came across, utilizing only their will and their toughness, wits, and those deadly stone hammers. Those doomed species that fell under those hammers included their fellow man. Dangling from the posts that formed the barricade wall were the skeletal remains of human beings. As they marched closer to the entry gates, Jimbo noted that the bones were cleverly kept intact using leather thongs securing them where tendons once connected the limbs. The remains all had one common trait. They were all headless.

Nothing in the history books recorded anything like this. According to the experts, these blue men shouldn't be here.

North and South America were devoid of any human life, let alone highly organized societies using tools, agriculture, and basic engineering skills. Of course, there was nothing about cannibal monkey men or hot topless chicks either. Recorded history covered less than two percent of mankind's estimated million-plus years on this planet. That's a lot of guessing and goshing. Any damn thing could have happened in the hundreds of millennia before the Sumerians first scratched the names of their gods on some rocks.

They passed under the arch above the entry gate, fashioned from a pair of massive mammoth tusks, in the center of a mass of their captors and comrades. The blue warriors all held their stone bludgeons aloft and joined in unison in a sound that started in their bellies as a low hum and rose to a deafening sustained howl. They were answered by crowds of people emerging from between huts made of thatch and timber posts separated by narrow lanes. In some of these lanes, the carcasses of fish hung to dry. Impossibly big bass, catfish, muskellunge, and carp. Everywhere the bones of fish were heaped in messy piles.

It explained the stink of their captors.

The women were small and slender with silky black hair worn long or ratted out to create a colossal mane atop their heads. They wore only skimpy skins knotted around their hips. Some were decorated with strings of beads, animal teeth, claws, and the tiny skulls of birds and rodents. Stones gleamed dully on some of the necklaces. They wore wristlets and anklets hammered from the same material.

Gold.

The same imperfect brand of soft gold that Jimbo and the Rangers had pulled from the cave, *would* pull from the cave, a day's march south and one hundred thousand years from now.

This place could be the source of the golden fertility idol, Jimbo thought. Was it possible that the skinnies had raided here and carried the idol away long ago? Or were there other settlements just like this all over the West? Some unknown early Asian migration? Or were these the original native Americans?

Whoever the hell they were, Jimbo decided he didn't like them.

The children running alongside the procession wore no clothing at all, and they seemed to outnumber the adults three to one. Only the adult men were dyed blue. The women and children had unmarked mocha latte skin except for a few of the women who decorated their faces with lime wash and their eyes with what appeared to be black ash. The effect was primal and creepy. To Jimbo, they looked like vampire geishas.

The kids were like kids any place and any time. They laughed as they pitched handfuls of mud and fish guts at the strange men and woman arriving trussed like turkeys into their village. The adults seemed as amused at this as proud Little League parents would be at little Jason's first time on base.

Bucky took a clod of muck in the face. He decided he'd had enough and chased the kids away with a swing of his bludgeon. They persisted, throwing mud until Bucky caught one of them with an upward swing that lifted a child, who couldn't have been more than four, clean off the ground. The kid fell lifeless to the dirt, jaw at a sickening angle. No one took any notice other than the kids who ran away laughing. Just another day at the mall.

The procession moved on, leaving the little figure lying unmourned behind.

Bat let out a sob. Jimbo turned to see tears cutting through the filth on her face.

"Son of a bitch. Where the fuck are we?" she mouthed.

"It's going to be okay. Lee and Chaz are still out there," Jimbo said, walking close to her to be heard over the din around them.

"And what can they do? We're fucked royally. Even if we were still alive when they found us." She turned and looked at him, fury in her eyes.

He had nothing to say to that. They followed the urging of Bucky and the others closer into the shadows beneath the dome. They were going to see whoever was in charge here—the boss of the skin palace. Jimbo had a strong inkling that things would not get better from there.

As they entered the huge structure, he looked up to see that it was roofed by plates of hammered metal attached somehow to curved joists. The metal reflected the light of a blazing fire set atop a cairn of rocks at the center of the building with a shimmering sheen of buttery ambiance.

Gold.

The entire massive prehistoric palace was roofed with gold.

## 36

## THE KING OF THE WORLD

The powers that be were not prepared to receive visitors just yet.

The four captives were tossed into a pit at the foot of the stone cairn. It was dug to hold prisoners of the size usually captured by the blue men, maybe six feet deep, easily scalable by Jimbo at six foot two inches. He could see over the top of it. In a better situation, it would have been laughable.

They were left unguarded except for the company of an incredibly wrinkled old woman, who stood smacking her toothless gums and studying them through narrowed eyes. Tied as they were, they could not climb out anyway.

They moved as best they could, and each sat with their back to the wall of the pit to give their legs and spines a rest.

"Everybody holding up?" Jimbo asked.

"I could use an iced tea," Rick croaked.

"Shit." Bat shook her head, laughing.

"Bruce? You okay?" Jimbo asked the Macedonian seated with his head pressed back against the earthen wall.

"We are damned," he said to no one and everyone.

"Fucked. We are fucked," Bat put in.

"Yes. Damned and fucked." Byrus nodded in agreement as much as the thong about his neck would allow.

"Anyone see Neeta? You think they have her?" Rick asked. His usual gruff demeanor was gone.

"I didn't see her," Jimbo said. "We weren't that far behind her. If they had her they'd have brought her along with our party, right? Or she'd be in this hole with us."

"Yeah. That makes sense. She's still on the loose," Rick said.

"So, we fucked up the rescue. Now it's time to save ourselves. We need to have a plan," Jimbo said.

"Yeah. First, let me pull the knife out of my ass, and I'll cut us free." The old Renzi was back.

"I have a knife," Bat said.

The others fell silent, turning their heads to her.

Shadows fell over them from above. Bucky and Biff dropped into the pit and got the prisoners to their feet with kicks and slaps. A ladder was levered down, and they were led up to the surface again. A gang of the blue bully boys dragged and prodded them past the stone cairn toward a building constructed of pillars of stacked stone and roofed over with a tent of sewn skins. More skins hung between the columns hiding the interior in shadow.

Piled unceremoniously to one side of the hut was their gear. The packs, drone case, ammo, and weapons had been dropped there as trophies or offerings. Enough firepower to ruin the day of every fucker in this parish just out of reach. The Rangers looked at them longingly.

Blue smoke rose lazily from an opening in the tent roof. Jimbo sniffed then shifted his gaze to meet Rick's eyes. Renzi shrugged.

The sickly-sweet herbal aroma of marijuana rose thick as fog through the rooftop.

A flat tinkle like a wind chime reached them from within. The indigo men all around them dropped to their knees at the sound. Jimbo felt a club strike the back of his legs and he dropped to his knees as well. Bat and the other two captives did the same. Bucky and Biff and their pals touched their foreheads to the ground. Jimbo kept his back straight. The ligature about his neck didn't allow for prostrating himself.

The first to emerge from the opening to the house within a house was the same wrinkly old woman who had been so keenly interested in them earlier. She came swaying into view, tits down to her crotch and giggling. The old bitch was high as bejesus on whatever they were huffing in the stone hut. She shook a curved coup stick hung with hundreds of tiny fish bones, the source of the tinkling sound. The ancient woman stumbled to a stop and unceremoniously dropped to take a seat on the dirt, where she dozed off instantly.

Next to come out of the hut were four indigo men carrying a bier on their shoulders with a seated figure atop it. They walked with a slow and solemn stride toward where the captives knelt. A reedy command from atop the bier and they lowered their burden to the ground with a practiced gentleness. This was all part of some deep ritual.

They weren't just in the presence of the leader of the blue men, Jimbo realized. The Rangers and Bat and Byrus were about to meet their gods.

Seated on the bier, now at eye level with the captives, was a pathetic creature made all the more so by a crown of colorful feathers and gold beading that adorned his head. It was a man of indeterminate age who was afflicted with a variety of congenital defects. His chest was sunken above a grotesquely swollen belly. His right arm was a spindly thing more bone than flesh. His left was withered and ended just below the elbow in a twisted three-fingered claw. All this made his head seem outsized. Large wet eyes gleamed with the burnished iron reflection of severe cataracts. His mouth hung open, revealing blackened teeth widely spaced, and a tongue that flickered over his lips like a reptile's. His afflictions continued below his waist to an undeveloped pelvis and legs that were withered and bent.

This creature regarded them with near-blind eyes. A snot-encrusted nose sniffed wetly at them.

"Who's the retard?" Rick said.

The broken man-child tilted its head slightly at this sound and closed its mouth with a snap. It mewled softly in a hoarse whisper. Bucky, head pressed to the dirt, answered with a quavering voice. He was scared shitless by this sad cripple. They had an exchange. The thing on the bier speaking and Bucky answering. Whatever was being said here would determine their fate, Jimbo realized. This was a reckoning, and they were the topic of the day. It was for damned certain they wouldn't like the outcome no matter what was decided. He thought of the headless skeletons lining the rampart walls.

The thing on the bier raised its one good hand in the air and chittered away in the high falsetto they'd heard earlier. Bucky and his gang groveled lower, knees shifting, asses up and bellies on the ground. The carriers lifted their burden once again and backed away into the shadows of the smoke-filled hut. On the return trip, the creature on the bier raised a plaintive cry that sounded like a single word. At this, the wrinkled crone stirred, rose to her feet, and followed the procession into the hut.

Once the chief, shaman or chairman of the board was out of sight, a dry rattle of bones sounded from within. That was the signal for Bucky, Biff, and the rest of the thugs that the audience was ended. They leaped to their feet to roughly drag their prisoners back away from the skin palace and past the holding pit. Standing deeper in the shadows of the golden rooftop was a stout cage of crossed birch poles tied in place by bundled thongs. A gate was swung open, and the four captives were shoved inside. The gate was then closed and secured with a length of knotted straps. Bucky and the others departed, leaving only Biff behind as guard.

The cage was about the size of a double-wide trailer home, obviously constructed to hold many more captives. The floor was a raised platform of interlaced bamboo shafts and crusted with feces from previous occupants. The stench of shit and piss was overpowering. The floor was a shifting black carpet of millions of flies suspended over a cesspit.

There were twenty or more occupants already enclosed inside. A huddle of men and women and a couple of kids gathered back in the far corner. They looked up at the newcomers with little interest. There was an empty, vacant look in their eyes. These were the eyes of people in shock, who'd seen pure horror and deep loss and were broken by it.

Jimbo had seen that look before. In the faces of villagers in the Helmond after the Taliban had been through. In Haditha and Tikrit in the wake of Al Qaeda occupations.

Their fellow captives had jet-black hair and olive skin. "They're from Neeta's village. This is what's left of them," Jimbo said.

"Your in-laws, Renzi," Bat said.

"Fuck them. What about us?" Rick said.

"The little lady tells us where her knife is hidden, and we go get our guns back," Jimbo said.

## 37

## BROTHERS IN THE WOODS

"Can you talk to us, Neeta? Tell us where Ricky is? Ricky?" Lee said.

N'itha recovered with the help of some sips of water and a cool cloth on her forehead. She looked like hell. Muddy as a drowned rat with bleeding cuts to her arms and legs where she had run through miles of brambles to catch up with them.

She could sure talk. Only she was as little help conscious as she had been in a faint. The language problem was an insurmountable barrier. Whatever way she had of communicating with Rick Renzi was intuitive and relied a lot on their year of closely shared company. To the pair of Rangers, it was just a bunch of hand-waving and babble spiced with a few choice Renzi-isms.

"Big shit! Biiiig shit! Men! Holy fuck! Men!" she shouted and pulled at them before falling back into the rapid-fire gibberish of what passed for her language.

"Slow down, Neeta. What men? Some men took Rick?" Chaz gently touched her arm.

"Rikki! Gone! Men!" N'itha slapped Chaz's hand. He withdrew it, but she grabbed his wrist and stroked the back of his hand with her fingers.

"Men! Men! Men!" she said, touching his hand as she repeated it.

"Men? Like me? Black men?"

She nodded her head with enthusiasm.

"Damn. There's *brothers* here? Black men?" Chaz said, astonished.

She nodded, pulling on his wrist and pointing north along the trail they were following in pursuit of their friends. All the jabber was riling up the skinnies who kept running down the trail and back, urging the Rangers on with hoots and grunts. Whether or not they understood N'itha was an open question, but they surely picked something up from her tone.

"She saw *something* anyway," Lee said.

"No shit. But it doesn't do us much good if we can't understand her." Chaz brushed away Homer, who was anxiously pawing at his arm.

"They understand her somehow." Lee nodded at the agitated skinnies, who were acting like penned hounds with the scent of the fox in their snouts.

"Great. We can't talk to them either."

Lee offered N'itha the hose of his CamelBak once more. She drank deeply then took the protein bar he offered. She took one bite and ran off north down the trail with the skinnies following on her six, eating as she ran.

"We gonna let a beat-up, barefoot girl beat us to the fight?" Chaz said and took off after her.

"Fuck," Lee snarled and gave chase.

---

It was late afternoon by the time they reached the foot of the causeway. Chaz had to take N'itha around the waist and lift her bodily off the ground to keep her from haring off across the causeway and taking their platoon of skinnies with her.

"Slow down, girl. You have guts. Now we use our brains and Ranger logic," he said in her ear as soothing as he could. Chaz used the same voice he used when he was a kid to calm the milk cows back on Uncle Red's farm. It worked. She was still humming with a desire to bolt but seemed to grasp his cautioning tone.

The Rangers urged the skinnies into concealment in the tall reeds and gestured for the agitated man-eaters to stay quiet by holding their hands over their mouths. The boggy apron of the causeway was covered in fresh human tracks, some booted. A pair of size thirteens another size eleven and the smaller imprint of Bat's boots and Byrus' sneakers. They were alive when they passed this point not that long ago. All the other prints told them this place was heavily trafficked by whoever it was who took their friends.

The skinnies complied and squatted down out of sight below the tops of the razor grass and cattails at the edge of the marsh. Most of them curled up and fell asleep, heaped together like house cats all around the big .50 caliber they'd humped all this way. N'itha argued with Chaz in an urgent whisper and finally sat down and was soon asleep, legs crossed and head drooped forward.

"You keep watch here," Lee said. "I'm going to find some high ground." He made his way through the rushes heading for a collection of rocks visible above them along the tree line. It formed a level knob with a view of the marsh and the causeway surface.

Chaz munched a HOOAH! bar washed down with filtered water mixed with an instant coffee packet. The cold joe was nasty, but he needed to stay awake. After nearly twelve hours of pushing hard and only a couple hours' sleep before that, he was beat. If he lowered his head for a second, he'd be gone as fast as the skinnies snoring away all around him. Only Homer was awake, sucking on a Marlboro, eyes half-lidded and bloodshot.

---

Lee lay atop the rise and read the land.

The half-mile-long causeway was God's own chokepoint, the only way to their target other than humping around the marsh that surrounded the lake. And there was no assurance that there was a way to the settlement around the other side. On a sweep of the lakeshore with the 30x, he spotted a splash of white water and spreading ripples. Further study revealed a wide muddy slide free of vegetation, a sure sign of crocs or gators. As he watched, he saw subtle movement on the shore. What he thought was a hummock of mud at first, with a focus adjustment, revealed itself to be a long crocodilian of some species separating itself from a pile of maybe a dozen other gators slumbering in the sunlight. Further study showed him even more scaly horrors lying slathered in muck along the water's edge.

He turned the glass back to the settlement. The post-and-wicker fence wall was pure cheeseball. He could probably kick down a section with his boots. What lay beyond was more troubling. Columns of smoke rose from cook fires among the rooftops packed cheek by jowl inside the fence line. Lots of columns. Lots of cook fires. When the wind shifted, he could smell the fish frying even over the rich funk of the swamp. There were no canoes pulled up on the shore. These weren't water-going folks. Couldn't blame them, with a lake full of gators on the shores and God alone knew what else below the surface.

Wading the marsh might have been a quick and dirty way in and out but for those seen and unseen dangers. Scaling the sleeping monsters to the length of the cattails near them he saw they were easily twenty footers or more. He'd been a lot closer to these kind of bastards on an op in Sarawak than he ever cared to be. They owned the water here, and he'd let them have it.

The village sat near the foot of a range of tall red cliffs. Beautiful high ground but on the wrong side of the target zone for him. And humping to the peak would take days. Lee didn't think Bat, Jimbo, and the others had that kind of time. If the Rangers and company were going to be pulled out of there, it would have to be tonight while they were hopefully still alive and all together in one place.

Lee turned his gaze back to the fenced compound. It was extensive. Twenty acres of densely packed rooftops around a large central structure. None of it looked very sturdy. It was all certainly flammable. A little napalm and a few 20mm grenades in the right place, and it would be one giant barbecue with the locals trapped inside. Worse come to worst, payback would be easy. That gave him cold comfort. A rescue was still the mission priority.

The big structure at the center of the village made him curious. It was like a sports dome designed by Tarzan except for the roof. The surface of it was rippled, the details clear in the 30x scope borrowed from Jimbo's rifle. It shimmered in the afternoon sunlight. A burnished yellow glow. Like gold. Gold. The roof of the big hooch was gold. A ton of it.

Two tons. Maybe three.

However this ended, he'd be back in a hundred thousand years or so to check this place out again.

Lee crawled backward off the ledge and down to Chaz to work out what came next.

38

THE HIDDEN BLADE

Bat Jaffe's hideaway knife was cleverly concealed in the heel of one of her boots. Even close examination didn't reveal the tiny indentation of a fingernail-deep hold at the rear of the heel. She and Jimbo maneuvered themselves to be back to back. She directed him where to touch for it. He worked his nearly numbed fingers as she directed his hands.

The blade slid free, and Jimbo concentrated on maintaining his grip on the narrow, rubberized handle. He couldn't manage to bend his swollen wrists to an angle that would allow him to saw through his own bonds. There was too much risk of losing his grip. Drop the knife, and it might fall through the crisscross bamboo flooring into the tub of shit beneath them. He moved closer to touch the point of the blade to the thongs around Bat's wrists. The blood loss to his constricted hands caused him to lose his finer sense of touch.

"That's me," she said in a hush. "Sorry. We good now?" he whispered.

"Yes. You're on the leather. Just press. Don't saw. Let the blade do the work. I'll tell you if you're cutting me."

Biff was seated against the door of the cage and fast asleep with his chin on one knee. His stone hammer lay in his lap.

The blade was razor-sharp and parted the stiff leather with little effort. Even so, the Pima's face and neck were running with fresh sweat before he felt the last strand snap free and heard Bat sigh in grateful relief. She drew away from him and stood up, rubbing life back into her hands. They dripped with her own blood where the blade had nicked her. She took the spade-shaped tool from Jimbo's fingers and cut him loose before slicing off the choker around her own neck and casting it aside. Rick and Byrus were soon free, and all were flexing to restore feeling to their blood-starved fingers. Pins and needles flooded through their knuckles, growing to sharp stabbing pains as constricted vessels filled with blood once more, giving life to sleeping nerves.

"Hurts so good," Rick said. Byrus grunted in assent.

Jimbo made shushing noises to Ricky and Byrus. No need to wake up Biff.

It was growing dark outside the skin palace. The only light reaching them was from the guttering pyre atop the cairn. It had to be fed by pitch or tar of some kind to keep burning this long without being fed. There was no movement visible through the thick weave of the cage walls other than insects fluttering in the gloom.

Bat gripped the knife and, without a word to the others, crept over the creaking bamboo floor and leaned close to the gate, her face against the surface. She drew her arm back and drove the point of the blade hard through a narrow space between two birch poles. Three rapid punches inside of a second. Her boot sole squeaked on the flooring as she reset her footing for one final plunge. There was a gurgling exhalation from outside the lattice wall. She stepped back, her arm gleaming crimson to the elbow.

Biff tumbled over in a heap with three strikes to the base of his skull, stone dead.

The knife sliced through the leather ties keeping the gate secured in place. Jimbo and Byrus put their shoulders to it and shoved against the sentry's corpse. Biff's dead weight rolled aside, clearing the way to open the gate wide. Jimbo picked up the stone-headed bludgeon from where it lay by Biff. The blue man wore an expression of dull surprise that would be frozen forever on his face.

Bat turned back to the group of their fellow captives huddled in the rear of the cage. They'd made no move, no sound as the newcomers freed themselves, killed their guard, and opened the cage. Bat gestured to them to come on. They were not bound in any way. They were free to leave. But these were prisoners in mind as well as body. They were resigned to die with no wish to hasten that time. They regarded her dully as though uncomprehending. Bat turned and left them behind.

Without a shared word the pair of Rangers, Byrus and Bat moved, keeping to the darkest shadows and any available cover, for the front of the skin palace where they had last seen their weapons and gear.

An indigo figure emerged with a rush from the darkness before them. Jimbo brought him down with a line-drive to the side of the head that sent blood and skull fragments flying in a spray.

They all turned at a high keening cry. The naked crone stood with toothless mouth wide and rheumy eyes bulging. A wavering finger pointed their way like the judgment of God.

"Fuck this," Rick said and broke into a hobbling run on a beeline for the skin palace. The others raced after.

All around them voices rose in call and answer. The village was up and hot for blood.

Jimbo was the first to round the front of the skin palace and into the wavering glow from atop the stone cairn.

Out of the gloom all around charged a brace of the blue brothers howling like wolves and swinging their stone hammers overhead. It would be a race for the weapons stash. Whoever reached it first lived. Second place was the grave.

Except the weapons and packs were no longer stacked before the skin palace.

They were gone.

39

## THE FIVE-STAR CELL

Morris Tauber's captivity was considerably more pleasant. He had free range of the multi-room suite Taan had provided for him. In fact, he had free range of the entire city of Shanghai and the surrounding province should he choose to travel. Basically, China was his prison. Mr. Taan's only insistence was that he take along a translator as well as security. For his own safety, of course.

The condo had high speed, uncensored, internet that he was free to use as well as satellite feed with an astonishing number of channels of television, movies, and music. The telephone was open to his use even though Morris knew that it, as well as all his internet communications, would be monitored.

Food service was unlimited as well. He could order anything from Kobe beef to a real Philadelphia cheesesteak at any hour of the day or night by simply picking up a phone, and it would be sent up from the fully staffed kitchen on the condo's ground floor. The menu was updated daily with new items. A walk-in closet was stocked with clothing in his size and taste, and there were shoes to go with them. Khaki pants in tan and dark green, and button-down shirts from Willis and Geiger in white, black, and loden. Apparently, Mr. Taan's organization had access to his purchase history as Kenneth Armbruster of Halifax, Nova Scotia.

Even the bathroom was stocked with his usual brand of soap, shampoo, and toothpaste.

His own personal full-time concierge suggested events Morris might want to attend or sights that would be worth visiting. He also implied, in the most discreet manner imaginable, that feminine companionship could be obtained were Dr. Tauber interested. Morris declined politely and emphatically, and the subject was never mentioned again.

Despite all of these comforts and distractions, he was bored out of his mind. Being left with nothing to do but choose his next amusement left him adrift. He missed work. His work. It was his life, and he was dedicated to it. It was why he got out of bed in the morning and stayed out of bed after breakfast. The Tauber Tube took up most of his mind's activity, and now he was being kept from his programs and files and notes. Most painful of all, his study of the books and files provided by Samuel Renzi had been truncated by this abduction. His suffering was acute.

This unwanted sabbatical from his regular work, this damned vacation, was Morris' by choice. He was allowed remote access to the database aboard the *Ocean Raj*. He could continue his examination and studies. But he was determined that Taan and his corporate pirates would not get a door into his and Caroline's encrypted files.

His memory was quite good if hardly eidetic. All he could do was play with the theorems and constructs that he could recall in his mind. He couldn't record his thoughts or even take notes on paper lest they fall into the hands of his captors. It was maddening. Possessed of a highly analytical mind, he still longed to record and organize his thoughts in some medium other than his brain.

For now, the only card Morris held was Taan's ignorance of the location of the Tauber Tube and Team Tauber—as Morris referred to the Rangers in his mind. And Morris himself was an indispensable asset due to the contents of his mind.

I guess that's actually two cards, Morris thought.

Taan just had to be patient before he could get his way. He seemed to have a well of patience as infinitely deep as his confidence. The smugness of the man infuriated Morris. At least Taan understood that they could not accede to his wishes until the team was reassembled in one place and time. Morris didn't fully understand the reasons for the delays himself.

He tried to inquire about the postponements during his frequent satellite calls to Caroline. She was more cryptic than informative.

"There have been some complications," Caroline had said the night before.

"Hardware or software?" Morris asked. It was well after midnight in Shanghai. He watched the lights winking through the haze lying on the surface of the harbor. Big ships maneuvered in their slow-motion dance for space along the piers.

"Hardware. Humanware. We've lost contact. The long-range communications are down on the away end, Mo."

"When was last contact?"

"Our time? A week. Their time? They were at Day Six the last time we received from them."

"What was their situation then?"

"Primary objective obtained. They were getting ready to return to the extraction point. Something must have happened. They either lost long-range comms or comms altogether."

"The channel is still live?"

"Five by five, as the man says."

"The man" would be Dwayne Roenbach, his brother-in-law. Caroline wasn't using names.

"That means you can measure elapsed time downfield," Morris said.

"Two days. They've been out of contact for two days," she said after conferring with someone in the room with her.

"Do you have any game plan?"

"We're working on it. I'll let you know when we have some answers. Then we can deal with your situation. Are you okay?"

"I'm in danger of being pampered to death. Don't worry about me. I have a very understanding jailer. As long as you maintain regular contact that he and his minions can listen in on, I think they'll keep the thumbscrews and waterboard in the attic." That was for Taan and any minions that happened to be listening. Morris' own tiny effort at rebellion.

"Good. I'll keep you posted. Take care, Mo. We miss you," she said and hung up. There was something in her voice. A note of tension. Well, she had a lot on her plate with a baby on board, a missing brother, and contact lost with the Rangers somewhere back in prehistoric Nevada.

———

"He doesn't know. He has no idea," Caroline said, setting the sat phone down on the table in the galley.

"He's better off that way. You think they're treating him okay or is he putting up a brave front?" Dwayne took from his ear the earbud he'd been using to listen to the conversation.

"Mo sounds bored off his ass. It's for real. They're babying him," she said and rose to pour a mug of coffee she didn't want. She just wanted an excuse to pace.

"For now."

"Yeah. He has no idea what he's in the middle of. To Morris, it's all academic. He's more concerned with his work than anything else. They've managed to convince him that they mean him no harm." She stirred a spoon in the mug in a listless circle.

"They covered their tracks. That kid who had the fossil with

Bat's boot print vanished. Probably taco filling now. They could do that to all of us."

"And we thought we were in trouble with Sir Neal."

"We'll work it out. We always do. We have what they want. It's not in this Taan's interests to hurt any of us now. But we need a plan."

"I haven't asked you to sign on for this, Dwayne," she said.

"Well, we *are* signed on." He touched her hand.

"You can't speak for the others. This Taan could be sending you into a situation you won't come back from."

"If it makes you feel better, we'll all take a vote when they get back."

"*If* they get back. *If* we haven't lost them." She met his eyes.

"Boats and me are working on something. Give it a week or so, and we'll open the field again for a recon."

"You're going back there?"

"What choice do we have? We know where they were when we heard from them last."

"Just you and Boats? You two barely made it back this last time."

"The ribs are healing. They'll be knit solid by the time we head back."

"But all that way on foot. Just the pair of you." It was her turn to grip his hand.

"Boats and I have a few ideas. A workaround. Cut the travel time down to a day at the most."

"What are your ideas?"

"Actually, Chaz thought of it first." Dwayne smiled.

## 40

## KIND TO BE CRUEL

The indigo men came on in an encircling mass. Horns sounded. The old bitch shrieked and stabbed an accusing finger at the escapees.

The Rangers, the Macedonian, and Xena of East Highland Park tried to withdraw, only to find their line of retreat blocked by yapping blue fuckers whirling hammers over their heads. A storm of thrown stone clubs was followed by a charge closing on them from all around.

Rick was struck in the back and dropped to his knees, gasping with pain. Jimbo stood by him, swinging his borrowed club backhand and forehand. He brained one warrior, sending teeth hurling away. He crushed the throat of another with a thrust, the stone end of the club taking the man just below the chin with an audible crunch. Hands grabbed at him, and he shrugged them off, whirling the club in an arc that connected with bone and flesh.

Byrus was off on Jimbo's flank, covering the Pima's blind side.

The little man was striking out with fists and teeth, falling back on his days as a pit fighter. He expertly hooked a thumb in the open mouth of a screaming blue man and tore the lower half of the man's face from his jaw like ripping paper. The man dropped, shrieking and spewing blood. Byrus drove the heel of his hand into the face of a second man, snapping the septum up into the howling warrior's brain with a single vicious blow. The guy dropped like a sack of wet sand.

More bastards leaped over their dead comrade to launch themselves at the Macedonian. He lost his footing. They dragged him to the dirt and pinned his wrists to his body. Byrus shook his head violently back and forth until he got his teeth on the ear of one of his attackers. He jerked his head to the left, neck muscles straining and felt the ear lobe tear from the head of his victim in a long strip of flesh. His mouth filled with the sweet coppery ambrosia of an enemy's blood. The splash of warm excrescence blinded him. His back struck the ground, and the air was driven from his lungs by a crush of knees all over him from thighs to shoulders.

Deadliest of all was Bat Jaffe. She held the spade-shaped dagger in her fist and punched out with it. Any poor blue meanie who got close enough got three hard strikes to the abdomen or neck delivered with the speed of a piston. The dagger tore them open like piñatas. She had a heap of dead growing before her. Bat was hissing between clenched teeth with each breath. Her heart raced, and her mind sang with fury. They would not tie her hands again.

A warrior leaped at her, flinging his club. She ducked under his throw and reached out to slice open his femoral artery. A spray of dark blood splashed over her as the man tumbled back into his comrades and clutched at his thigh in a futile attempt to stem the flushing of his lifeblood onto the ground. She was backing toward Byrus, punching and slicing. Another thrown hammer struck her knife hand. An arm reached around her neck and yanked her off her feet. Others moved in, reaching for her. She slashed out with the blade, slicing fingers to stumps and flaying forearms. Her foot caught another warrior with a toe kick to the face, crushing the man's eye socket to red jelly. Sheer numbers brought her down at last. A vice-like grip twisted her wrist.

The blade fell from her fingers. A scream of rage rose up from deep within her as she felt her arm pulled painfully behind her and fresh loops of leather looped about her wrists. Though the binding process was agony, they were making an effort not to harm her. That was a bad thing, she decided. A very bad thing.

They were saving her for something.

The four captives were bound and hauled upright. Bucky paced before them, seething. He had a hand clamped to his head. Rivulets of blood flowed between his fingers. It was his ear that Byrus had done a Mike Tyson on. The little Macedonian grinned defiantly at the blue man, blood glistening on his teeth. Bucky stood before him huffing and puffing, eyes like twin blazes of cold fire from his wine-dark face.

"They got plans for us, bro," Rick said. "Yeah," was all Jimbo could manage.

The mob of blue warriors was joined by the rest of the village. It looked like the entire population was out for a night on the town. They muttered with excitement. Some kids pitched rocks at the prisoners until they were run off by Bucky spitting and barking.

The whole party moved back in the direction of the cage, shoving Jimbo and the others before them. From pitched battle to celebration, it was all taking on a Mardi Gras feel with laughter and shouting from the mob. Horns were blown, and fingers tapped small drums of animal hide stretched over rings of warped birch branches. They reached the cage where the score or so of locals were hauled out and pushed into place to join the company of Jimbo, Rick, Bat, and Byrus. Bucky led the way, with old noodle tits crab-walking beside him and giggling like a mental patient. The noisy parade moved out through an opening in the rear of the skin palace and along a trail of beaten earth in the direction of the cliffs standing black against a sky of fast-moving clouds.

Whatever they were being saved for lay ahead of them at those cliffs. From the excitement building in the crowd, Jimbo surmised that this was a welcome event. Party time for the blue crew with the Rangers and their friends the guests of honor.

Jimbo recalled those headless skeletons that decorated the fence surrounding the village. Well, that particular mystery would be solved soon, he thought.

## 41

# COOLIDGE LEFT

Lee Hammond had made it through sniper school at Fort Benning more through persistence than anything else. He called it "the tyranny of will." Two times he'd gone from Harmony Church to FTX, washing out before the final shot. The wind had not been with him. The third time he'd made it through the grueling course to the end. He struck the final shot at one thousand yards by sheer luck. The metallic clang of his round hitting home was the sweetest sound he'd ever heard. The stress, abuse, and four-hundred-yard crawls through freezing mud. Three times to make the cut. Three times to get that sniper patch.

He'd never be the natural marksman that Jimmy Smalls was even if he used that man's rifle. The Pima had some sixth or seventh sense that let him up close to his target on some spiritual level Lee could never achieve. Once in the crosshairs of the one-eyed Indian, the targets could probably hear an astrally-projected whisper in their ear before the killing round ended all their worries forever. Or some mystic shit like that, Lee imagined.

Or maybe the son of a bitch just had eyesight like Catfish Hunter.

But within five hundred yards Hammond could drive nails with a Model 70 eight times out of ten. Good enough for him.

And that's where he was positioned. Downrange in the deepening dark of the causeway with the night-vision scope sweeping the front façade of the wicker fence before the village where his friends were being held. He was standing for the best view. The dark of night was his hide. Behind him, fifty yards or more, Chaz was holding back the skinnies, waiting for Lee's sign to come forward. That was a job in itself. Homer and the others smelled blood and were twitchy to get some action of their own.

The moon was low in an overcast sky. Clouds were building, and a warm wind made the cattails dance and the rushes murmur.

The air was alive with every bug in the hemisphere. Mosquitos the size of sparrows. Cicadas as big as pigeons buzzing and fluttering. The water on either side of the causeway was a source of high white noise. Toads chirruped. Lizards croaked. Frogs wah-wahed. Something cackled in sudden bursts now and then. It was a mad rave of animal noise rising and falling in a discordant rhythm that could drive anyone insane if they listened long enough, the brain trying to make sense of a senseless cacophony.

Brain-numbing, and it covered all noise of their approach like a warm and fuzzy audio blanket of sound.

In the greenish field visible through the lens, ghost-like figures meandered in the flickering light of pitch torches mounted on the fence wall. The meandering ghosts threw crazed emerald shadows on the sand.

Five targets. Male. Near naked. Little guys but clearly human. One of them turned to look right at Lee in the 30x view, eyes aglow like a raccoon caught in a headlight.

A squeeze on the trigger.

The thick, wet air absorbed the suppressed cough of the big

rifle. The creatures of the night had a sudden hiccup in their riff but filled the gap of silence back in within a half-second.

Lee brought the scope back down level. His target lay still on the ground. Two of his buddies ambled over to see why their pal suddenly dropped to the mat as if thunderstruck.

The crosshairs shifted to center mass of the largest of the curious duo. Squeeze. The man slumped to the sand. Shift. Squeeze. A skull turned to vapor. The remaining pair of dummies realized something was up but stayed on the shore, searching blindly into the surrounding dark.

Squeeze. One of the peepers dropped as though pole-axed.

The last clueless bastard realized that he was next for the chop. He turned to sprint for the open gateway. Lee's finger pressed on the ridged surface of the trigger ever so slowly. A few foot-pounds of pressure and

the final sentry stumbled to a stop and dropped face-down, arms spread, three paces from the gateway.

His trainer at Benning would say they were weak cheese shots. But this country was the baddest of the bad bush, and here there were no weak cheese shots. No milk runs. No easy days. He was five for five, and the way was clear for insertion into the hot zone.

Lee turned and cut the surrounding din with a two-finger whistle.

Chaz led the skinnies across the causeway toward him at the trot. Bart and Millhouse were closest to him, carrying bandoliers of extra mags for the M4s. Homer followed close and took the Winchester back from Lee. He winced at the scorching touch of the hot barrel. N'itha was silent and staring from among the pack of softly hooting and cooing skinnies. This was as quiet as they could be. This was monkey noise discipline and the best the Rangers could hope for.

Restoring his M4 to his combat sling, Lee turned to his merry band of brothers.

"Gate's clear. Wide open for infil. Any thoughts on tactics?"

"Once we're inside the skinnies will do what they do. It's up to you and me to locate our people and pull them out of there. I'll keep Neeta close since I can't keep her back."

"Love," Lee snorted.

Chaz nodded. "Fucking A."

"As a plan, it sucks dick," Lee said, drawing back the cocking handle on his rifle back to chamber a round.

"Bad plan's better than no plan."

"And love is free, but sex is twenty bucks."

"Hoo-ah, asshole."

"Rikki?" N'itha said, eyes shining like pewter in the muted moonlight.

"Yes. Ricky," Chaz said and smiled, hoping the confidence he was faking was some comfort to her.

"Let's go twenty-first century on their prehistoric asses," Lee said and trotted toward the glow of the fires. Rain began to fall in fat gobbets.

The platoon of naked man-apes followed their calls growing louder with their excitement. They knew jack shit about war. All they understood was that here was live meat on the other side of the water, and it was theirs for the taking.

4 2

# THE PIT AND THE HAMMER

The carnival throng of blue men and their wild entourage hiked under torchlight along a ledge that followed around the base of the red cliffs on a curving path. Their prisoners were shoved and pulled before them, leaders of the parade. The rock ledge was less than ten feet across at the narrowest spot causing the revelers and their unwilling guests to contract into a long column marching away from the village into the shadows of the sheer rock wall towering above. The surface of the pathway was slick with fresh rain beginning to lash down in big drops. An equatorial rain, heavy and hot.

Bucky yapped away and jabbed upwards with his stone bludgeon. A group of warriors broke from the line to clamber up a slender path that sloped up the wall at a thirty-degree angle. There was only room for them to move in single file, but they did so with practiced ease, moving at a run while staying on the hand-width trail high up into the greater dark.

Jimbo craned his neck to the extent the choker about his throat would allow. He watched the twenty or so blue fuckers climb out of sight above them. It was all a part of a ritual that he was in no hurry to see any more of. His mind worked furiously.

They were bound and weaponless. In addition to that, they were outnumbered with no place to run. To one side of the path was a near-vertical rock wall. To the other, a drop into a shadowy pit roughly oval in shape.

Out of that pit rose the heavy funk of rotting flesh. The sweet, cloying smell of decomposition. Jimbo risked a look over the lip of the ledge as he tramped along. In the pit below grew thick stands of flowering sumac. A flash of lightning ripped the sky in half and momentarily illuminated the floor of the depths.

The flickering blue radiance flashed off the white of bones. The remains of thousands of souls. Human rib cages, femurs, spines, and scapulae. A vast collection of bones from years and years of victims. Generations of dead captives that went before them up this ledge. The source of the decorations that lined the fence without. Every manner of skeletal remnants lay below but one.

Not a single skull.

These victims were tossed to this mass grave without heads.

A second flash of lightning came on the heels of a crack of thunder that resounded off the surrounding rocks with a fearful resonance. This second glimpse into the pit revealed dead who'd been disposed of more recently. The black shapes of carrion eaters of some unknown species crawled over the gray-white flesh of corpses littering the slopes of the crater. Men and women. Children and infants. All discarded like so much rubbish. A landfill of the forgotten, now food for vermin.

And each without a head. It was an unwanted preview of what lay ahead.

"We're not going down easy," Jimbo said loud enough for the others to hear over the sing-song chants and jeers of the following mob.

"Fucking A," Rick growled low then repeated it in a shout at the top of his lungs. Blue men around him laughed at the sound.

"It is all booshit," Byrus said, understanding the sentiment if not the nuance.

"Say the word, Jimmy. I'm ready to take some of these assholes over the side with me," Bat said, jaw clamped tight to keep her teeth from chattering.

The final rush. Jimbo could feel a flush through his limbs, rising warm from his belly. Adrenalin, born of fear, infused him. Next would come the calm, the easy feeling of knowing that death was likely and close. He'd felt it before. Back on Highway One in Afghanistan in an MRAP that was flipped by a roadside bomb. He lay listening to the strike of rounds on the armor and the screams of his platoon mates. The most recent time he had this sensation of battle Nirvana was above a dry wash in Judea when men were coming for him and Byrus with spear and sword.

He wished the Pimas had a death chant. At least there was none he knew of. His tribe weren't those kinds of Indians. Not like the Cherokee or the Crow. The Pima were a happier people than their more dour brothers to the north and east. The only thing close to a death song that came to him was the Johnny Cash tune, "The Ballad of Ira Hayes," that everyone in his tribe knew by heart. The story of Hayes, a Pima who joined the Marines in World War Two and was one of the jarheads who raised the flag atop Suribachi.

*There they battled up Iwo Jima's hill,*
*Two Hundred and fifty men*
*But only twenty-seven lived to walk back down again.*
*And when the fight was over*
*And when Old Glory raised*
*Among the men who held it high*
*Was the Indian, Ira Hayes.*

Jimbo laughed when he thought of it. Going to the happy hunting grounds and my death song was written by a white guy, he thought. Well, it was the Man in Black anyway. Can't do much better than that.

The ledge widened gradually until it grew to a shelf of rock broad enough for much of the accompanying crowd to gather in a half-circle. Others watched from farther back up the trail. The younger among them climbed to the vantage posts of natural mantels in the rock where they sat with legs swinging or stood clinging to the cliff face, eyes eager for what came next. This was the big show. No one wanted to miss what was coming except the victims.

The center of all the attention was a niche in the face of the red cliffs that ran all the way up into the dark above. It may have started as a natural formation but showed signs of being deepened and widened in places with tools of some kind. The interior was a yard across. The surface shone with rainwater that ran down its smooth surface like a natural downspout. The most unusual feature was a rounded stone resting at the bottom of the niche. It was six foot in height and an arm's breadth around at its widest point. It looked to weigh a half-ton. There were ropes of wound hemp fortified with leather and bound around it in a sturdy netting. A wrist-thick rope rose as a cinch above it to run up the vertical channel to where it vanished into the gloom above. The rope was hemp or sinew and wrapped around with bands of leather to prevent breaking. The rope was made to hold the full weight of the thousand-pound stone.

The bottom of the hemp-wrapped stone and the floor of the channel were stained black to a height of three feet with a black rivulet running down the slight slope to the shelf of rock upon which they all stood. It was blood. A permanent stain. The stink gave it away.

Jimbo was getting a sense of the significance of all this when the naked old bitch came creeping up to them with a gaggle of topless women behind her. Each of the women carried wooden bowls filled with a powdery substance the consistency of flour. There was red, yellow and blue silt and the women pitched handfuls of the stuff on the prisoners standing in a loose rank. Dried and crushed flower petals pounded into a fine dust. Jimbo recognized the sweet smell of cornflowers and marigolds. This was all part of a familiar ritual, and the women wore faces frozen in solemnity. The crowd waited silently until all the prisoners were coated head to foot with the flung Technicolor residue that was quickly mixing into a mud-colored mess under the increasing rainfall.

At this the mob let out a whoop, raising and lowering their arms in unison like a drunken baseball crowd failing at performing The Wave. They whooped and waved until the bleats of a horn called them to quiet. The capacity crowd parted to allow the bier-carriers passage. The blue men bore the twisted form of the god-king onto the shelf and up to the line of prisoners. They wore ceremonial skirts of long feathers now drenched and slick with rain.

The freak waved the fingers of his one whole hand in some kind of gesture of damnation or benediction, or maybe it was a palsy. The crowd lowered their eyes. Many dropped to the ground as if they'd been flung down. They bopped their foreheads on the stone in regular rhythm.

N'itha's people lowered their eyes as well. They feared this malformed curiosity as much as his loyal followers loved him. They had reason to be scared. This fucked up mutant was the undisputed Caesar and Jesus here. He was about to give the people what they wanted.

Bucky threw his head back and bawled a command that reverbed off the rocks. From high above, there was an answering call followed by numerous grunts. These were the blue guys Jimbo had seen parting company with the rest and climbing up the cliff wall on that skinny sill in the rock.

The hemp rope was pulled taut from above. Water sprayed from it as the fibers tightened and thrummed. With each succeeding grunt, the pillar of rock was hauled a few more feet up the channel. It rose, grinding on the interior of the channel until it was lost to sight in the gloom. The cadence of grunts continued until the thousand-pound weight was drawn, by Jimbo's guess, at least a hundred feet above the base of the red cliff.

A shout echoed down from above. Bucky called back and turned to the line of captives before him. He walked down the rank, tapping each prisoner on the chest lightly with the rounded stone at the end of his club. A grin split his face when he stopped before a young girl who looked to be no older than twelve. Bucky touched her face with his fingers then yanked her chin up, forcing her to look him in the face. The irises of her eyes quivered with the fear rising within her. He took a handful of her hair and pulled her from the line.

Indigo warriors stepped up and took hold of her as she bucked and scratched and kicked to be released from Bucky's grip. They carried her bodily to the foot of the vertical pipe. They laid her down on her back with her head positioned within the niche atop the blood-stained rock. Blue men sat on her chest and legs to hold her in place. The crowd took in an audible breath of anticipation as Bucky raised his hammer and howled a command.

The thousand-pound stone thundered down from above. A rising scream could be heard above the growing grind of the falling weight dropping down the stone throat of the shaft. The girl shrieked at the sight of the crushing weight racing down toward her. The stone struck with an impact that could be felt as well as heard, cutting off the girl's scream in an instant. The blue men seated atop the girl were showered with blood, bone chips, and globs of brain matter.

A second of silence followed only to be shattered by the throng's sudden roar of joyous approval. The noise shook Jimbo out of the stunned torpor that riveted him in the wake of this new horror.

The rope grew taut again, and the stone was hauled back up the channel for another round.

The girl's body was dragged from its place. Her head was now gone. Only a mess of blood, brain matter, and bone fragments splashed on the face of the rock and the bodies of her handlers remained. Grinning, teeth yellow against the greasy crimson mess dripping from their faces, they dragged her across the rock shelf and tossed her off the edge into the pit below.

The mob was mindless with glee, cheering and calling and stamping their feet in mad jigs. Some women dropped to their hands and knees in orgasmic seizures, and some of the blue men accommodated them, mounting them from behind to copulate with violence and without shame. As each man swiftly exhausted himself another took his place. The look on the women's faces was a horror of pain and pleasure painted with running lime, the ash black around their eyes, creating ebon tears. This was the human race as a feral pack. Sex and death all wrapped in a ceremony that satisfied their lusts for both.

Those who weren't indulging in an orgy of animal sex were chanting for the next victim.

The deformed freak atop the bier let out an extended squeal while raising a shuddering hand.

It was time for the stone to fall once more.

## GONE RABID

Bat was next.

The juddering fingers of the gibbering man child pointed to her, and Bucky made for her.

Jimbo and Rick launched themselves simultaneously. Jimbo won the sprint and, after a hop to give him some loft, drove his head down into the stunned Bucky's face with all the force he could muster. The thong cut into his throat, shutting off his breath as he bent his jackknifed body to strike downward. He stumbled past Bucky, fighting to stay on his feet. To fall was to die. To fall was the end of the fight.

Bucky's two front teeth snapped off at the gum line and were lost in the jet of blood gushing from his crushed nose. They were going to have to change the little bastard's nickname. He fell hard on his ass, eyes white and spinning in their sockets. His ear and two teeth gone in one night.

The blue men got over their initial shock and rushed the four from all around. Bat leaped and kicked, and many fell to their knees, sucking air and clutching testicles mashed by her steel-toed boots. Byrus simply hurled himself headlong into the mass like a gristle missile. He rammed a screaming blue meanie in the midsection, using his head as a blunt instrument at a full run. He was staying to Jimbo's blind side, protecting his closest friend in all the world. The impact of Byrus' attack drove his victim back into a clutch of others, and all fell in a heap with the Macedonian kicking and biting atop them.

Jimbo rushed the surrounding warriors, ducking under their club swings to break through the ring around them. He hammered out an opening, sending men to the ground, only to see the gap instantly filled in again. Rick followed close behind him, stamping his booted foot down on the heads and throats of the fallen.

The twisted little king shrieked atop his throne. His bearers dropped him without ceremony and rushed into the fight. The kids picked up rocks and clods of dirt and began winging them, striking friend and foe alike.

Jimbo and Rick found themselves separated from Bat and Byrus in the confusion. The pair of Rangers stood back-to-back in an ever-shrinking circle of ground. A hand gripped the thong at Jimbo's back and yanked. His throat closed painfully. His vision went gray, then red around the edges, and he was down with knees on the ground, then at the bottom of a pile-on of fists and feet. He heard Rick spitting curses then go silent. The ligature around his neck slackened, and the blows stopped raining down. He lay gasping for air, ears ringing.

They hauled the Pima to his feet, a half dozen of the blue warriors keeping a firm hold on him. Jimbo turned his head to see Rick wriggling helplessly in the grasp of another clutch of men. Rick was bleeding from gashes, and a big purple bruise was growing over one side of his face around a cut to his cheek. Bat was hauled forward with Bucky's fist in her hair, and his other hand drawing the thong back like a bowstring to cut off her air. Her tongue stuck between her teeth, blowing spittle as she struggled to breathe.

Byrus had the worst of it. Three blue fuckers dragged him

back to the line. His dirty blonde mop of hair was stained black with blood. One eye was closed by an angry swelling that was spreading up from his jaw. The flesh of one thigh had a ragged tear sending a steady sheet of blood down his leg. He looked to be conscious but only barely. He was being held upright as much as he was being held fast.

Badly as they'd been beaten, the locals took the worst of it. Bucky's nose was a flattened black mass that looked like a blob of wet tar spread over his mouth. When he spoke, he sprayed thick gobs of blood from an upper lip with a ragged tear in it. Other warriors limped or crawled with a good number clutching their balls in sorrowful agony. At least one looked like he'd never go anywhere again, lying in a pool of blood dappled with falling rain. His jaw was nearly torn from his face, and one eye dangled at the end of a sinewy stalk.

Through all this, the captives from N'itha's village stood like sheep, uncomprehending and submissive.

Jimbo was jerked and pulled in his captor's grip. A shot to the kidneys with the end of a club buckled his knees. They dragged him back into line as Bucky hauled Bat toward the bottom of the bloody niche and the waiting hands of a gauntlet of pissed off blue guys. Bat still had fight in her and kicked and struggled with a new flush of panic. Her handlers were determined and latched onto her, locking her legs together as they lifted her from the ground. They bore her toward the niche with Bucky in the lead barking orders, spewing flecks of blood from the mess his mouth had become under Jimbo's savage head butt.

The man-child was back up on his perch atop the shoulders of his bearers and keening a string of high-pitched demands. The brawl over, the crowd was getting back into the rhythm of their chant, anxious for the next decapitation and thirsty for blood.

Bat spasmed and stiffened her body, making her handlers fight for every inch as they brought her to the plate of rock before the foot of the vertical channel. They bent at the knees to lower her in place. She planted her feet and somehow made it take the total effort of six strong men to try to shove her into place.

Her head was still just outside the niche when a grinding sound came from above, growing in volume. The pillar of granite fell down the shaft to land on the rock with a sharp crack that sent chips of stone everywhere. The pull rope fell with it, tumbling down to gather in a messy heap atop the stone leaning in the niche, its base only inches from the top of Bat's head.

The drop of the stone was followed by the bodies of screaming men raining down from above. The blue warriors sent up the narrow ramp to pull the stone aloft were crashing down on their brothers with devastating effect.

Jimbo craned his neck to look up. Against the stormy sky, he saw the green trails of tracers flashing above him toward the rock face. Over the bewildered moans of the spectators and the angered shouts of the warriors, he could now pick out the sharp claps of rifle fire.

With a renewed vigor fueled by mad hope, combined with the confusion of his handlers, Jimbo was able to break away from his handlers and stumble free. A blue man snarled and reached for the Pima only to have the top of his head vanish in a red haze. More warriors were falling. Two of the twisted king's bearers fell with exit wounds blossoming on their indigo flesh. The bier crashed down, sending the little freak tumbling to the ground, squeaking with indignation.

Panic set in. The warriors released their captives to run about waving their clubs with an impotent fury that barely concealed the utter terror they were feeling. Something invisible was striking at them, the wrath of their gods or the trickery of demons. The mystery of it was making them simple with fear.

That panic turned to total pandemonium when some of the mob saw a reddish glow reflected from the clouds hanging low to the south. Their village was on fire. A dense column of smoke was rising to join the roiling sky filled with storm clouds. White embers ascended into the air like clouds of fireflies, whipped upwards by the heat of the blaze.

Their home was burning. More than that, the fire, if it grew, would seal them in this cul-de-sac until they were roasted alive against the cliff face. The bloody sacrificial ceremony forgotten, the mob and the warriors rushed down from the shelf of rock to the narrow ledge that would take them away. Some came too close to the edge of the path. They were shoved, screaming into the crater to join their earlier victims. Their yelping king was borne away unceremoniously on the shoulders of one of his bearers. His mama shambled after at best speed calling out, begging to be taken along.

Only Bucky remained behind, too pissed off to be frightened. With a roar of rage, he charged through the remaining captives from N'itha's village, laying about himself with the club and braining adult and child alike. Those who weren't dropped by his vicious assault took off after the rest of the terrified throng.

Bucky charged on a direct path toward Jimbo raising his club, now matted with fresh blood and hair.

Lee and Chaz were out there in the dark somewhere, but the rifle fire had stopped. Maybe their angle of fire was all wrong, or they were dealing with the sudden exodus of thousands of freaked out primitives. In any case, there was no more gunfire coming. The four captives were bound and beaten and on their own.

Bucky grinned madly, the whites of his eyes gleaming out of that ruined face as he rushed for Jimbo, the focus of his rage, with club upraised for the lethal blow.

He didn't see Byrus rolling into his path.

The Macedonian tangled his legs in Bucky's and took him to the dirt. Bucky went down on one knee and brought the stone club around for a strike to Byrus' unprotected skull.

Jimbo hurled himself across the intervening space to body

check Bucky between the shoulders. The blue bastard crashed to the rock with Jimbo atop him. He still had the club in his grasp and was twisting to bring it to bear on the Pima. Rick Renzi had trotted forward and brought his booted foot down on Bucky's wrist with a meaty snap. A fresh spray of blood jetted from the warrior's mouth as he shrieked his pain to the night.

Somehow, Bat was up now and kicking at Bucky's head. They all took places around the fallen war chief and systematically drove their only weapons, their boots, into him until he moved no more. Bat was the last to admit victory. The Rangers prodded her away with their shoulders as she kept on driving her boot into the pulpy ruin of what was once her tormentor's skull. Tears cut swathes down her filthy cheeks. Her breath came in wet gasps.

They left Bucky's still and broken body to move through the litter of corpses that had fallen to the fire of the invisible gunmen.

Byrus dropped to his knees by a dead warrior. With an awkward effort, his numbed fingers found the bone handle of a flint knife. He pulled it from a sheath that hung about the corpse's waist on a thong. The Macedonian sliced through his bonds then trotted to the others still panting from their exertions.

"I will free you, baas. As you freed me." He grinned, happy as a child through a distorted face black with crusted blood.

## 44

## GOING DOWNTOWN

It was a target-rich environment while it lasted.

Lee Hammond had to give up his position on the narrow section of ledge when the frenzied mob came rushing down toward him. He was on a narrow part of the trail where it curved around the crater. From his vantage point, he could aim directly across to where his friends were about to be fed into some kind of Flintstones' version of a pile driver.

He chose to head up the trail around the pit when Chaz and the skinnies found the village below empty of anyone. Chaz got busy setting the village to the torch to give them a distraction for their exfil once, and if, they found the rest of their unit alive. The skinnies were digging the action and rushing around tossing burning brands into thatch hooches that went up like kindling. The flames spread quickly, even in the downpour.

Lee heard the chanting ahead and found the target area through his scope just as his friends' final act of defiance was ending. Jimbo and the others put up as good a fight as they could without the use of their hands. He was relieved to see Bat very much alive and *krav maga*-ing caveman ass like a champ. But as he studied the sit-rep, he saw she was being dragged toward the foot of the contraption by six or more guys all painted head to toe in blue like they'd been bathing in a chemical toilet.

The zone was well inside his optimal kill distance. He made a quick study of the contraption with the rock channel, rope, and the deadly weight. He trained the scope up to find the gang of rope pullers on a sloped section of rock high above the revelers. The scope on the M4 was a 20x with NODs option and up to the job. He sprayed the fuckers in three round bursts and brought them and their lethal hammer down. Those that didn't fall the height of the cliff were splattered on ledges on the way down. He didn't even need to hit them all. Once the killing started, they tried to rabbit off the ledge in a bunch. A good score of them simply plummeted to their demise, sliding off into space after being shoved aside by their pals.

After the big rock dropped and the party broke up, Lee chose targets of opportunity to bring down the men closest to Bat. He followed up by kakking anyone near the line-up of prisoners that included his friends. His view of them was blocked as the crowd came between him and the kill zone. The party was over, and there was only one way out of this dead end, and no place to hide on the exposed ledge.

The terrified horde was practically on his heels when he came off the foot of the curving trail. Lee dived into the cover of some pine trees and watched the passing parade of panic. Women, kids, and those buck naked blue fuckers came down the narrow trail, filling it from side to side. Where the path got too constricted, folks were jostled out of the way, usually by the blue guys sprinting along and bashing aside anyone who got between them and where they wanted to be. Not fast enough or big enough and it was over the side into the pit with your ass. He saw a woman get her brains dashed out with a single swing from one of these heroes. She and the squalling baby she carried were knocked to the ground and crushed to paste under the feet of more than a thousand of their neighbors bugging out for home.

The goddamn weirdest sights of a night of truly weird sights was a dude painted up for the Blue Man Group piggybacking some kind of dwarf who was howling like a cat with its tail caught in a car door and a shriveled up old bat with tubular tits swinging like a pair of pendulums chasing after. It was all lent a hellish touch by the rising glow of flames, as the fire in the village reached flashpoint. A hot wind was blowing embers toward the woods at the foot of the cliff face. Even in the driving rain, these pines could catch fire in a heartbeat. Lee needed to haul ass up that trail and get any survivors the fuck out of there.

Behind him, something erupted. He turned to see a blast go skyward with a white flash at its heart. Everything went black and white for a half-second, followed by a series of pops that went on and on, sending greenish arcs into the sky. That was ordnance. The fire had found the weaponry taken off the abducted Rangers.

The fleeing villagers hesitated. A gust of hot air washed over them, driven by the concussive wave of Semtex going off in close series below. But they were being shoved from behind by their cousins, and the procession was at a run once more. They moved swiftly past Lee's hide until there were just a few stragglers left moping down the trail.

"Fuck this," he hissed, stepping from the brush. Lee wasn't waiting anymore. He trotted up the trail, meeting some kids younger than four picking their way down from above. They were stepping around a lot of trampled bodies mashed to meat jelly laying all over the rocks. He showed the kids his teeth, and they picked up the pace to take off past him, legs pumping, to find their mamas.

Following behind them were some sad sacks of shit nursing wounds. Blue guys. Like the ones who were trying to feed his girlfriend into their stone age guillotine. They were hurting. Some from bullet wounds thanks to him. Others from injuries taken when Jimbo and the others put up what they thought was their last fight.

He walked up close to each one and served a double-tap center mass to each. Maybe ten in all by the time he made his way around the circular pathway to where he met his friends coming down. Enough shots that he had to slap in a fresh mag.

Jimbo was carrying Byrus on his shoulders. Rick was limping, using a pole for support. Bat was trying to help. They were all in a condition that shocked Lee. Spattered in blood of their own and others—what was left of their clothes was stiff with it. Foul as hell and sporting bruises and cuts. Harshest of all was the dead look from their eyes. It was the glaze that's left when the adrenaline is gone. They were in the wake of the rush. When the fear has risen to high tide and then fallen away, leaving one surprised to be alive. Walking shock. If post-traumatic stress disorder was the price of survival, this was the moment in which it was forged.

The glaze left Bat's eyes when she saw Lee double-timing for them. For a fleeting instant, her eyes went from staring into the abyss to recognition to the dancing lights of the woman he knew in his heart he loved.

She tore herself from Rick's side and practically skipped into his arms. Lee Hammond, life-taking, heart-breaking, hard-charging Ranger, crushed her to him, never wanting to let her go.

King Chaos rained down in the village.

The skin palace was collapsing into itself as flames consumed the dome of dried skins and timbers. Explosions continued to shake the ground from within what remained of the structure. Cakes of Semtex ignited when the heat reached them. The air was peppered by stray rounds going off at all angles with the ammo inside weapons and magazines cooking off.

Some of the hooches were fully ablaze. More were smoldering in the driving rain. Smoke hung heavy over the enclosure, filling the air with a noxious reek of burnt leather and hair. At least it covered the fish stink.

The blue men and their kin were frantically scooping up wet mud to put out fires. There wasn't much order to it, and many gave up on the effort as shacks turned to pyres. Others were rushing into their homes to retrieve treasured possessions. Still more were taking goodies from homes not their own. Fights broke out over what belonged to who. In addition, the rounds flying everywhere as ammo cooked off were dropping any citizens who got too close to the skin palace.

True pandemonium arrived with the first sightings of apemen within the compound. Homer and his crew were moving through the village in a wandering pack looking for trouble and finding it. They roamed the periphery of the hooches picking out isolated villagers and falling on them like wolves, clubbing and tearing. Awareness of their presence in the hood spread to others who fled in all directions to escape the wrath of the flesh-eaters.

"Yabba dabba doo, motherfuckers," Chaz Raleigh said. He was stalking toward the sounds of rifle fire he'd heard earlier. With N'itha by his side, he picked his way well around the center of the village away from the explosive inferno of the largest structure. He picked off adult males, dudes who looked Chinese trying to pass for brothers. These were the guys N'itha was talking about. At close range, the rifle rounds took the wild looking assholes and lifted them off the ground. Shots over the heads of kids and women were enough to send them running if the sight of a giant black man didn't already have them flying in the opposite direction.

Closer to the center of the village, the original Beastie Boys sensed the tide turning.

Once Homer and the skinnies grasped the extent of the fear, they inspired in the populace they raced into the lanes between the hooches in numbers. The blue men retreated before the unexpected onrush of claws and teeth. Those who remained to defy the skinnies were brought down and torn to bits by gangs of the smaller hominids. The skinnies were closer to animals than men with the proportionate strength and fearless ferocity of beasts.

Homer led them into the routed villagers, swinging the Winchester Model 70 by the barrel as a flail.

Bart and Millhouse chased a terrified indigo warrior who was shrieking, probably, for his god or his mother. Bart snagged his legs while Millhouse landed hard on his shoulders, and the poor bastard went down in the mud. Millhouse sank fangs into his neck while Bart tore an arm off at the shoulder like a drumstick off a roasted chicken. Working together the pair pulled ropes of greasy viscera from where they'd torn open the corpse's abdomen. They squatted over their impromptu picnic, munching with contentment in the rain as their cousins rushed past for their own servings.

These were man-eaters by nature, and here was more prey than they'd ever seen in one place in their lives. Their hunger drove them, and so their hunger sated slowed them. As enough victims were brought down the skinnies, who'd been on the run without full bellies for more than twenty-four hours, stopped their attack long enough to feed. These were gorgers, and soon they were full, their bellies stuffed and fur slick with clotting blood.

The blue warriors realized that the momentum of the flesh-eaters' assault had slowed to a stop. They regrouped under the barked orders and kicks of a self-appointed war chief, a broad-shouldered bastard a head taller than most of his troops. He whipped them into a loose wedge formation, and they went on the counter-attack.

Homer and the others, thinking the fighting was over and the buffet begun, were taken by surprise. A few fell to thrown clubs, and the rest ran away into the shadows. The crew tasked with carrying the Ma Deuce decided that it wasn't all that sacred after all and rabbited away. The skinnies could easily outrun their pursuers. Even logy as they were with the weight of fresh meat in their stomachs, they made it to the gate and through to the causeway with no further casualties. The mob of chattering skinnies fled down the causeway forgetting their alliance of convenience with their gods.

So much for religious faith.

## 45

# TOGETHER AGAIN

Lee Hammond distributed all his available weapons to the others. Bat got his big Smith 500 revolver. Byrus, recovered enough to stand on his own, got his tomahawk. Ricky took the Gil Hibben, a broad-bladed Bowie knife with a honed razor edge.

"Sorry, Jimmy. Nothing for you unless you want my Zippo," Lee said.

"Thought you'd give me the tomahawk," Jimbo said, stooping to pick up a fresh pair of discarded stone clubs.

"I didn't want to seem racially insensitive." Lee shrugged.

"Neeta. Have you seen Neeta?" Ricky said through teeth clenched with pain. Bad off as he was, he was more concerned with the girl than himself. Lee realized they really were seeing a brand new Rick Renzi.

"She's with Raleigh. Neeta's the one who brought us here," Lee said, embellishing the girl's role a little.

They stuck close to the remainder of the trail back to the village. They used smoke and shadow for cover. Lee led them on a circuitous path toward the exfil point he and Chaz had chosen earlier, but the way was blocked by a mob of armed blue warriors milling around the gateway in the wake of their pursuit of Homer and the mob of fleeing skinnies. The ragged group changed course and made their way along muddy lanes between scorched hooches toward a far point in the encircling fence wall.

They made best speed, meeting little resistance along the way. The villagers they did meet fled before them. Finally, they came to the wall of posts and woven buckthorn.

"Step back," Lee said, loading a fat frag round into the chamber of the launcher underslung on the rail in front of the forestock of his rifle. They withdrew into the uncertain shelter of some thatch hooches. A loud pop was followed by a sharp crack and a cloud of the chemical stink of cowshit and turpentine that came in the aftermath of a C-4 blast.

Lee stood by a fresh gap in the fence wall. Two stout posts were torn off at ground level, taking three sections of woven branches with them.

"Wait until you hear two more bloopers and run like hell for the causeway." He pulled the smoking 20mm spent canister from the open chamber of the launcher.

The group hustled through.

Lee figured the Kentucky windage and sent off two grenade rounds, a frag for carnage and an HE for effect. The frag arced over the village, landing with a dull thump where he imagined the gateway was. A chorus of shrieks reached him to let him know he'd caused some shock and awe. He launched the high explosives round on the same course. It raised a gout of muddy water he could see over the rooftops of the hooches. Probably a miss but enough to scare the blue fuckers shitless.

He was moving to follow the others and stopped at a call.

"Hoo-ah!"

Lee turned to see Chaz Raleigh coming at a run out of the crazed shadows caused by flames still rising from the skin palace behind him. Little N'itha was close on his heels.

"These people need Jesus," Chaz said, panting hard.

"I'm surprised you're not carrying a new television set, muh brothuh," Lee said.

"Fuck you, white trash." Chaz grinned.

They exited through the fence to find their comrades waiting in the dark. Their forward progress was slowed only by Ricky and N'itha sharing a brief embrace before setting off for their next encounter.

The two grenade rounds did their job. The gateway at the head of the causeway was clear of opposing forces. The only sign that there had ever been a clutch of warriors there were a few bodies lying on the smoking shale. No way to tell how many. There were bloody pieces everywhere. A few dozen 9mm BBs spreading out at ballistic lethality will do that.

The troop moved on to the causeway and only slowed when they lost sight of the fence line behind them. All were exhausted. The captives were beat from their long run away from Bedrock and their suffering at the hands of the blue meanies. Their rescuers reached the ragged end of their stamina from an almost non-stop twenty-four slog done at best speed. They took a moment to rest and handle necessary logistics.

First things first. Chaz handed his Dan Wesson over to Jimbo and his tomahawk to Rick. N'itha had his combat knife already. Jimbo kept one of the war clubs, shoving it under his belt. Water was shared along with protein bars.

"Where's my Winnie?" Jimbo asked.

"Homer's carrying it with your ammo. Beats the shit outta me where he is now," Chaz said.

"We'll run into him down the road. Need to keep moving,

people. Take your calories walking." Lee rose from a crouch to gesture them along.

"Think they'll follow?" Rick asked. The flesh around his lips was white from the pain he was suffering in his bad leg.

"You got to know them better than me. They pissed off enough to dog us?"

"They're persistent pricks," Jimbo said. "We burnt down their holy place and fucked with their party. They'll give pursuit for a day or more. Until then they'll be on our ass like dingleberries."

"Okay, then. We have until daybreak to build as much of a lead as we can. They'll be after us when the sun is up."

"At least it's not raining," Chaz said, shouting to be heard over the bucketing downpour.

They came upon the platoon of skinnies sleeping in piles in the woods beyond the foot of the causeway. They lay about, dead to the world in the undergrowth of ferns on the forest floor. Farting and snoring, with bellies distended from their hasty meal of raw flesh.

Jimbo fired the big-bore revolver in the air. They leaped to their feet, fangs bared. He handed off the Dan Wesson to Rick. Homer looked petulant, all sad eyes and protruding lower lip when Jimbo gestured for the return of his rifle.

The skinny chief handed it over with reluctance, along with the belts of ammo pouches he'd been wearing like a primordial Pancho Villa. He only paused to retrieve his last packs of Marlboros from one of the pouches. He expertly peeled the cellophane away with his teeth and tapped a butt clear to stick between his lips. He gestured for a light from Lee. He blew a stream of blue smoke skyward, mollified by the nicotine over having to surrender the rifle.

The Winchester was operable but probably way off alignment

after being used as a club. The Rynex stock survived the beating, although the butt end was dented and clotted with dried blood and brain matter. Lee offered the 30x scope for Jimbo to reattach.

"Keep it on you. The barrel's probably so out of true the scope's worthless. No time to zero it." Jimbo slung the rifle over his shoulder.

"No time for anything but a shit and a piss. We need to get humping," Lee said.

"That's my boyfriend, everyone," Bat said with a weary smile.

"Chaz and I will walk drag," Lee said. "You make the best time you can. And I mean the best time, Rangers. Walk off the pain. We're going to have trouble on our six in the morning."

"Which way?" Jimbo said.

"Back around Cannibal Lake and hook a right for Malibu. We're going home."

## 46

## THE LONG WALK BACK

Lee and Chaz hung behind, walking a long drag.

Tired as they were, their every fiber screamed for them to move at a run. To put distance between them and the carnage they'd created. Instead, they held their pace down to a crawl, maintaining an interval between them and their slow-moving comrades. They watched and listened for pursuit, ready to set up a rearguard action to delay anyone coming after them. The trail behind was free of howling blue men through the night.

In the hour before dawn, the two Rangers rejoined their company at N'itha's ruined village. They were all at their limit. Some beyond it. Except for the skinnies, who were still acting like kids on a field trip. Just watching Bart and Millhouse run around the scorched huts looking for goodies made Lee feel even more tired than he was.

In addition to fatigue, there were the wounded. All had cuts, bruises, and sprains. Those they could work around. Bat and Jimbo managed to stop the bleeding from Byrus' leg wound. He was looking pale from blood loss but willing to soldier on.

Worst off among them was Rick Renzi. His leg below the knee was swollen three times its size and an angry red color. He was grinding his teeth. N'itha knelt by him, hugging his arm and speaking softly. Words of comfort, words of love, or words of prayer. The tone was like music.

The girl was alone in the world. All around lay the remains of her people. The last of them had died under that stone hammer or in the panic that followed Lee's attack. N'itha was the sole survivor of her entire culture. The language she spoke, her gods, her way of life, ended with her. She lay holding on to the last familiar thing she had left to her.

"We're going to have to rig something up to carry you, bro," Chaz said. "You keep putting weight on that leg, and you're looking at an embolism or something."

"I'm becoming a goddamn inconvenience," Rick said.

"Becoming?"

"Fuck you."

"There's my man, Renzi." Chaz gave Rick's face a gentle slap.

Lee watched their back trail while Chaz and Jimbo lashed up a travois from poles found in the debris field that was all that remained of the village. When it was ready, they moved out with the skinnies leading the way.

The sun was full up when they came to the shores of Cannibal Lake.

"We have a choice," Lee said to the group gathered on the beach.

"I've been weighing things too," Jimbo said.

"We hook a right here and keep on back to our ex-fil site. Or we go to Bedrock and fort up. Maybe the blue fuckers will be scared to come into skinny country. One is a dick-busting hump, and the other gives us a chance to rest up and recharge."

"We're bringing Neeta with us, right? That discussion is closed, right?" Rick said from where he lay raised on an elbow on the travois.

"She's coming with," Lee said.

"Then let's get the fuck out of here," Rick said and lay back down.

Most of the skinnies had already run off along the beach toward home. Homer and a score or more remained behind. They looked to be waiting for the company to move on, and they would follow. Lee stepped up to them and pointed.

"Head back to Bedrock," Lee said. Bat stood by him, holding out a handful of protein bars as a parting gift.

Homer's brows knitted. His eyes shifted from under beetled brows.

"Move! You are dismissed!" Lee put a hand to Homer's chest and shoved.

Homer bared his teeth. Some of his bruisers stepped up to defend their chief. Lee fired three rounds into the mud before them. The skinnies backed off, startled. Some turned tail and ran full out into the trees.

"Go! Go home!" Lee stabbed his finger in the direction of Bedrock.

The skinnies spun and made their way over the shale beach and away. Homer was the last to join them, turning from Lee and the others, looking for all the world like a child being sent to bed early. Though the ciggie hanging from his lower lip diluted the effect.

"I feel bad for them," Bat said.

"Save it. We'd do them no favor letting them tag along over strange country. They'd never find their way back," Lee said.

"You couldn't have reached us without them," she said.

"They had their fun," he said and rejoined the group.

***

The company allowed themselves an hour's break. Bat and Byrus dropped off where they lay. N'itha reclined on the travois close to Rick, and both were sound asleep in seconds.

Jimbo sat with Lee, watching their back trail. Chaz was up in the tree line where he had a better view of the north shore of the lake.

"Can't sleep?" Lee said.

"Too worked up still. And my eye itches."

"Wherever the hell that is."

"I was thinking about Morris Tauber," Jimbo said.

"That's messed up, bro. Should be thinking about cold beer or pussy."

"We left a lot of shit out there. Anomalies all over the AO. The Ma Deuce, ordnance, lots of brass."

"Couldn't be helped. Most of your shit got blown up."

"Still lots of plastic scrap and wires laying around. Parts of weapons. Parts of the drone. Mo will freak."

"Let him. It's all Big Foot anyway. Someone finds an iPod in King Tut's tomb. So what? Who cares? Who'd listen? No way to explain it, so the world moves on." Lee shrugged.

"He'll still bitch us out."

"That dude needs to get laid. Hour's up." Lee rose to wake the sleepers.

They filled the remaining two CamelBaks from the lake and rucked up as best they could. Bat and Jimbo dragged the travois with Chaz walking point. Byrus and N'itha could pull when they got tired. Lee walked drag.

The company was well into the trees above the lake on the return route west when they heard a high braying sound echoing over the waters below.

A hunting horn.

## 47

## THE HARDEST MILE

Choices.

There were always choices to be made.

Make the right one and live. Live a while longer anyway.

Make the wrong one and die.

Their pursuers were going to catch up to them. It was only a matter of where and when. They couldn't really choose the time, but they could choose the place.

"We move to higher ground. Make them come for us," Lee said, walking with Jimbo. It was N'itha and Byrus' turn pulling Rick on the travois.

They were on high ground in the trees above the lakeshore, heading for the place where the dry riverbed met the muddy marsh. The route kept them out of sight from below, but the going was rough on the sloping terrain.

"Defend a static position? Not very Ranger. I don't like it," Jimbo said. His voice was hoarse. His eyes were red. He was near his limit.

"A stand-off. We drop enough of them, they have to give up. There has to be less than a hundred left. I say they've already had enough."

"That's what we thought last time. Remember? Turned out the skinnies were an extended community. These assholes could be at brigade strength by now. We just don't know if these fuckers are all there are."

Lee nodded. "Yeah. You're right."

"Could explain why they took their time coming after us. Might have spent the morning making up a coalition," Jimbo said.

"I already said you're right, okay?"

"And I don't want to veer off our return route. We don't have the drone anymore, so we should stick to the land we know."

"You mean follow that dry riverbed back?" Lee said.

"Draw them out on it to the choke point," Jimbo said.

"We'll have high ground and a free-fire zone with scarce cover for them and room for us to maneuver."

"That means a hard push for you and the others, Cochise. An all-day hump. We do not want these fuckers catching us out on that riverbed."

"Then it means a hard push. If we don't, we'll have them on our ass all the way to the San Gabriels. We can't make that in the shape we're in carrying wounded."

"Makes sense. It sucks, but it makes sense. Me and Chaz will cover your ass. But you need to get to that dam even if it's on your knees." Lee turned to trot back to where Chaz walked drag.

Jimbo joined the others struggling with the travois. They were having a hard time navigating between the trees over uneven ground.

"Good news. We're moving downhill to level ground," Jimbo said and took the ends of the trailing poles to lift Ricky from the ground.

"Bad news? There's always bad news," Bat said. "We're going to have to stop half-assing it and make some time." Jimbo tried to smile. It came off like a controlled snarl on his drawn face. "Shit," Bat said.

She and N'itha took the weight of the crossed poles where they were lashed together at the apex of the triangular platform. They lifted the poles on their shoulders. Byrus grabbed the other trailing end and, together, the four lifted the burden and picked their way downslope for the silvery band running along the middle of the dry bed below.

The going was easier on the flat surface of the riverbed. They dragged the travois on the highest part of the bank where the ground was firmer. The center channel was broader now, swollen with the rain from the night before. The ground was swampy to either side of it. It was hotter out in the open and away from the shade of the forest. Jimbo rigged up a canopy from a groundsheet so Rick wouldn't broil, exposed as he was.

Rick was unconscious but not feverish. He surrendered to the exhaustion of their two-day march and slept. They only awakened him to take sips of water when they stopped to drink. He dropped back into deep slumber within seconds.

Except for stops to rehydrate, the four moved on, sharing their burden at a steady, mile-eating pace. To Jimbo, this was a hump, plain and simple. The easiest mile was behind you. The hardest mile was the next one.

His mind dropped into the nether zone he developed on long marches in training at Benning in Georgia and Elgin down in Florida. Tramping under full loads through forests, over mountains, and across swamps. He had learned to shut out the pain and fatigue while keeping his situational awareness, his combat radar, on high alert. The compartmentalization of his own physical suffering had been drilled into him by tireless instructors. Men a generation older than him and seemingly made of cold steel and hardwood. Near the end of those fire route marches, his lungs had been on fire, his leg muscles twisted, and his back aflame with pain. Yet those instructors, old enough to be his father, were still moving double-time, back and forth along the ragged columns and screaming abuse at the top of their voices. A youth spent running in the high desert around the Pima reservation had made him tough but not Ranger tough.

All that hardship made him capable of humping forty miles in full battle rattle, engaging in a firefight, and asking for seconds. Over in Iraq and Helmand, he and his unit, including the men with him today, performed the tasks that soldiers have engaged in since the time of the ancients. They marched hard, killed the enemy, and held the ground.

This slog to the base of the dam and their tactical chokepoint was harder than any he could recall. He was hurting and beat. An instructor at Benning had told them that he once met a vet from the French Foreign Legion—some tough bastards, that bunch. This guy told the instructor that the philosophy of *le Legion* was that when a man thought he'd given his all, he'd actually only given seventy percent of his all. That stayed with Jimbo, and he thought of it often when on extended hikes under heavy loads.

He was nearing ninety percent of his tolerance by his own estimation. The others were probably as bad off. Bat wore the mask, burying her weariness and ache deep. Byrus stayed to Jimbo's right and still offered his familiar grin whenever their gazes met. N'itha was only concerned for Rick and pushed harder than the rest. The girl was probably the toughest of them all. It took a degree of mean-dog orneriness to survive in this world of giant predators and blood-crazed primitives. She'd been born Ranger hard.

Their spirit buoyed him, and he made a new commitment to make their destination well ahead of their pursuers. And if the inspiration of his comrades wasn't enough to spur him on, Jimbo could hear more and more hunting horns growing closer from the trees behind them.

The first of them emerged from the woods along the north bank of the riverbed. There was no order to their advance. These weren't scouts, just the fastest arriving first with the rest following behind. First one then another came down out of the tree line and onto the broad muddy path snaking west. There were a dozen or more milling around looking for any sign of human passage.

A few were the blue-dyed men from the village where the captives had been taken. But there were fewer familiar varieties here. Some dudes with bushes of matted hair atop their heads and masks of black ash painted across their eyes. Another tribe or some kind of sect. Cousins to the blue bastards. Some of these carried the same stone hammers as their brethren. Most had spears six feet or more in length with spade-shaped blades of hammered iron.

A third, smaller, portion of the group distinguished itself with a coat of lime over every inch of their naked hides and faces painted black with charcoal. This branch of the family wore rows of animal teeth and claws about their necks. They carried no weapons. They moved oddly, crouched and sometimes on all fours in imitation of beasts though they were clearly men. They made a show of sniffing and studying the ground as they loped over the mud and splashed through the stream at the center of the bed.

These were the trackers.

It was one of these who found the twin furrows left by the travois. He barked for the others and hopped around, waiting for them to gather.

Lee's first shot took the tracker through the head.

The others jumped away as the spray of blood and bone spattered them. The blue men were the first to run. They'd seen this before. The black masks and lime-asses, as Lee took to thinking of them, stood dumbly looking down at their near-headless pal twitching out his last at their feet.

Lee dropped another with an intentional wounding shot to the hip. In another hide, farther along his side of the riverbed, Chaz opened up, bringing down two more with center mass shots. The rest got the idea and went haring back to the trees on the other side. Lee took the last one in the thigh. That left behind two wounded but not ambulatory to shriek out their pain for the others to hear.

And that was enough. They were low on ammo. Maybe three hundred rounds between them for the M4s. They needed to conserve. Each shot had to count now.

The idea was to slow the fuckers down, make them think twice. Maybe scare them off.

Lee watched and listened. No movement on the other side. Just a damp wind through the leaves. The two poor suckers rolled around and screamed for their buddies. Their cousins had either wised up or just didn't give a shit. Sorry, bro. Nobody's coming to save your blue ass today.

Calls began rising from inside the trees. Answering calls came from deeper within. The long bleat of a hunting horn came from upslope. A second and then a third sounding further off with each reply.

The hunt was on for real.

That was the signal for the Rangers to move. Lee rose from his hide and, picking his way low through the shadows of the trees, followed the bank of riverbed westward. Ahead of him, Chaz would be doing the same thing.

Stick and move, stick and move. Halt the enemy where they could, harassing them, keeping them off their pace.

If it worked, it would buy Jimbo, Bat, and the others time enough to reach the choke point ahead of him and Chaz. If not . .
.

Well, there was no use thinking about that.

## SHANGHAI BLUES

"I'm bored. Tell me something I can think about," Morris said.

"Samuel visited us," Caroline said over the sat phone.

"Whuh—where you are?" Morris almost mentioned the *Ocean Raj*, the ship they called home.

"He had some words of advice for us all."

"You're killing me here, Sis."

"You asked me to tell you something you could think about, Mo."

"But not something to drive me crazier than I'm already going."

"We'll have the team back soon. We're pushing the schedule up as much as we can. Then we'll come to terms with this Taan guy."

"He wants us to work for him."

"I know that."

"Will the team agree?"

"Dwayne says they'll put it to vote. He's pretty sure how it'll come out. We've all come this far, right?"

"Right," Morris agreed though he wasn't convinced. It just

seemed too much to ask these men to take another risk for his sake.

"This is what they do. It's not like any of them were going to retire," Caroline said.

"Yeah."

"Stephen's awake. I'll give him a kiss from his uncle." The line went dead before he could respond.

---

Morris was playing the back nine at Augusta on a virtual golf course set up in the media room of his suite. Though he never had any interest in the game before, he was getting pretty good at it. He was trying to break ninety and might just manage it if he could get on the green in two on the eleventh.

Two men entered the room unannounced. Another pair of Taan's army of muscular toughs. These guys were dressed in black Armani like the others with buttoned-up white dress shirts and no ties. One removed the golf club from Morris' hands. The other held the door open. Neither said a word, but the intent was clear.

They all took a ride down in the elevator to the garage level where a stretch limo waited. A third tough opened the rear door and nodded his head for Morris to enter.

Taan was seated in the deep leather seat that curved along the rear of the luxury car. The two toughs who had retrieved Morris pushed him down on the bench seat across from Taan then took seats on either side of Morris. This was new. Something was up. Mr. Taan waited until the door was pressed shut before he spoke.

"I think you would agree that I am a patient man," Taan said.

"Gracious even," Morris offered with a weak smile.

"But all things have a limit. I feel your sister and her associates are not treating this situation with the gravity it requires. In short, they are stalling."

"They're not, Mr. Taan. There are complications that you can't—"

Mr. Tann lowered his eyes and raised an open hand. "Your sister is clever, maybe more so than you. We have tried to triangulate her current location during your many telephone calls. It would not surprise you, I'm sure, to learn that she routes those calls through many satellites and earth stations."

Morris felt beads of sweat forming in his hairline despite the pleasantly cool interior of the limo.

"And so, I regret, we must increase pressure in the only way we can." Taan frowned with what looked like honest regret in his eyes.

The car engine hummed to life, its gentle vibrations felt through the plush carpet beneath Morris' feet.

"Um, where are we going, Mr. Taan?" Morris said, poorly feigning idle curiosity.

"I am going nowhere." The door was pulled open, and Mr. Taan exited the limo. The door was slammed closed after him.

# THE PACK

N'itha saw them first and froze.

She was at the lead of her group rounding a sharp bend in the river. Before her, the pack was resting and drinking around a broad pool formed by the rain the night before. Jet black with silver fur about their mouths. A full pack with their cubs napping by mothers sunning on rocks along the banks. N'itha had no name for them though she had seen the skin of one worn by a hunter in her village.

Jimbo recognized them from one of the picture books. Dire wolves. A hundred or more within a hundred yards of them and blocking their way.

Jimbo took N'itha's wrist and, together, they began backing away slowly, returning the way they'd come toward the shelter of a huge deadfall trapped against the curve in the bank.

Too late.

It was a cub that spotted them first. It raced toward them yapping, rousing the adults in the pack who stood with ears peaked atop broad skulls. Their wide-set eyes studied the open riverbed, and the pup rushing toward a pair of figures, moving away now at a run.

The wolves were up and streaming toward the unexpected prey. They rushed headlong in a rough wedge, the pack leader snarling and snapping to take his place at the lead, drawing blood from brother and sister alike in his fight to be the first to the kill. They rounded the deadfall in a baying torrent of fur and fangs, yelping and grunting.

Jimbo shot the lead wolf through the chest, spilling the big animal to the ground. The .458 Win Mag round blew an exit hole the size of a fist through the big canine. It fell stone dead, spraying blood and bone fragments over the racing pack. Some of the wolves following close behind stumbled over the collapsed form of their leader. The rest either leaped the collision or eddied around it intent, on fresh meat and hot blood.

He stood and chambered another round to bring down a second wolf. Its skull opened like a bloody flower. The only effect was to spur the others on to greater speed. The pack split around the second carcass as it skidded on the mud to a rest. They joined together once again to aim for Jimbo like the point of a spear.

Running was of no use. They'd only drag him down after a few steps. And Bat and the others were still making their way up the slope into the woods above carrying the burden of an unconscious Rick Renzi. He worked the bolt and took down another wolf with a shot from the hip. The creature spun like a top, colliding with others rushing up behind. These were big animals. Lean in the body like coyotes but broader in the chest like a mastiff. Their jaws were wider, more gape-mouthed than the wolves he knew. The eyes were pale as moonlight against ebon coats. They were seconds away from tearing him apart unless he could change their minds.

He chambered the last round in the magazine and put the hammer down on the nearest wolf. It went end over end before falling to the slurry kicking and convulsing, its spine shattered. Jimbo took the rifle by the barrel and flung it at the snarling mass now spreading out to rush about his flanks for the kill. A wolf yipped when the heavy rifle impacted on its skull, but the onrush did not slow in the least.

Jimbo drew the stone hammer he'd stuck in his belt earlier and crouched to receive the charge, wishing once again that the Pimas had a death chant. The mass of slavering jaws grew larger, tongues lolling wet, eyes hungry.

He sensed something off to his blind side. A hand touched his wrist, sliding something between his fingers. The rubberized grip of the .500 revolver. Jimbo turned his head to confirm what he already knew. Byrus stood braced with the tomahawk in his fist. His good eye was here to watch his flank. The Macedonian would never leave his side in a fight. The big wheel gun bucked in his hand as he sent one fat load after another into the mass of the pack. One, two, three animals were down. The point of the pack closed the gap in three leaps. He felt a heavy mass strike him in the chest, and he was bowled over. A vice-like pressure gripped his arm, making him drop the club.

The revolver was pressed between him and the beast pinning him to the ground. He kicked out a booted foot and felt the bone of a second attacker snap under the blow. Dangerous as it was, he depressed the trigger on the .500. The heat of the blast scorched him across the mid-section with a muffled roar. The body atop him was lifted off with the force of the point-blank blast. Jimbo kicked clear, conscious of sharp pain in his left forearm. Hot blood seeped through his clothes to the skin. Some of it was his own, he knew.

By him, Byrus was swinging the tomahawk to ward off the snapping jaws of the last two wolves remaining on the attack. A third lay feebly spasming in the mud at his feet. The rest of the pack had done the math and were running off, tails down, as fast as they could, back the way they'd come.

Byrus caught one of the two animals still dogging him across the snout sending teeth and blood dashing away in a shower. The second beast saw its opening and leaped. Firing freehand from a recumbent position, Jimbo caught the animal in mid-air with a shot that ripped through its midsection. The wolf landed on its side, snapping and snarling at the greasy mess of entrails cascading from its rent gut sack. The Macedonian dropped to straddle the remaining wolf. He raised and dropped the toma-hawk until he was covered in blood and flesh and the brute lay unmoving in the river muck.

Vision swimming Jimbo rose to his feet. The pain from the bite to his arm was taking hold now and sending fingers of white-hot fire the length of his arm and into his chest. He hobbled to where the thrown rifle lay and shoved the hot revolver into his waistband to free his good arm to lift it. He almost fell again and felt something gripping him around the ribs.

It was Bat. She was smiling up at him, but her eyes wavered with fear and tension.

"You are out of your fucking mind," she breathed.

She and Byrus helped him to the shoreline where they put him down by Rick's travois. N'itha crouched there, knife in hand to defend her man to the last breath. Byrus left them to run down the hill. He returned weighed down with the carcass of the largest wolf across his shoulders as well as the discarded Winchester. No one asked him why he wanted the dead wolf. They were all too damned tired to be curious.

"There goes Plan A, fucked in the ass," the Pima managed before passing out on ground as soft to him as a hotel mattress.

## PLAN B

The team was together again by late afternoon. There was nothing happy about the reunion. Two members, Rick and now Jimbo, were down.

Chaz found the sad collection forted up above the southern bank of the riverbed. He followed a trail of blood from a litter of wolf carcasses lying center stream near a deadfall to a level spot above the turn in the river's course.

There Byrus had pulled together a sort of redoubt using thorn brambles arranged in a rough circle. The Macedonian was a born tactician and tireless soldier. The makeshift hedge hid the group as well as serving to slow any potential attacks.

Inside the ring of thorns, Rick lay barely conscious. N'itha dabbed his lips with a wet rag. Jimbo's left arm was in a sling made by Bat from his own t-shirt. His good eye betrayed the pain the bite was giving him. The cloth of the sling was stained black from the wolf bite. They all looked pale with fatigue.

"I got a morphine shot if you want it," Chaz said, taking a knee by the Pima.

"No, thanks. Need to stay sharp. We're going to need every gun," Jimbo said in a hoarse voice.

"Stay sharp, bro? One eye. One arm. You're no good to us anyway."

"I'd rather not sleep through what comes next."

"Your call," Chaz said.

"What's pursuit like?" Bat asked.

"Getting heavier. The blue fuckers have friends they brought along. Lee and I capped a few to keep them to their side of the river. But we're running low on ammo."

"You think they're up for a stand-up fight?" Jimbo said.

"They look pissed. God knows they're fresher than us. As far as organization, there isn't much. They won't come in one rush. It's more like war bands of twenty or so. Small independent units. But if one or more broke across and got around behind us it could go bad for us," Chaz said. He stood and scanned the banks for Lee.

Hammond surprised them all by seeming to materialize out of the forest gloom above them.

"This our Alamo?" Lee said.

"I prefer Rorke's Drift," Jimbo said in reference to the stand-off during the Zulu Wars in which less than two hundred British soldiers successfully stood off repeated assaults by thousands of Zulu *impi*. "

Lee shrugged. That movie did have the happier ending."

"How far are they behind you?" Chaz said.

"Not far enough. And we're six or seven klicks short of the dam from here," Lee said.

No one said anything for a few moments. Lee didn't ask if they could make it. He could see that they couldn't. Make a run for the choke point, and the odds had them out in the open when the blue crew and their cousins caught them up. It would be a melee on ground not of their choosing. If they were all in prime condition, it would be worth the risk. But Rick was *hors de combat,* and Jimbo was close to the same. Byrus and the girls weren't much better off.

"We need to keep the bad guys on the other side of the river away from us," Chaz said.

"Look at our Dollar Store von Clausewitz," Lee smirked.

"Fuck you. We're low on ammo," Chaz said. "We can't hold them off. And sooner or later they're going to get over their fear and work their way across. We can't watch the whole river. There's only one way to make them keep their distance long term." He scraped an imaginary river in the dirt at his feet with a stick. "Okay," Lee said.

"Blow the beaver dam," Chaz said and stabbed the stick in the dirt at the head of the river he'd drawn.

"That'll be me." Lee began shucking out of his Molle vest, belt, and t-shirt until he was down to his BDU pants and boots.

"Why you?" Chaz challenged.

"Because I'm faster than you. Always have been," Lee said and handed his M4 off to Bat. He held his hand out for the Smith and Wesson .500. Bat handed it over, and Lee stuck it in his waistband. She gave him the handful of shells that remained. He pocketed them. He crouched and rooted around in his pack until he found their last two bricks of Semtex and two detonator sticks. He was surprised when Bat locked him in a hug as he stood.

"Just a little run, babe. Back before you have a chance to miss me," Lee said with a hand in her hair.

"Sure," she said into his shoulder and tightened her grip for just a second before letting go and stepping back.

He stopped just long enough to secure the bricks in one cargo pocket and the detonator sticks in another.

"See you when I see you," Lee said and moved off at a trot through the trees and down the dry bed.

---

Their vantage point from within the thorn ring was optimal. It was inside and above the elbow turn of the river. The approach from the trees on the far bank and the whole expanse of the riverbed were both visible for a quarter mile or more. Clear fields of fire from high ground. The climb to their makeshift redoubt was a steep one. The opposite bank formed a natural glacis. Anyone coming down it to the riverbed would be fully exposed and well inside accurate range.

"You chose your ground well, girl," Chaz said. "Location. Location. Location." Bat smiled back. "You're going to hold here. I'm going to work the hillside. You have the M4 and Jimmy's long gun. There're three twenty-mil grenades left. Save 'em for when things get tight." Chaz touched the fat lozenges where they lay inside the loops of a bandolier.

"I'll use the Winchester until the ammo runs out. I'm good at distances."

"Lebanon, right?"

"And a few other places," she said, suddenly more tired than before.

Chaz divided the remaining magazines between himself and Bat. She noticed that he gave her six full magazines of thirty rounds and kept only three for himself. The significance wasn't lost on her. If he got nailed out there, she'd need the bulk of the ammo to make their last stand.

"Just stay out of my sightlines," she said.

"Roger that. I'll be to the east moving and sticking. Maybe I can divide them if they come in a bunch. If not, I'll pick 'em off around the edges. Blunt their momentum. In theory."

"It's solid." She nodded, and the black man was away through a gap in the thorns.

She glanced over at Byrus. He smiled at her, a feral leer from a face painted crimson with drying wolf's blood. The Macedonian had skinned the lupine carcass he brought back with him from the slaughter below. He wore the wolf's hollowed-out head atop his own, the fangs of the upper jaw shadowing his brow. The rest of the skin formed a bloody cloak over his shoulders. With the stone club and tomahawk in his fists, he looked more dangerous and wild than the men who were after them. Bat took some comfort in that. Only the New Balances on his feet spoiled the image.

"You look like Hercules, Bruce," she said. He looked puzzled.

"Hercules," she repeated and reached out to touch the ear of the wolf 's head.

"Hyaculeaz?" Byrus asked.

"Hercules. Yes. The son of Zeus."

His smile broadened like a child's.

## 51

## THORNS

Lee Hammond sprinted flat out along the harder ground closer to shore. He ran with the big revolver held tight in his fist. There was no time for mini-moves and stealth. This was a race. At most, seven kilometers more to where he recalled the dam to be. A quarter marathon.

Movement to his right. Dark shapes loping low in the tree line. He saw the black forms of dire wolves in the shadows there. The pack had enough for one day and only watched silently as he ran past.

The stream at the center of the bed was a natural watering place. He startled flocks of birds into moving away to allow him passage. Smaller mammals slinked off before he could identify their species. Might be those midget horses Jimbo talked about. At one stretch of the river, a herd of large, antlered animals filled the bed from bank to bank. They were the size of caribou with cream-colored stripes running through chocolate-colored fur along their flanks. They blocked his way. An alpha male lowered his head in challenge as Lee ran headlong for the herd.

He raised the big revolver and fired two shots in the air. The twin booms were enough to startle the herd to movement. They turned and bolted up a hillside of broken shale toward the trees above. Lee ran on without breaking stride. After five klicks, he was dizzy with the exertion. He paused long enough to drink water from the stream and duck his head into the water. Raising his head to shake the excess from his scalp, he saw glittering eyes regarding him coldly. From a muddy wallow along the bank, an alligator the size of an SUV lay studying him. Around it swarmed dozens of baby gators. Its brood.

Mama gator either had a full belly or was just not interested in the two-legged morsel squatting frozen not thirty feet in front of her. The babies were curious though and began scurrying over the mud in Lee's direction. Needing no more inspiration than that, the Ranger was sprinting west, legs and arms pumping.

His lungs felt like he was sucking in sand and his legs were on fire when he sighted the bulk of the dam rising before him across the span of the river.

An echo of distant thunder reached him from the east. Gunfire. The big-bore Model 70. Whatever was going to happen back, there was starting right now. With the last of his reserve, he ran for the base of the massive barrier of tangled brush and mud.

---

Bat fixed her gaze on the trees on the opposite bank. She swept left and right, keeping her eyes relaxed, leaving her peripherals open for any movement that was out of place. On overwatch, you needed to cast your visual net wide and let it *all* in. Desert, urban, or the deep, deep woods, it was all about looking for what shouldn't be there.

Something filled in the place between two shadows for a fleeting second. The broad frond of a fern along the bank moved in a way counter to the wind. She dropped the front post of the Winchester on the spot, both eyes open and watching.

A ghostly creature stepped out of the deep green shade and into the sunlight beaming down on the open riverbed.

A naked man covered head to toe in white powder. Lime caked on all his skin except his face, which was covered in dark black streaks of charcoal ash. He moved in imitation of a more primal being, knees bent and hands brushing the mud. The man stopped for a moment and raised his head to sniff the air as a beast might. Satisfied, he moved farther from the shelter of the overhanging branches and into the center of the river where the stream flowed.

Bat sighted on him, her finger resting on the outside of the trigger guard. The tang of the sight hovered over his chest. She watched the man, well inside a range of one hundred yards and below her, as he capered into the water. From behind him, more men emerged out of the trees, peering around cautiously. Some were more of their blue-dyed tormenters. Others were of a different brand, bushy manes atop their heads and masks of black coal drawn across their eyes. These last carried spears with broad blades secured at the point. They looked more like stabbing weapons since the hafts were longer than their carriers were tall.

That meant they'd have to come within the length of those poles to strike.

Throwing spears, arrows, or even slings would have changed the equation radically in their favor. As long as Bat and Chaz's fire could keep them at a distance, there was a chance for Plan B to work out. But a concerted rush and all bets were off.

No sound from Chaz's rifle. He'd be waiting for her to decide what was best for the position she and the others were in.

"Lady's choice," she whispered and put her finger inside the guard and squeezed the ridged surface of the trigger home.

The big Win Mag lifted the plaster-white scout clean off his feet. He actually flipped a one-eighty in the air, coming back to earth with a crash, stone dead.

Rather than retreat back the way they came, the rest, maybe thirty in number, charged, splashing through the stream toward the near bank below Bat's position just outside the thorn ring. Let them keep on like that, and they'd be out of sight down the hillside below her.

She worked the bolt without moving the rifle from where it was pressed into her shoulder. Bat dropped first a blue man, then one of his woolly-headed compadres. The sharp report of Chaz's M4 sounded, and three more fell spinning and clawing in the shallow water. Bat stood for a better angle and knocked a fourth then a fifth man into the water. The last took the round downward through the chest to exit low in his abdomen which sprouted a thick tangle of entrails like some hideous bloom.

The bolt open, she jammed in three more rounds and slid a fourth into the smoking chamber and slammed the bolt home again. The sights were up, and she nailed a sixth and seventh. Chaz got a few while she was reloading. Eighteen targets lay either unmoving or writhing in the final spasms of death down on the dry bed. The rest were out of sight. By her quick calculations, that left a dozen or more unaccounted for on the wrong side of the river. They were out of sight on her side. She stood swinging the rifle side for side, watching for movement in the thick foliage below her. The M4 barked somewhere downstream. Whether it was targeted fire or suppression, she couldn't tell.

A horn sounded from the far bank of the river. More men. Fifty or more emerged all along the bank and rushed across the mud, racing through the center stream before she could even sight on a target. She picked one particularly nasty specimen and blew his head off at the neck. Bat was pulling back the bolt to chamber a fresh round when a sudden movement crossed her sight to the left. She whirled, taking her finger from the trigger in time to prevent putting a bullet into Byrus who was bounding past her, weapons raised. The pit fighter let out a piercing shriek and leaped down the hillside, the grisly cape made of untanned dire wolf skin flapping behind him. He was out of sight in seconds, the shriek rising and falling from somewhere below. It was joined by the animal cries of pain or terror from whatever unlucky bastards he'd run into in his rush to battle.

Bat was damned glad he was on their side, but she cursed him for getting downrange of her. She picked up the M4 and bandolier of grenades to move laterally along the slope, seeking the cover of a thicket of birches. It would give her a better firing line over an open strip of ground between her and the carpet of ferns closer to the bank. The better to tell friend from foe. It had the added advantage of drawing attackers away from N'itha and the two injured Rangers lying low inside the thorn refuge.

Down on the riverbed, men were crossing the stream for the near bank. Some rushed all out. Some bunched together, moving in halting steps as if crossing through traffic on a busy street. Their faces were turned to the sky as though watching for signs of celestial vengeance. Somewhere out of her sight, Chaz was picking off targets in an attempt to slow the advance. Bodies lay still or thrashing in the thick mud. Their shrieks of pain were spooking the less motivated.

She picked up the M4 and slid the receiver of the grenade launcher forward to open the breach. The fat 20mm dropped home. She snapped it back and pressed the safety latch off. Standing up, she fired on a lateral trajectory at the largest clump of reluctant warriors standing midstream.

The anti-personnel round went off in the midst of them.

Thousands of feet of kinked steel wire fragmented, turning the living into ribbons of flesh in a deadly circle all around. A score or more turned to a mist that sprayed over an acre and a half as a fine crimson rain. At the farthest extent of the kill zone, still more dropped to the muck with missing limbs or heads. A gray fog dropped down to hang low over the riverbed.

Bat was dismayed to see the numbers of attackers grow rather than abate in the wake of the blast. Over the dying echoes of the explosion, she could hear a high, shrill voice from within the trees on the other side. It was a voice she'd never forget. The twisted freak these assholes worshipped was somewhere out of sight on the far bank. He was issuing commands at the top of his lungs. They were, as unfathomable as it seemed to Bat, still more afraid of that drooling man-child than they were of bullets and bombs.

She listened hard for that keening voice, trying to determine its position and ignoring the onrush of savages now in the foliage just below her. Figuring the windage, she adjusted the angle of the M4 and reloaded the grenade tube. The launcher fired with a heavy bloop. The chubby grenade spun in a high arc out toward the tree line on the other bank. It created a muted wallop that sent shredded foliage and black soil into the sky in a high plume.

When the resonance died away, the reedy voice was still there, shouting even more emphatically than before.

"Shit," she said at the waste of a round and turned the M4 toward the shapes clawing up the sheer slope toward her, using branches and vines for handholds. Their eyes burned with feral lust.

Bat fought down the urge to spray them with a full mag. Byrus was still down there someplace. Her shooting had to remain steady and deliberate. There were more bad guys here than she had rounds for. It was combat economy, plain and shitty. She sighted on the closest man and recited a prayer, the *Birkhat HaGomel* as she squeezed the trigger.

> *"Blessed are You, Lord our God, King of the Universe,*
> *Who bestows good things upon the unworthy, and*
> *Has bestowed upon me every goodness."*

## 52

## AT THE CHOKE POINT

He waded into the pool of runoff water that bled from the face of the dam. It trickled down in sheets, filtering through the dense skein of branches and deadfall built by the giant beavers. The dam acted more to greatly reduce the water rather than stop it entirely. It stretched two stories above him. An engineering marvel that had taken months of work and denuding a forest to create. The water of the pool reached up to his chest.

He wedged the two bricks of Semtex into a gap in the complex wicker of branches at the center of the face of the dam. There was a pocket there that allowed his arm in up to the elbow. When the bricks were firmly seated, he removed the mercury fuses from his cargo pocket after poking a starter hole in the plastic wrap about the bricks with a clasp knife. With even pressure, he poked each of the fuses into the gritty clay of the plastic explosives.

Using one hand to secure the fuse in place, he pulled the detonation ring from the housing to allow the binary mix within the chemical fuse to start its reaction. The stick fuse had a one hundred and eighty-second delay. That's what the literature said.

All Lee knew was that he wanted to be as far away and above the dam as his tired-ass legs could carry him in three minutes.

He threw aside the pull rings and turned to push out from the lake of muddy water and haul ass.

From somewhere above, a chittering sound reached him. Lee turned to see a beaver the size of a grizzly bear sliding on its belly down the muddy bank. It was all spiky fur and slashing teeth as it plunged into the pool toward him at an astonishing speed.

He brought the big revolver up and sent a plea to Horace Smith and Daniel Wesson that the barrel wasn't clogged with river mud.

---

Chaz rushed uphill with howling pursuit close on his boot heels. So close that a flung stone hammer crashed through the branches above him. Twigs and leaves rained down.

The blue guys and the bushy guys and the whiter-than-white guys were coming over the riverbed in force. A few forded above Chaz and came down on his flank. They'd have had him if one of them didn't let out a whoop upon sighting him. Chaz took the whooper with a double-tap. The rest came out of the foliage, wailing and throwing hammers from all directions at once. The Ranger broke through with a few well-placed bursts and was rushing away uphill in an attempt to get above them, leading them away from the others.

"Come on, motherfuckers! Follow my black ass if you have the balls!" he called back to them.

---

Bat plugged the last of her grenades into the launcher and tossed the empty bandolier aside. She had a magazine in the M4 and one spare in a pouch on her Molle vest. The reports from Chaz's rifle were getting farther away. It was time to fall back toward the thorn refuge. That would be the last stand. She wasn't about to let these animals get at N'itha and the wounded Rangers without a fight. She trotted, rifle up and sights transiting along a path that would bring her above the thorn circle.

A figure burst from the brambles below her. This one was painted bright red. She laid the tang of the M4's front sight center mass. She was moving her finger from the trigger guard to the trigger when she recognized the panting figure sprinting toward her.

"Bruce, you're alive," she breathed.

"Fucking A," he gasped. His toothy smile was hideous in the gory mess covering his face. The wolf's head he wore was matted with blood. He still had the tomahawk in one hand and a stone hammer in the other. Both were clotted with blood and matter.

She raised her sights toward whoever was following noisily behind him.

A trio of the lime-daubed warriors scrambled out of the hedge of bushes, clawing after Byrus. Bat dropped them with a long, expensive burst of rounds. She and the Macedonian took off running without looking back. The tortured screams rose behind them, the sounds of dying men.

---

N'itha crouched between Rick and Jimbo. She had a tomahawk in her fists. The sounds of explosions and the shrieks of their enemies filled the air beyond the barrier of thorn branches. They were coming closer. They would come here and find them.

She had been game for any fate on the night she slipped from the house of her father. Her spurning of Koto and defiance of the Earth Mother's wishes had been done at great risk. She'd understood from the start that her rebellious rejection of the great honor of being the annual sacrifice to the sky gods might end in her death. Each day following her exodus was a gift. She had no regrets.

If it ended today, she considered herself fortunate. She'd spent many days and nights with a man she truly wanted to be with. She'd seen many wonders she would never have been a part of had she meekly surrendered to the destiny chosen for her. And should it end today, it would end with them together. With Rick Renzi. She would stand and defend her mate just as he had saved her. With the last beat of her heart, she would strike at their enemy. They would not take her man easily. And they would need to kill her as well. She would not go back to that wicked place with them. She would not die as her people had. Like rabbits in a trap, too frightened to try and save themselves.

One of the shiny metal objects that Rikki and his kind used to slay their enemies lay by the other fallen man, the one-eyed man with hair as black as hers. That weapon might be of more lethal use than the tomahawk. She tried to understand how it worked. To her, it seemed like all Rikki, and the others did was point it, and it spat flame and death by a kind of magic.

She knew that was wrong. Rikki had tried to show her how his weapon worked, even encouraging her to learn how to use it herself. She'd been frightened and ran away. He'd laughed at her, and she grew angry and flung a rock that struck him in the face. He only laughed harder, seated on the ground holding a bloody hand to his nose. But he'd never tried to show her how the fire weapon worked again, and now she was regretting it.

Fingers trembling, she reached for the smooth metal of the .44 magnum revolver. A hand clamped on her wrist.

"I can take it from here, girl," Jimbo said, sitting up.

---

It was like a bad, bad dream.

Lee once heard a range instructor call it ballistic performance anxiety.

It was all happening in slow motion. He was backing out of the water, boots fighting for traction on rocks slippery with algae. The black shape rocketed toward him across the murky lake at the foot of the dam face.

Lee's arm was out with the big .500 in his fist as he backed off. It was trained at the looming beast gliding at him behind a swollen bow wave. If the muddy water obstructed the big-bore barrel, he wouldn't have to worry about being gnawed to death by a beaver. The trapped gases within the revolver would blow his arm off. He'd bleed out before the monster rodent could get to him. Then they'd both ride two bricks of high explosives into whatever came next.

So there was an upside.

He pulled the trigger again and again in rapid succession. The revolver kicked and bucked back. The high caliber blasts created waves of their own in the water. Thick gouts of blood leaped from the slick fur on the beaver's back. Lee's foot went out from under him. The bulk of the animal struck him. He brought down the butt of the revolver on the monster's skull before becoming submerged beneath the weight of it.

Lee fought back to sunlight with a snort. He reached and pulled, reached and pulled, until he was in the shallows. One look back at the massive beaver floating still on its back in a spreading stain of red and he was off running. Knees up, arms pumping. Twenty seconds lost splashing around with the buck-toothed beast. Maybe more. He had a minute to get clear.

His pace took him fifty yards downstream before he hooked hard right to climb up the bank on all fours. He reached a collection of boulders and dove behind the cover of them. The ground came up to meet him—the two packs of Semtex went up as one. The sky clouded over in a rush. Chunks of wood and clots of mud rained down as well as a drenching mist of water.

Aching over every inch of his body, Lee pulled himself up to peer over the edge of his rocky shelter. The sight was underwhelming. The smoke cleared to show him a smoking vertical crater in the tangled wall of the dam face. But the dam appeared to hold.

"Son of a bitch." Lee slammed a fist down on the rock.

The gambit didn't pay off. He had run off from Bat and his buddies to save the day. Now they'd die without him being there. He pushed himself off the rocks, surprised to see the .500 revolver still in his hand. The jumble of shells still rattled in his pocket. He could get back in time to be with the Rangers— to be with Bat. Lee started to run along the bank.

A cracking, splintering sound grew louder and louder.

Lee turned.

The dam face was collapsing in on itself, the whole structure sagging in toward the weak spot created by the blast. Water burst from the gaps the explosives had made. Muddy water streamed from the weak places in the dam like the spray from a fire hose. With a sudden, violent motion the entire span collapsed, followed by a churning wall of water sweeping logs and debris before it in a racing, frothing mass. Lee scrambled higher and higher up the bank as the flood climbed to reach him, the river swollen and roiling. Those miles and miles of flooded land were free to find a new course for the billions of gallons held contained behind the dam. That much water would go wherever gravity and the lay of the land took it. And the bulk of it was racing downstream like some kind of tidal memory had taken hold of the waters to take them home.

He stood on a flat promontory and watched the torrent rushing east. It found its own track, engulfing what were once turns and bends in the river in a pitching tsunami of dirty brown wash that rose in colossal hummocks and fell back level when the land beneath had been battered flat or slashed away under the weight of the deluge. The water found its own path. Trees fell in its wake, torn loose to become a part of the onslaught. The water climbed up the banks, ripping away earth, creating a rising mist before it as water turned to vapor upon impact with anything in its path.

Shaking his head in awe at the power of what he'd unleashed, Lee sank to his knees, spent.

## 53

# GÖTTERDÄMMERUNG

Chaz tapped his last magazine on a rock before reloading his rifle.

Thirty rounds.

Through the trees, he could see at least a hundred men crossing the stream toward the bank below. No idea how many were behind them. He had no count on the number already in the woods and brush around him. By necessity, he slacked off on suppression fire. He was picking targets with more discretion. One shot, one kill. He couldn't stop them, but he could make them pay.

A yipping sound reached him. It sounded like one of those purse pooches with its paw stuck in a trap. Chaz sighted along the riverbed to find six men carrying the twisted freak on his bier. Napoleon riding out to show the troops support. The little fucker was bouncing up and down on the platform and screeching like this was a field trip to Disney. Probably never been this far from home.

Chaz drew a bead on him. If their god died, maybe these assholes would all go home. He let out his breath and pressed the trigger home.

The angle was tricky. The bullet dropped to take one of the carriers in the head. The guy pitched to the mud with the top of his skull missing. The freak nearly tumbled off his seat as the bier tilted. He let out a howl of fury or fear or both. He wiped greasy brain matter from his face. A new guy took the place of the fallen, and the bier moved on.

Chaz stood for a better angle. He brought the rifle down and set the front tang on the pathetic creature's chest. Rising from cover exposed him to a war band rushing from below. Stone hammers whistled past overhead.

A growing sound came from upstream. A thunderous roar gaining in volume with every passing second. A fine white mist climbed through the trees in a sudden rush. A fast-moving fog flowed to fill the valley like smoke. Chaz could see the waters of the stream widen below. Within seconds even the dry portions of the riverbed were ankle-deep and then knee-deep. The advance of warriors across the bed broke up. Some headed to the near shore while others turned to run back the way they'd come. The little freak on his perch waggled his hand and shouted in a dumb show. His commands were drowned out by the all-consuming noise. Confused, his bearers could only manage to stumble around in circles in the swirling water. Out of the west, the constant roar became deafening, wiping away even thought.

The war band below Chaz turned from him to look at the river below. Chaz took the opportunity to nail a few of them. His eyes were also drawn to the rushing current rising to a torrent as the riverbed filled from bank to bank dragging, blue-dyed and white-painted warriors along with it. The bier carriers were ripped off their feet, and the wooden platform splashed into the swell. The little freak screamed soundlessly as he bobbed along for a few seconds before the bier capsized and vanished, sucked below the surface in an instant.

The thick white mist raced downstream before the tide to cover all in an obscuring haze. It was followed by a filthy wall of water that rose up the slopes on either bank, clawing away at the earth to find a new course to lower ground. Trees fell into the churning waters as the ground beneath them was dashed away by millions of tons of liquid force. The bank eroded, collapsing under the force tearing away at the foundations of the river valley. Great spouts of spray exploded upward when the flood struck obstacles and finally battered them down with the relentless power of the surge's momentum.

Chaz was up and running for the thorn hide. His path carried him close past bands of blue warriors. They were either too busy climbing the slope to escape the killing current or standing in stupefied shock at the immensity of it all to pay attention to him. The waters of the earth had risen up to swallow their god. They were lost.

He came across a sad procession climbing the slope away from the white-water rapids roaring by below.

Bat and Byrus were struggling to support an unconscious Rick Renzi in a two-man carry. Jimbo was ambulatory with N'itha's help, but the Pima was pale from blood loss. He moved as if each step was an Olympic event.

Chaz took Rick in a fireman's carry over his shoulder and did a quick sit-rep.

Bat had twenty rounds for her M4. Chaz had about the same. Bat had tossed the Winchester after firing her last rounds from it. Jimbo had the Dan Wesson with a few dozen rounds. The rest were armed with edged weapons of one sort or another.

"Where are the packs?" Chaz asked.

"Lost them. The water came up so fast. There was no time," Bat said.

"Radio?"

"Gone."

"Shit. We're still in deep. The bush is loaded with unfriendlies on this side. Best plan, head west to link with Hammond. Can I get an 'amen?'" Chaz shooed them along without waiting for a reply.

---

Lee Hammond was seated atop a shelf of rock well above the swirling chaos he'd created. He was getting over his amazement at what he'd accomplished with a little bit of thought and a whole lot of bang. Every inch of him throbbed with a deep ache. All he asked was for a quiet moment or two to catch his breath.

The dam was gone. The rush of water that carried it away had slowed to a steady stream as the miles of marsh above drained out, its contents seeking lower ground, seeking level. The flow roughly followed the original course of the river. In places, he could see where it swamped turns in the channel. He pictured it filling Cannibal Lake back to the depth it was at when he first saw it. Maybe the surge would flood out the skinnies. He hoped it would do that to the blue fuckers and their cousins. Wash the whole sick horde away like flushing God's own toilet.

The level of flow dropped down from the banks following the initial flood. Lee could see dark shapes drifting in the churning mud. A mess of the big beavers. Some rode the current, body surfing along downriver. A few climbed out on either shore, shaking the wet from their fur. They prowled the banks, sniffing and snorting and generally trying to figure out what the hell happened.

Not being sure what an Escalade-sized beaver was capable of, Lee retreated from the ledge to move on a trail that led east toward the sounds of intermittent gunfire.

Lee broke into a limping trot, then a run. He hoped, in his attempt to save his friends and the woman he loved, that he hadn't doomed them all.

## 54

## JUNGLE NURSE

L ee shrugged. "We're going to have to live off the land on the way back. Well, the Indian will be happy anyway."

Jimbo forced a smile. It was meant to be sarcastic. It came off more shark than snark.

The reunion was without drama. They'd had enough of that. Lee simply saw the ragged troop crawling along a lower trail and called to them.

"We ain't going nowhere for a few days," Chaz said.

"You suggest we go camping?" Lee said. "I don't see a Marriott around here."

"We're running on vapors here, Lee. You included. And we have two injured," Bat said.

"Yeah." Lee gave in.

"We'll get to higher ground and find a place we can secure. I think those blue fucks have had enough, but you never know," Chaz said. He stooped to grab Rick's arms and lift him into a carry. Rick's only response was a hollow groan.

They found a rocky knob at the crest of a hill. A long-ago forest fire had leaped over the ridgeline and scorched everything down to the bare soil. Wind and rain had carried away the top layer leaving naked stone behind. It had clear sightlines in every direction down to hedges of berry bushes that had claimed the terrain in the absence of the big trees that had burnt away. The place was a natural fortification. There was even a cold spring nearby splashing out of the hillside to overflow into a natural tank. Lee found it without Jimbo's help.

The troop could rest and recuperate here in relative safety. No one thought anyone from the skin palace would be after them at this point. Their twisted man-god had been washed away in the deluge. And no one in the company was in any shape to give a damn anymore.

Chaz and Lee split the overnight watch. The rest fell out where they were and slept dusk to dawn.

Lee went for a hunt the following morning. N'itha joined him, unasked. She was wearing Chaz's boonie hat. Lee didn't ask about that either.

"Good eye, Neeta," Lee said when she pointed out a nice fat caribou at the edge of a herd munching leaves and berries in the thicket below their camp.

He brought it down with one shot to the head. Lee gutted it then laid it with head down the incline to bleed out. While he was at that, N'itha gathered berries and wild scallions, placing them in the boonie hat she used as an improvised bowl.

Lee sent her back up to the camp for Chaz. She must have understood because Chaz and Bat both came down to help bring breakfast up to their firebase. By Chaz's guess, the beast dressed out to five hundred pounds even after gutting and chopping off the forelegs. They dragged it up using a line run around the antlers. It was sloppy work but got the job done, and soon caribou steaks were cooking over a fire Byrus prepared.

N'itha made a broth for Rick but he puked it up as soon she got it down him.

"He's running a fever. We have to get it down. And that leg is looking nasty," Chaz said, shaking his head.

Rick's leg was swollen and red around the bad break that had healed all wrong five years back. The continued pressure had strained his leg and stirred up something that resulted in infection. If it hadn't already eaten down to the bone, it would soon. Then there was nothing they could do for Ricky. His skin was paper-dry and hot to the touch, especially in the area around the swelling.

"Help me carry him to that spring, Lee," Chaz said. "Jimbo, you put a fresh edge on a knife and sterilize it."

They brought Rick down to the spring where ice-cold water ran out of the rocks and into a shallow pool. N'itha came with them and waded into the water as they lowered him down, leaving only his face exposed. Rick fought them feebly. Chaz told him to stop being a pussy and let them save his life before dunking him under the surface. They pulled Rick up, sputtering.

When Chaz was satisfied that Rick's temps were lowered a bit, they hauled him out and carried him back to camp. Jimbo had Lee's clasp knife sharpened and ready. The tip glowed dull orange where he'd had it in the fire.

"I won't lie to you. This is gonna hurt like a bitch," Chaz said.

"Shame we went through the Jack Daniels already," Rick croaked.

"You mean *you* went through the Jack, motherfucker. Hold his ass down," Chaz said.

Byrus and Jimbo put their full weight on either of Renzi's arms. Lee pressed his legs flat above the knees. N'itha grabbed Rick by the hair in both hands and held his head immobile. This was a whole world of tough love coming down, Chaz thought. He shoved the hot point of the knife up into the base of the swollen mass, creating a slit an inch wide and six inches deep on the outside the leg away from main arteries.

When Chaz withdrew the blade, watery pus exploded out in a stream. Ricky bucked and tossed, but the foursome holding him to the ground stayed firm. He renewed the fight when Chaz put pressure on the angry bulge in his leg. Thick, foul-smelling ichor jetted from the incision. Bat, standing by playing nurse, leaped out of the way of the nauseating spray. Chaz kept up the pressure until he saw bright red blood leaking from the cut.

Ricky was punchy from the pain and whispering curses at them all.

"Let it go, brother. Let it go," Jimbo said.

As if obeying an order, Ricky slumped back into a deep sleep.

"We need to keep that as clean as we can. If this worked, his fever should crash. Bring him to the fire and let's see if we can break it," Chaz said.

Once they had him situated by the fire, N'itha left them to run down the slope into the hedge of bushes. She was wearing Chaz's boonie hat once more.

"Maybe she went to hurl. I sure feel like it," Bat said.

"Neeta's got a stronger stomach than any of us, I'll bet," Chaz said.

She returned within the hour and sat by Renzi. The boonie hat was loaded with goodies. With a rounded stone, N'itha crushed the objects she'd found into a thick paste that she smeared on Rick's leg all around the incision and over the whole infected area. Chaz dipped fingers in the mess and took a whiff.

"Honey and wild garlic. A natural antibiotic." He nodded in approval.

"She can open one of those hippie holistic clinics back in The Now," Jimbo said.

"So we're really taking her back with us?" Chaz asked.

"I think, right now, we should worry about how we get our own asses back before we start making any other plans," Lee said.

## THE ECLIPSE

Rick Renzi was ready for travel after five days. His temp was normal, and he was taking solids and fluids again. He had a wasted look to him. None of them were looking very good after all their time in the field.

It wasn't all rest for the team. Jimbo, with N'itha's help, made them water skins from the bladders of a roebuck and a deer that Lee and Bat brought back. The wolf bite to the arm was troubling the Pima. He submitted to Chaz cleaning and cauterizing the bites. N'itha wrapped it in her honey and garlic poultice soaked into strips of cloth torn from Chaz's t-shirt. She then crushed tree bark to powder and made a tea for Ricky and Jimbo.

"Homebrew aspirin," Jimbo said, sipping the bitter mix.

"That's my girl," Rick said.

Byrus lashed up a new, sturdier travois to carry Rick. He did a rough job of tanning skins to make a bed stretched between the poles. After everyone complained of the stink, the Macedonian washed and tanned his wolf headpiece. They wanted him to toss it far away, but after Bat said it reminded her of Hercules, there was no convincing him. He stretched it on a frame and scrubbed it with sand and ash mixed with his own urine. When he was done drying and scraping the sinew from the ragged fur cape, it still smelled bad but in a different, more tolerable way.

Lee jerked strips of game meat in the sun for the trip back to the coast. Bat and N'itha found nuts, berries, apples, and scallions growing wild in the thicket around their camp. Chaz went along to watch for predators, human, pre-human, animal or otherwise. By day, they saw caribou, deer, sloths, a herd of Jimbo's tiny porkers, and more different species of birds than they could count. The flooding of the river valley drove them out of the valley for drier ground. The higher elevation took the team above the worst of the biting insects.

Evening brought a pleasant breeze over the ridgeline that at least stirred the humid air a little. The wind also carried the sounds of monsters. Deep roars emerged from the surrounding dark. A chorus of howls from a thousand throats was lifted toward the Moon. Jimbo was recovered enough to take a rifle so the team could keep a pair on watch through the night. One sat overwatch at the highest point of the knobby hilltop. The other walked the perimeter.

They had only two night-vision arrays between them. Whoever stood watch wore them and scanned the surrounding slopes for any suspicious movement.

On the first night, Lee saw something out in the trees that looked at first like a bear but moved more like a dog. It came partway through the hedge of berry bushes and lay down on its belly. It watched the camp until close to dawn before moving off. It couldn't make up its mind about the strange animals around the campfire any more than Lee could figure out what the hell it was. He asked Jimbo the next day.

The Pima shrugged. "Don't know what you saw, bro. Fossil record's not complete."

Their fourth night, Jimbo had overwatch. A collection of

ghostly images trotted between the trees gathering in greater and greater numbers, eyes glowing white, bodies silvery through the enhanced illumination of the NODs gear. Dire wolves. Probably the same pack he'd tangled with, now with a new alpha male in the lead. They moved silently in a clockwise pattern around the camp in, what they believed, was the sheltering dark behind the glow of the campfire. The pack was following Chaz on his perimeter watch, keeping to below the brow of the hilltop where the Ranger could not see them. He sure didn't look like he could hear them loping along in a swirling column thirty yards from his position.

Jimbo sighted on the largest of the animals and put a round center mass. The big wolf went tumbling and kicking to the ground. The rest of the pack headed off in all directions. Chaz stopped in his tracks, whirling his gun about at the sudden crash of foliage being crushed beneath hundreds of the retreating paws.

The blast of the M4 cut the silence. The whole camp was up, weapons in hand.

"Wolves. They're gone now," Jimbo called out. No one got much sleep the rest of that night.

The morning of the sixth day they saddled up for home. They took turns pulling the travois carrying Rick who bitched about it endlessly.

"I can walk. Let me walk," he whined. Chaz read him his orders.

"When we get on flat ground, I'm gonna pull you off that rig and make you walk. You're gonna need to put weight on it. But there's no damned way I'm risking you falling down on this rough ground, you broke-leg fucker." Chaz kicked a pole of the travois.

"You'd make a great doctor. In a Mexican prison," Rick carped.

"We came all this way for your sorry ass. We're bringing you home, so we have something to show for this godforsaken trip," Chaz said.

"Might have more than Ricky to show, brother. You check out the roof of that big hooch back in Blue City?" Lee said, walking behind.

"I saw it. Solid gold."

"I say we find that place back in The Now and maybe dig around a little. That's a few million just lying around to be found."

"That rock face is probably still there. We know the rough position. Thirty-plus klicks almost dead north of Cannibal Lake."

"Part of that's mine," Renzi piped up.

"Consider it a wedding present," Chaz said, grinning.

***

Four days brought them along the highlands around the great marsh which was mostly drained now. Out of the high ground, they hiked down onto the broad grassy veldt. Renzi rose from his portable bed and walked part of the day, using a stick Byrus found him for support. Chaz ordered him back onto the travois before he overdid it. Renzi didn't argue. He looked done in.

Their easy progress over the level ground was halted out on the grasslands by an enormous herd of the long-horned bison of the type they'd encountered on their way inland. The herd stretched from horizon to horizon and as deep as the eye could see. Each was two tons of pure meanness on the hoof. A brain the size of a human fist programmed for fear or rage and nothing in between those two extremes. The San Gabriels were just a grayish smear far to the west. Three days march at their current speed.

"We could try and walk around it," Lee offered.

"Would add days to the trip," Jimbo said. "And if they shifted in the direction of our detour we could be all the way to Tijuana before we found a way around."

"And we're sure as shit not marching *through* them," Chaz confirmed for them all.

"A stampede and *we'd* be part of the fossil record," Jimbo said. "A shift in weather could move them on. I say we give them a day and see if they clear out."

They made camp on a hummock of ground thick with birch trees and waited the herd out.

Jimbo sat first watch that evening, the rifle across his knees. Chaz sat by him, both watching the sun drop behind the distant range.

"Hard to believe this was ever like this. Even harder to believe that it all ends. There'll be highways and gas stations and supermarkets out where those buffalo roam," Jimbo said.

"Sounds like you'll miss it," Chaz said.

"No. Like I said before, no horses. None you can ride. I'm glad I saw it. Just a little sad, you know, bro? This was the world once. Then it passes. Someday we'll pass. Time is a bitch."

"Yeah, bro. But we've got time by the ass, remember?"

"Do we?" Jimbo asked.

Chaz left his friend alone. When the Pima got weird like this, it was time to be somewhere else.

The following day weather came in from the north. A hard, pelting rain backed by black thunderheads that ripped the sky apart in ribbons of blinding light. The herd began moving as the barometer dropped. By afternoon, they were trotting by at speed in a vain attempt to stay ahead of the storm front. The bison passed by hour after hour, with no end to them in sight. They raised a cloud of dust behind that swirled into the sky until the rain came and beat it down.

It was getting dark by the time the last of the herd, calves and old cows, made their way past. These were pursued by predators. Big cats brought down the old and lame left to straggle behind the main body of the herd. The cats lay down near their kills after filling their bellies. There were dozens of slaughtered carcasses in view all surrounded by sabretooth monsters.

"Shit. The buffalo were bad. These are worse," Lee said.

"Good thing they have something to eat besides us," Bat said.

"We can't hike by night anyway. Too many predators. The cats will probably move on by morning. We'll head out then," Jimbo said.

"Make fire. Big fire," Byrus said, eyes locked on what he was certain were demons out of his own legends.

Lee was on watch that evening with Bat. The weather cleared up, the storm blowing away south left a cloudless sky. In a world without electric lighting, the dark created a dense canopy of stars above. A full moon rose over the grass tops waving in the night wind. It was easy to forget the mankillers lying sated and asleep not a hundred meters from their hill camp.

"I've never seen the moon so big," Bat said, laying back with the rifle across her belly.

"It's the dense air. Acts like a lens and magnifies the moon. I've seen it on jungle ops around the equator," Lee said.

"Shut up, Hammond."

"Yeah. It's romantic, I guess."

"Too late, mood spoiler," she said, but Bat was smiling at him.

---

He sat by her, and they both watched the moon. It was probably the only constant in all their travels together and apart. They could look up and see the same moon that had been there for billions of years and would be there when they returned to their own time, perpetual and unchanged. Lee was about to say something to that effect when Bat sat up suddenly.

"The moon," she said.

"Yeah. I was just going to say that."

"What is that crossing the moon?"

Lee squinted up. Against the moon's opalescent surface was a black oblong shape that grew in size as they stared at it. It was something moving through the sky in their general direction.

As it grew nearer, they could hear the unmistakable purr of motors.

## 56

## "IS IT TOMORROW OR JUST THE END OF TIME?"

L ee roused the camp. "Get more wood on that fire!"

Byrus dragged branches and logs to the campfire with Chaz's help. The blaze grew bright and high.

"It's my blimp! That was my idea!" Chaz was shouting.

"It's some kind of airship. How do we know it's friendly?" Jimbo stood looking up at the elongated egg shape as it moved away from the moon's glow on a northerly course away from them.

"Who else would be flying a goddamn zeppelin around here?" Lee called, tossing a stout log to the center of the pyre. Glowing embers exploded upward.

"That Harnesh guy? He has his own manifestation tubes, remember? The last radio transmission was pretty damn cryptic. Maybe they ran into trouble up in The Now," Jimbo said.

"All I know is that I'm looking at something that doesn't *belong* here. *We* don't belong here. And those cats are going to take an interest in us soon. I'll play the odds that Dwayne and that crazy SEAL are flying that thing." Lee walked from the glare of the fire.

He fired controlled bursts from his rifle into the air. Tracers streamed, drawing long contrails of light against the dark. Bat joined him, sending another flurry of tracers upward.

"Shit," Chaz said. The blimp was still moving away for a destination farther inland. The motor sounds faded in the distance.

"Wait. What's happening to it?" Bat said. The shape of the flying object was changing.

"It's turning. Adjusting course." Jimbo had his 30x to his remaining eye.

"Turning back?" Chaz said.

"Looks like it," Jimbo said, eye on the distant object turning from a ball-shape to an ovoid and back to a ball as it changed direction back toward them in a graceful one-eighty. The sound of the motors rose in volume as it neared.

"It's got to be Dwayne and Boats," Chaz said, eyes on the black blob against the stars growing larger.

"If it's not we're fucked," Jimbo said.

"We're already fucked. Those cats know we're here now," Lee said. Eyes glowed white in the gloom outside the towering blaze of their signal fire. The beasts were closer now. Myriad points of reflected light arrayed in a deadly constellation all around them.

The team withdrew to stand about the fire. The pairs of watching eyes came no nearer but grew in number until scores of sabretooths closed around them in an invisible ring. Then the tigers were visible in a sudden cone of light trained on the peak of the hill from above. Brilliant lights suspended below the hovering airship turned the surrounding ten acres to high noon in an instant. The lights exposed a nightmare vision. The entire pride of fanged horrors was exposed by the intense illumination from above. The beasts looked upward into the light, roaring in defiance. Their deafening bellows rumbled over the team.

Bat felt the sound of their rage in her chest. The M4 shook in her hands where she struggled to hold it trained on a big male leaping up on hind legs to claw at the air in an attempt to spend his fury on the source of the blinding light. She wondered how many rounds remained in the final magazine now in the rifle.

The airship's engines flared above them in a rising whine. The sound was joined by a piercing squeal following by a rhythmic thumping of seismic levels booming down from above in an inescapable sonic wave. As one, the cats spun on their back legs and vanished into the encircling dark.

Rick Renzi held a hand clapped to one ear.

"Who's the Hendrix fan?" He shouted to be heard over the din pounding from the airship.

Lee shouted back to be heard over *Purple Haze*. "It's that bugfuck-crazy SEAL."

---

The driving beat of the music died away. The airship settled to the ground into a broad lake of light projected from the halogen bundles mounted on stanchions around the gondola slung beneath it. It dropped gently, the whirring rotors of the engines mounted either side creating twin cyclones brushing back the tops of the grass all around. Four landing legs touched down on a level spot on the veldt.

The ship was approximately a hundred meters bow to stern and a third of that at its widest center point. The lights reflected off the silvery outer skin of the inflatable portion, which was lined with the black squares of solar panels. Beneath this was a gondola that formed the belly of the craft. The gondola was six feet above the turf once it settled down onto the hydraulics of the landing gear at the end of spindly legs like a spider coming to rest.

A hatch opened followed by a set of ladder steps swinging out to squash the grass flat.

"Roenbach, you son of a bitch! You took my idea!" Chaz

shouted as he raced into the nimbus of harsh artificial light to embrace his brother Ranger.

"Trust me, we were all out of *good* ideas," Dwayne said, pounding Chaz's back.

"Everybody here?" Boats said, climbing down out of the cabin.

"Everybody plus one," Lee said, stepping into the glare with Bat by his side and the rest of the company behind. Rick limped forward with some help from N'itha.

"Who the fuck?" the SEAL said.

"The new Mrs. Renzi." Chaz grinned.

"A lot has changed back in The Now. We made a few upgrades. And we have a situation that needs to be rectified," Dwayne said.

"I don't care if it's World War Three as long we're going back to where the beer's cold and the showers are hot," Chaz said.

"This thing going to carry us all?" Lee said, nodding up at the curve of the airship looming over them.

"It'll be tight," Boats said. "It's rated to lift a ton of weight. But the helium gauges have been dropping in this goddamn heat."

"We're going to have to leave any non-essential gear behind," Dwayne said.

"Won't Morris have a shit fit about that?" Jimbo said.

"Then, when you see him, don't tell him," Dwayne said. Jimbo didn't ask what he meant by that.

All remaining gear, weapons, CamelBaks, rations, and the scant little else that was left from their trek were dumped in a pile away from the airship by Lee and Chaz. Boats tossed a thermite grenade on the heap, and it went up in a flash of heat hotter than the sun. What wasn't vaporized was turned into an unrecognizable liquid mess of molten steel.

"Suck on that, Indiana Jones," the SEAL grunted as the three made their way back to the airship.

"Did you guys super-size the Tube while we were gone?" Jimbo said, seated in a comfortable chair.

Chairs were bolted down in two rows lining the port and starboard walls of the fuselage of the main cabin. The cabin was spartan. Bare metal walls and deck. Four seats down either side of a center aisle and an open pilot's deck two steps down at the bow. A console of dials and screens glowed. There were view-ports down either side. At the rear of the cabin was a storage cage, where several rifles and shotguns stood upright in racks.

Dwayne handed out bottled water and wrapped sandwiches, cheese and turkey, from a mini-fridge. There was a container of sliced fruit as well.

"Brought this beast through in crates," Boats said. "Five trips. Then we assembled it down on the beach where we first landed. Geteye and two of the *Raj's* crew came through with us and helped us assemble it. Took a week."

"You've been here a week?" Bat said.

Dwayne said, "Last time we saw you, for us, was three weeks ago. As soon as we lost contact, Boats and I started planning how to come get you. We remembered what Chaz was saying about a blimp. Ordered one from a place in Van Nuys that manufactures them. Paid triple price for rush delivery and no questions. This whole thing came in one cargo container."

"Cost us a goddamn fortune to have it ferried out to the *Raj*," Boats bitched, still smarting over the cost.

"We assembled the cabin on board the *Raj*. That was the most involved build. Rigged up a raft to haul it through the tube behind the Titan. It took some work with torches to cut a bigger working area in the Tube chamber. Then we hauled through the frame for the envelope and the engines. Geteye and the guys worked on the upper while Boats and I bolted on the maneu-vering engines," Dwayne said.

"And since when are you guys pilots?" Lee said.

"Hey, I went to chopper school in the Navy," the SEAL said.

"And, if I remember right, you told us you washed out twice," Lee said.

"Anyway. Blimps are more forgiving." Boats shrugged.

"You said you wanted us back in a hurry last time we had contact. By your calendar that's been more than a month," Jimbo said to Dwayne.

"You've been through the shitter. Let's get you back to The Now. Plenty of time to update you there," Dwayne said and made his way to the pilot deck.

"Take a deep breath and pucker your assholes, ladies and gentlemen. Next stop, the future." Boats grinned and went forward to take his place in the pilot's chair.

## 57

# TURNING TO THE NOW

The motors growled to life, sending a vibration through the aluminum gondola that betrayed the fragile nature of the craft. It was an excursion model, a millionaire's toy. It had a fraction of the helium capacity or lift properties of larger cargo craft used in construction projects.

Boats pulled a lever on the console to release a ton of sand held in a ballast chamber in the belly of the gondola. As the sand bled out through several open cocks, the airship rose gently at first and then, with a jerk that settled them all back in their seats, lifted one hundred feet in seconds. The motors settled down to a steady beat. It was a noisier ride than any of them expected. Also less graceful than it appeared from outside the craft as it responded to every crosswind and updraft, no matter how slight.

"The skin's a little damp from a gusher we flew through. We'll have more lift as she dries out," Boats called back from the pilot's chair where he was turning the wheel and working levers to keep them level and on course.

At this remark, the passengers looked from their ports to see that they were cruising along at less than two hundred feet over the plain below. The sun was rising behind them, and the grass looked like burnished copper passing by below in a dizzying blur. Dark shapes darted through the grass and out from under the long gray shadow cast beneath them. Animals, startled by the appearance of this floating monstrosity, were rushing to get out from under its massive shape. They saw bison, caribou, and camels raising thick clouds of dust in their haste to be away.

The sun rose and began to dry the wet surface of the huge shell containing the helium nacelles that kept them aloft. They lifted higher to an altitude of one thousand feet, and the ride smoothed out except for course corrections that yanked them back and forth in their seats without any warning—except for the SEAL's cries of "bitch!" from the pilot deck. The sun also worked on the aluminum and magnesium shell of the gondola, raising the temperatures inside. No air-conditioning aboard the blimp but the ports could be unlatched and swung inward to allow cool air to blow across the passengers.

Within hours the airship crossed the open prairie and threaded the needle of a pass through the San Gabriels to the beach. By noon they were setting down on a level patch of sand within sight of the base camp created to construct the blimp. The mini firebase was covered by a pair of .50 machine guns on raised platforms manned by Geteye and two of his crew. A dome tent was set up by two Titan inflatables staked down and secured on the sand.

Dwayne radioed ahead while in transit to the coast to Caroline in The Now in order to schedule a field opening. They departed on the pair of power rafts after setting a thermite charge in the cabin of the airship that turned the craft into a swirling tower of flame. The aluminum and magnesium structure was practically vaporized in the blast furnace heat.

"She was a beauty," Boats said from the tiller of Titan One. He looked back at the collapsing column of white smoke spreading over the beach.

"Chronal integrity, bro," Chaz said from his bench seat.

"Except for all that shit we left behind at Blue City," Lee said.

"We'll keep that our little secret," Bat said. "Besides, who's ever going to find that stuff after all the time exposed to the weather and changes?"

Boats kept quiet. He concentrated on the horizon line, looking for the mist that would take them home.

The story continues with Sons of Heaven, book five in the Bad Times story from Chuck Dixon.

**Millions were dead.**
**Millions more would join them.**
The Rangers step back into the bloodiest civil war in history all at the orders of a man they'd rather see dead. Somewhere in an empire tearing itself to bloody shreds lies a secret worth killing and dying for. Lee, Chaz, Jimbo and the rest are willing to do the former and struggling like hell to avoid the latter.

*The fifth book in the epic Bad Times series by Chuck Dixon.*

Military action in a time travel scenario that blends realistic action with high concept science fiction for a tale populated with unforgettable characters and unique situations. This is the next chapter in the eon sprawling adventure of a team of U.S. Army Rangers lost in time and damned by fate.

Order now at Amazon and through Kindle Unlimited.

Chuck Dixon is the prolific author of thousands of comic book scripts for *Batman and Robin, the Punisher, Nightwing, Conan the Barbarian, Airboy, the Simpsons, Alien Legion,* and countless other titles.

Together with Graham Nolan, Chuck created the now iconic Batman villain Bane. He also wrote the international bestselling graphic novel adaptation of J.R.R Tolkien's *The Hobbit.*

His first foray into prose, the *SEAL Team 6* novels from Dynamite Entertainment, have become an ebook sensation. He currently scripts *GI Joe Special Missions* for IDW publishing as well as the *Pellucidar* weekly comic strip for ERB Inc.

He calls Florida home these days.

**You can connect with Chuck here:**

Facebook:
https://www.facebook.com/chuck.dixon.779

Website
http://dixonverse.blogspot.com/

Amazon
https://www.amazon.com/Chuck-Dixon/e/B001HOL26O